CW00506532

# CHRISTOPI
## THE CASE OF THE RUSSIAN CROSS

CHRISTOPHER BUSH was born Charlie Christmas Bush in Norfolk in 1885. His father was a farm labourer and his mother a milliner. In the early years of his childhood he lived with his aunt and uncle in London before returning to Norfolk aged seven, later winning a scholarship to Thetford Grammar School.

As an adult, Bush worked as a schoolmaster for 27 years, pausing only to fight in World War One, until retiring aged 46 in 1931 to be a full-time novelist. His first novel featuring the eccentric Ludovic Travers was published in 1926, and was followed by 62 additional Travers mysteries. These are all to be republished by Dean Street Press.

Christopher Bush fought again in World War Two, and was elected a member of the prestigious Detection Club. He died in 1973.

# CHRISTOPHER BUSH

## THE CASE OF THE RUSSIAN CROSS

With an introduction
by Curtis Evans

DEAN STREET PRESS

THE AUTHOR, having discovered that this
is his 50th novel of detection, dedicates it,
in sheer astonishment,
to
HIMSELF

# INTRODUCTION

## Ring out the Old, Ring in the New
### Christopher Bush and Mystery Fiction in the Fifties

"Mr. Bush has an urbane and intelligent way of dealing with mystery which makes his work much more attractive than the stampeding sensationalism of some of his rivals."
—Rupert Crofts-Cooke (acclaimed author of the Leo Bruce detective novels)

New fashions in mystery fiction were decidedly afoot in the 1950s, as authors increasingly turned to sensationalistic tales of international espionage, hard-boiled sex and violence, and psychological suspense. Yet there indubitably remained, seemingly imperishable and eternal, what Anthony Boucher, dean of American mystery reviewers, dubbed the "conventional type of British detective story." This more modestly decorous but still intriguing and enticing mystery fare was most famously and lucratively embodied by Crime Queen Agatha Christie, who rang in the new decade and her Golden Jubilee as a published author with the classic detective novel that was promoted as her fiftieth mystery: *A Murder Is Announced* (although this was in fact a misleading claim, as this tally also included her short story collections). Also representing the traditional British detective story during the 1950s were such crime fiction stalwarts (all of them Christie contemporaries and, like the Queen of Crime, longtime members of the Detection Club) as Edith Caroline Rivett (E.C.R Lorac and Carol Carnac), E.R. Punshon, Cecil John Charles Street (John Rhode and Miles Burton) and Christopher Bush. Punshon and Rivett passed away in the Fifties, pens still brandished in their hands, if you will, but Street and Bush, apparently indefatigable, kept at crime throughout the decade, typically publishing in both the United Kingdom and the United States two books a year (Street with both of his pseudonyms).

Not to be outdone even by Agatha Christie, Bush would celebrate his own Golden Jubilee with his fiftieth mystery, *The Case of the Russian Cross*, in 1957—and this was done, in contrast with Christie, without his publishers having to resort to any creative accounting. *Cross* is the fiftieth Christopher Bush Ludovic Travers detective novel reprinted by Dean Street Press in this, the Spring of 2020, the hundredth anniversary of the dawning of the Golden Age of detective fiction, following, in this latest installment, *The Case of the Counterfeit Colonel* (1952), *The Case of the Burnt Bohemian* (1953), *The Case of The Silken Petticoat* (1953), *The Case of the Red Brunette* (1954), *The Case of the Three Lost Letters* (1954), *The Case of the Benevolent Bookie* (1955), *The Case of the Amateur Actor* (1955), *The Case of the Extra Man* (1956) and *The Case of the Flowery Corpse* (1956).

Not surprisingly, given its being the occasion of Christopher Bush's Golden Jubilee, *The Case of the Russian Cross* met with a favorable reception from reviewers, who found the author's wry dedication especially ingratiating: "The author, having discovered that this is his fiftieth novel of detection, dedicates it in sheer astonishment to HIMSELF." Writing as Francis Iles, the name under which he reviewed crime fiction, Bush's Detection Club colleague Anthony Berkeley, himself one of the great Golden Age innovators in the genre, commented, "I share Mr. Bush's own surprise that *The Case of the Russian Cross* should be his fiftieth book; not so much at the fact itself as at the freshness both of plot and writing which is still as notable with fifty up as it was in in his opening overs. There must be many readers who still enjoy a straightforward, honest-to-goodness puzzle, and here it is." The late crime writer Anthony Lejeune, who would be admitted to the Detection Club in 1963, for his part cheered, "Hats off to Christopher Bush....[L]ike his detective, [he] is unostentatious but always absolutely reliable." Alan Hunter, who recently had published his first George Gently mystery and at the time was being lauded as the "British Simenon," offered similarly praiseful words, pronouncing of *The*

*Case of the Russian Cross* that Bush's sleuth Ludovic Travers "continues to be a wholly satisfying creation, the characters are intriguing and the plot full of virility. . . . the only trace of long-service lies in the maturity of the treatment."

The high praise for Bush's fiftieth detective novel only confirmed (if resoundingly) what had become clear from reviews of earlier novels from the decade: that in Britain Christopher Bush, who had turned sixty-five in 1950, had become a Grand Old Man of Mystery, an Elder Statesman of Murder. Bush's *The Case of the Three Lost Letters*, for example, was praised by Anthony Berkeley as "a model detective story on classical lines: an original central idea, with a complicated plot to clothe it, plenty of sound, straightforward detection by a mellowed Ludovic Travers and never a word that is not strictly relevant to the story"; while reviewer "Christopher Pym" (English journalist and author Cyril Rotenberg) found the same novel a "beautifully quiet, close-knit problem in deduction very fairly presented and impeccably solved." Berkeley also highly praised Bush's *The Case of the Burnt Bohemian*, pronouncing it "yet another sound piece of work . . . in that, alas!, almost extinct genre, the real detective story, with Ludovic Travers in his very best form."

In the United States Bush was especially praised in smaller newspapers across the country, where, one suspects, traditional detection most strongly still held sway. "Bush is one of the soundest of the English craftsmen in this field," declared Ben B. Johnston, an editor at the *Richmond Times Dispatch*, in his review of *The Case of the Burnt Bohemian*, while Lucy Templeton, doyenne of the *Knoxville Sentinel* (the first female staffer at that Tennessee newspaper, Templeton, a freshly minted graduate of the University of Tennessee, had been hired as a proofreader back in 1904), enthusiastically avowed, in her review of *The Case of the Flowery Corpse*, that the novel was "the best mystery novel I have read in the last six months." Bush "has always told a good story with interesting backgrounds and rich characterization," she added admiringly. Another southern reviewer, one "M." of the *Montgomery Advertiser*, deemed *The Case of the Amateur Actor* "another Travers mystery to delight the most critical of a reader audience," concluding in inimitable American lingo, "it's a swell story." Even Anthony Boucher, who in the Fifties hardly could be termed an unalloyed admirer of conventional British detection, from his prestigious post at the *New York Times Books Review* afforded words of praise to a number of Christopher Bush mysteries from the decade, including the cases of the *Benevolent Bookie* ("a provocative puzzle"), the *Amateur Actor* ("solid detective interest"), the *Flowery Corpse* ("many small ingenuities of detection") and, but naturally, the *Russian Cross* ("a pretty puzzle"). In his own self-effacing fashion, it seems that Ludovic Travers had entered the pantheon of Great Detectives, as another American commentator suggested in a review of Bush's *The Case of The Silken Petticoat*:

> Although Ludovic Travers does not possess the esoteric learning of Van Dine's Philo Vance, the rough and ready punch of Mickey Spillane's Mike Hammer, the Parisian [sic!] touch of Agatha Christie's Hercule Poirot, the appetite and orchids of Rex Stout's Nero Wolfe, the suave coolness of The Falcon or the eerie laugh and invisibility of The Shadow, he does have good qualities— especially the ability to note and interpret clues and a dogged persistence in remembering and following up an episode he could not understand. These paid off in his solution of *The Case of The Silken Petticoat*.

In some ways Christopher Bush, his traditionalism notwithstanding, attempted with his Fifties Ludovic Travers mysteries to keep up with the tenor of rapidly changing times. As owner of the controlling interest in the Broad Street Detective Agency, Ludovic Travers increasingly comes to resemble an American private investigator rather than the gentleman amateur detective he had been in the 1930s; and the novels in which he appears reflect some of the jaded cynicism of post-World War Two American hard-boiled crime fiction. *The Case of the Red Brunette*, one of my favorite examples from this batch of Bushes, looks at civic corruption in provincial England in a case concerning a town counsellor who dies in an apparent "badger game" or "honey trap" gone fatally wrong ("a web of mystery skillfully spun" noted Pat McDermott of Iowa's *Quad City Times*), while in *The Case of the Three Lost Letters*, Travers finds himself having to explain to his phlegmatic wife Bernice the pink lipstick strains on his collar (incurred strictly in the line of duty, of course). Travers also pays homage to the popular, genre altering Inspector Maigret novels of Georges Simenon in *The Case of Red Brunette*, when he decides that he will "try to get a feel of the city [of Mainford]: make a Maigret-like tour and achieve some kind of background. . . ."

Christopher Bush finally decided that Travers could manage entirely without his longtime partner in crime solving, the wily and calculatingly avuncular Chief Superintendent George Wharton, whom at times Travers, in the tradition of American hard-boiled crime fiction, appears positively to dislike. "I generally admire and respect Wharton, but there are times when he annoys me almost beyond measure," Travers confides in *The Case of the Amateur Actor*. "There are even moments, as when he assumes that cheap and leering superiority, when I can suddenly hate him." George Wharton appropriately makes his final, brief appearance in the Bush oeuvre in *The Case of the Russian Cross*, where Travers allows that despite their differences, the "Old General" is "the man who'd become in most ways my oldest friend."

"Ring out the old, ring in the new" may have been the motto of many when it came to mid-century mystery fiction, but as another saying goes, what once was old eventually becomes sparklingly new again. The truth of the latter adage is proven by this shining new set of Christopher Bush reissues. "Just like old crimes," vintage mystery fans may sigh contentedly, as once again they peruse the pages of a Bush, pursuing murderous malefactors in the ever pleasant company of Ludovic Travers, all the while armed with the happy knowledge that a butcher's dozen of thirteen of Travers' investigations yet remains to be reissued.

Curtis Evans

# THEME I
# BLACKMAIL

"A listener will be hopelessly at sea if he expects to find in the later symphonies of Sibelius the conventional use of symphonic material.

"Sibelius has no first and second themes, development and final assertion. He introduces various short themes which may seem wholly unconnected. It is only towards the end that these themes are fused together into a satisfying whole."

*Extract from Programme Notes.*

## 1
## NEW BROOM

GEORGE Wharton gave me the tip well before it happened. You may possibly know that for a considerable number of years I've worked with George—Chief-Superintendent—Wharton on murder cases out of the ordinary run. But let's get something clear from the start. Though I mention cases out of the ordinary run, that's very far from implying that I have extraordinary brains or any other God-given gift that's in any way unique. It's just that over the years George and I have happened to achieve a harmony out of opposing temperaments and have combined to make a piece of machinery that on the whole has worked uncommonly well. We've had our failures—who hasn't?—but we've also managed to unravel some highly involved complexities.

It's work that I like doing. I wouldn't have been called in by George Wharton on a Case if that Case weren't a problem that looked like being tough. And I like problems and hate the nagging of an unsolved mystery. The whole thing becomes a very personal issue. Not personal, mind you, because there may be in it some useful publicity for the Broad Street Detective Agency, for there's rarely any publicity at all. What I mean is that when

I'm engaged, as what is known as an unofficial expert, on one of those Cases with George, then I hate to be licked. The financial reward, which is little more than trivial, doesn't in any case enter into it. It's the problem, and the problem alone, that matters.

George, as I said, gave me the tip just when it became known that Forlin was to be the new Commander Crime at the Yard. I'd never run across Forlin professionally but George described him as a stickler in the matter of the proper and conventional. If anything arose on which he—George—might request my co-operation, he had a kind of foreboding that Forlin would make things difficult.

We were talking about all sorts of things that night when he sprang that sudden surprise. Bernice—my wife—was out and George and I had been having a quiet bachelor evening at the flat. There have been hundreds of times in our twenty-five years of association when I'd have liked to wring George's neck, but that kind of feeling always passes and I get back—as I was doing that night—to a kind of warming affection. I was thinking, for instance, how little the years had changed him. The huge shoulders had scarcely the beginnings of a stoop: the hair hardly a trace of grey, and that monstrous, overhanging moustache still retained its raffish flamboyance. All the tricks of speech and the mannerisms were still there, and the pig-headedness in argument and the heavy-footed attempts to pull my leg, but at the back of it all there was only the nostalgic figure of the man with whom I'd been associated for a third of a lifetime: the man who'd become in most ways my oldest friend.

"Mind you," George said, "I'm not saying that Forlin will have everything quite his own way. He may be my superior but that isn't to say I've got to take everything lying down."

"No, no, George," I said. "I'm not having you getting into any bad odour because of me. After all, it's about time I retired—"

George gave me one of his special sneers.

"Now, now: you tell that to the Marines."

"Tell what?" I said guilelessly.

"That you're getting too old and that you ought to devote more time to that agency of yours and all the rest of the poppycock. You're like me: you'll never be too old. And you haven't got to worry about money—lucky you!"

"What I've made out of the Yard wouldn't keep me in beer," I said, and refilled his glass. "But I'll be frank about this, George, if it really happens. I'll feel a bit hurt perhaps out of sheer vanity, and I'll feel very much out of things when a Case turns up that I might have been up to the neck in. But it certainly won't get me down. And it won't make any difference to you and me, as you and me. Or to the other good friends I've made at the Yard—Jewle, Matthews and all the rest of 'em. In any case nothing may happen after all, so why let it get us down?"

But it did happen, and by the sheerest bit of bad luck. A certain murderer whom George and I had managed to catch by the heels was up for his trial at the Old Bailey and I had to give evidence. Defending counsel was unknown to me and practically unknown to George. I'd anticipated that my statement would be taken, as it usually was, as sheer hard fact and that there'd be practically no cross-examination. I was wrong. I wasn't cross-examined: I was turned inside-out.

The object—legitimate enough, I suppose, when you consider the issues at stake—was to discredit both me and my evidence. The questions were put with quite a charming and ironic suavity: each with a little smile towards the jury as if inviting them to take me as a rather unpleasant kind of joke. So I was an unofficial expert. Just what sort of an expert, or perhaps he might be allowed to put it another way—an expert in what?

Either I had to do a deal of trumpet-blowing or beg the question. I don't think I raised my voice in the least when I said the question was one for my superiors. Counsel raised his eyebrows. A queer expert, surely, who was unaware of his own speciality? That sort of chit-chat lasted a good five minutes and then I was blandly asked if I wasn't the proprietor of a detective agency. Substitute for detective agency the word brothel, and you have some idea of the tone in which the question was put. There was another five minutes of that and then, when he was satisfied as to the general impression he had created in the minds of the jury, he set about my evidence. I was grilled for an hour. I think I can claim that I was reasonably imperturbable. Even that didn't do me any good since the view given to the jury was that they were listening to someone very hard-bitten, and to be hard-bitten is in many people's minds to be pretty unscrupulous.

There was a great splash in the evening papers, not that it all made much difference to the verdict of the following day. Our man always had been guilty and he was duly to be hanged, but that didn't undo the mischief that had been done. One of the yellower of the dailies had a leader on the Yard's unofficial experts in which I was hinted at from a range just beyond the laws of libel. George Wharton was furious, but there was nothing he could do about it. And, as I told him, if I'd spent ten thousand pounds on advertising I could never have got so much publicity for the Agency. An Agency run by someone who's even called in by the Yard! That one fact, hammered into the heads of the reading public, was worth a fortune. A slight exaggeration, of course, but when one is trying to conceal an annoyance, one is apt to talk with less restraint.

For I was annoyed, and I was hurt. A bit childish, perhaps, but there it was. When in a week or two the Harper Street Case broke and George was to tell me that there was no likelihood of my being called in, it didn't hurt any the less. I'll even own up to the fact that I was infinitely more childish, at least in my private thoughts. Believe it or not, and now I can wince when I think of it, I wished the Harper Street Case would be one of the Yard's greatest flops. I even had moments when I envisaged some spectacular revenge and the Commander Crime almost crawling on his belly to beg me to return to the inquisitorial fold.

I suppose in a way that sort of thing wasn't altogether unpardonable. You can't do a job for a third of a lifetime and then be suddenly ignored without feeling a certain rancour. But it was scarcely more than momentary. After all, I *was* busy at the Agency. And I did retain my friends. George and Chief-Inspector Jewle—principally, I now think, out of sheer kindness of heart—did see me surreptitiously about one or two Yard matters. And yet, deep down somewhere inside me, was a feeling of having lost face. It was a question, not so much of clutching the inviolable shade as of nursing the unconquerable hope when the thought would sneak in upon me that sooner or later I'd get my chance. Chance to do what, I didn't exactly know, except that it would mean a triumphant return to the old way of life and a lost status. All of which shows how absurd one can permit one's ageing self to be. Or does it?

All that nonsense began to come less and less to my mind. Perhaps it would be more correct to say that it began to be thrust deeper and deeper into an abeyance, for, as I said, I did occupy myself to a far greater extent with Agency affairs, though always with a due regard for the position of Norris, the general manager. There was always plenty for both of us to do, for that unfortunate publicity had brought in a lot of new business that had to be carefully scrutinized. Let me explain.

When we acquired the business the goodwill was about equally divided between work for private clients and the retainers from two large insurance companies and a few private firms. When we were lucky enough gradually to increase that latter side of the business, we could afford to become more discriminating about the former. We would never, in any case, handle divorce work, but there are still clients whose real objects and intentions are vastly different from those that are speciously confided to Norris or myself. Unless you are sure of your client and have grasped the full implications of his case, you would do better, whatever the fee, to drop the whole thing like a red-hot poker. If not there is always the chance that you may very soon find yourself in remarkably bad odour with both the police and the actual law. And that kind of reputation, and possibly the attendant publicity, is ruination to an agency which stands or falls in infinitely more important matters on its reputation for absolute integrity.

And so at last to the Case of the Russian Cross. Our method, when we are the least suspicious of a client, is for ostensibly admirable reasons to postpone a decision to take his case and to use the brief respite to investigate that same client. Better be safe than sorry. In the Case of the Russian Cross we were lucky enough to end up safe, but it can still give me the cold shudders to think how near we came to being irreparably sorry.

That Case actually began in the April of 1955. But there was then no question of any Russian Cross. To use a somewhat grandiloquent simile, it was as if a hydrogen bomb, unknown to the world, had been detonated somewhere in the Pacific and I'd happened to notice a rather larger wave than usual breaking on the coast of Cornwall. There was no more connection than that. I couldn't possibly suggest the origin of that wave, and the last thing in my thoughts would be that one day I might have to investigate the bomb itself.

It was a lovely April morning when I went to Beaulieu Crescent to see Martin Penford. He's a rather gaunt Midlander of about sixty who has come up the hard way and made a fortune in the process. Just before the last war his father left him a grocery business, and in spite of restrictions he gradually made that store into a chain, and he had in addition, by way of foothold, a large store in the suburbs. We'd investigated for him a disturbing loss of stock. It had been a three months' job and we'd been lucky enough to clear the whole thing up. Penford had rung the office to say how delighted he was, and he wanted me to call personally at Beaulieu Crescent to collect his cheque.

I'd met him only once but Norris had seen him several times and had also done a certain amount of private investigation before we'd even accepted the case. Naturally I wanted to make a good impression on Penford in view of a possibly permanent retainer, so I asked Norris about him.

"Well, he does look rather like a church deacon, as you yourself said," Norris told me, "but that's very much of a front. He's kicked up his heels in his time, and still can, so I'm told by someone who knows him pretty well. He's always liked the theatre, for one thing. That's how he met his wife."

I raised enquiring eyebrows.

"She began in the chorus and ended up with small parts in a touring repertory company. Penford met her some twenty years ago at the local theatre." He gave his dry smile. "Wonder what she'd have said to the crystal-gazer if she'd been told she'd end up as Lady Penford."

"He really is getting a knighthood?"

"That's what I'm told for a fact," Norris said. "For public services to his native city, including the gift of the old repertory theatre and an endowment."

"And what's Mrs. Penford actually like? I don't suppose for a moment I'll be seeing her, but it's just as well to know."

"Not what you'd think," Norris said. "I only saw her once but she struck me as a remarkably level-headed woman—or lady. A bit on the plump side, but still quite good-looking. And well-spoken. You'd never guess she was once in the back row of the chorus."

All that didn't help very much in the matter of approach, not that I was at all flurried when the taxi dropped me at the staid-looking house in Beaulieu Crescent. It was quite a large place: the sort of house you find in most of the West-End squares, and when the door opened at my ring I was expecting to see a butler. But it was an elderly maid. She said that Penford was awaiting me and showed me at once into what she called the morning room: a pleasant room with French windows that opened on a sunny courtyard with flower beds and a tiny fountain.

Penford, who'd been looking at that garden, turned as the door opened and came forward with outstretched hand. He still looked like a deacon but one remarkably pleased with the collection. In the tall wing-collar his Adam's-apple looked more prominent than ever, and the wrists that protruded beyond the starched cuffs were as incredibly bony. He wore his Midland accent as one wears an old tweed coat, but I make no effort to reproduce it.

It was only eleven o'clock but he insisted that I should take a drink. When I chose sherry he further insisted that it should be accompanied in the old-fashioned way by a slice of plum cake. I didn't demur. I like plum cake and if he'd suggested cold plum-pudding it wouldn't have been policy to suggest a possible weight on the stomach. So the bell was pushed and the elderly maid brought in the cake, and remarkably good it was.

"I'm all for the old-fashioned ways," Penford told me as he poured the sherries at the mahogany sideboard. "I'm not talking about business, Mr. Travers, but in what you might call every-day life. In the home and so on. Our fathers weren't all fools."

I agreed. I complimented him on the sherry. He said it ought to be good, and told me the price. A minute or two later he was producing our account from a drawer of a rather ugly mahogany bureau that stood to the left of the windows.

"I oughtn't to say it," he told me, "but I never parted with money with greater satisfaction, Mr. Travers. You did a very good job."

The thin lips clamped together and then spread to a grim sort of smile.

"Between ourselves, and considering what you look like saving us in the future, I wouldn't have grumbled at paying a good bit more."

I'd have liked to tell him that I'd remembered that, but I didn't. I mentioned the matter of a retainer and the advantages in every way to his firm. He seemed interested—very interested. And then suddenly the door opened. A woman came in, stopped at the sight of me, and looked for a moment as if she was as quickly going out again. Penford was on his feet.

"Come in, dear: come in. Is the head better?"

"A lot better," she said, and it was at me she was looking.

She was much younger than her husband: in the mid-forties. Somehow I hadn't reconciled Norris's brief description of her with the ex-chorus girl and small-part provincial actress of my own imagining, and that first minute of her gave me quite a jolt. She was tallish, slightly on the plump side, but with a figure that quite a lot of women would have envied. Her face had character. Her dress was quiet but even I knew that it had that indefinable thing called style. There was no obtrusion of make-up. She had a natural poise, remote from the brassy assurance of her husband, and her voice was quiet too, and pleasant, with never a trace of accent.

Penford was almost flustered. It was as if some distinguished caller had unexpectedly arrived.

"This is Mr. Travers," he told her, and she gave me a little bow and a quiet smile. "Sit down here, love. Have a glass of sherry. It'll do you good."

"No sherry, thank you, Martin."

I'd moved an easy chair alongside my own and she gave me another little smile of thanks.

"I've told the wife all about you, Mr. Travers," Penford was babbling on, and embarrassingly for myself. "Mr. Travers isn't what you'd call a detective. I wouldn't be surprised if it wasn't a kind of hobby with him, if you know what I mean."

A brief pause and I managed to ask her if she suffered to any extent from headaches. She said she didn't: it was just a kind of passing phase.

"I can't get her to go to the doctor," Penford told me. "Headaches don't come from nowhere. Don't you think I'm right?"

"I think we're prone to exaggerate them," I said. "My wife has had them for years. Nothing that an aspirin or two won't cure, and an hour or two's quiet."

"You see, Martin?" she said. "Mr. Travers agrees with me. But what have you been talking about?"

Penford's face lost its solicitude and took on the old business wariness as he mentioned that retainer. As we began discussing it, something else soon emerged—that her business knowledge wasn't far behind his own. When we'd settled the matter to our mutual advantage, I ventured to congratulate her.

"Ah!" Penford told me. "What the wife doesn't know isn't worth knowing. She's what you might call the power behind the throne. We've come up a long way together, you know. If it hadn't been for her we'd neither of us be where we are today, and I don't care who hears me say it."

"Now, now, Martin!" She gave him that quiet, affectionate smile. "Mr. Travers doesn't want to hear all that nonsense about me. Not that it hasn't made me change my mind. I think I'll have some sherry after all. Just a little, Martin; not much."

She had been carrying a tiny handbag. Penford got beamingly to his feet and the moment his back was towards us she opened the handbag and quickly passed me something. It looked like a visiting card. Her finger went quickly to her lips and she shook her head. I slipped the card into my waistcoat pocket. Penford came back with a glass of sherry.

"There you are, love. Some more for you, Mr. Travers?"

I said it was too early in the day for a second, excellent sherry though it was.

"It ought to be," he said, and he'd probably have told me the price again if his wife hadn't spoken.

"You're married, then, Mr. Travers. Have you any children?" We talked what one might call family affairs for a minute or two and then there was a tap at the door and the elderly maid looked in. She said the car was ready. Penford glanced at his watch—a handsome gold one on a gold chain—and got to his feet.

"No idea it was so late. We'll have to go, my dear. I've got that conference. Which way are you going, Mr. Travers?"

I said I was going back to Broad Street. He was going almost past the door and he said he'd drop me there. I said goodbye to Rose Penford. I told her I hoped she'd be able to meet my wife some time. I was sure they'd get on well together.

We went out to the car—a not so old Rolls which Penford kept at a neighbouring garage with the chauffeur garage-provided. He began telling me about his wife and how worried he'd been recently about her health.

"Never had a thing wrong with her till a month or two ago. Now she's been getting those blinding headaches. Migraine, they call them. You don't tell me that going to a doctor wouldn't put it right."

All I could do was sympathise and then try to turn the conversation back to business. When at last he dropped me at the end of Broad Street, we'd agreed that he was to have a copy of the proposed retainer to submit to his board of directors.

"Just a formality," he said. "If it's all right with me, Mr. Travers, you can bet your life it'll be all right with them."

A grasp of his bony hand and that was that. The Rolls moved off. I walked a few yards along Broad Street and then took that visiting card from my waistcoat pocket. It was one of her own: just the name—Mrs. M. Penford—and the town address. It was what was on the back that made me stop in my tracks, and my fingers, in that old, nervous, instinctive trick of mine, were suddenly at my horn-rims. When I moved on, it was slowly, and because I wanted to think.

It wasn't long before I thought I could see the pattern. Rose Penford had known all about that job we had done for her husband's firm and had been impressed, as he had been, by what we'd achieved. I also gathered that he'd made his own surreptitious enquiries about us from time to time, hence that remark about my not being an ordinary detective: that is to say, the kind of enquiry agent of the popular mind. There's always a deal of snobbery in those like Penford who've come up the hard way.

And those sudden headaches of hers, with my diagnosis of the cause. That diagnosis had apparently been right. Worry of some sort, and, in view of what was written on the back of that visiting card, probably blackmail. As for the rest of it, she'd known of my visit and had written that card beforehand and had it ready in her bag. Maybe she'd listened outside the door to some of our conversation, and then she'd entered the room in order to give me a thorough scrutiny. If I hadn't passed muster, then that card would have stayed in her bag.

And what of the two people—Rose Penford and her husband? That he idolised her was as obvious as that he was proud of her. That she had been a major factor in their rise to wealth was as obvious, as was the fact that if her feelings towards him were well this side of idolatry they included that deep and somehow accepted affection that comes with the years of a happy marriage. Why then had she not confided in him? And especially as I had judged her to be, in her quiet unobtrusive way, the dominating figure.

Then I thought of something, or rather, remembered it: that knighthood that was said to be on the horizon. That Rose Penford would make an admirable Lady Penford I had no doubts. Did the threat, then, concern that likely knighthood? I didn't know. I could even smile ruefully and tell myself that there was nothing that I knew. Everything was sheer surmise. And that was when

I halted in my tracks once more at the Agency door and read again what was written on the back of that card.

> *Most Confidential.* Unless I am rung to the contrary I would urgently like you to be in the lounge of the Empress Hotel at eleven o'clock tomorrow morning.

# 2

# THE COWARD'S WAY

As I stood in the foyer at the Empress Hotel waiting for Rose Penford, an assistant manager all at once appeared.

"Mr. Travers?"

"Yes?" I said.

"Mrs. Penford is in the west lounge. This way, sir. And may I take your hat?"

It was a brisk morning and she was in the far corner by the fire. Hermes, who'd so suavely ushered me in, had as unobtrusively disappeared.

"How nice to see you again so soon," I said. She was looking the least bit nervous and it seemed up to me to put her at ease. "You often come here?"

"Martin's a director," she said as I drew one of those deep-sprung chairs alongside hers. "I often bring friends here."

"If you mean that I'm now one of them, then that's very charmingly put."

She gave me that quiet smile. Coffee would be coming at once, she said, and would I please smoke if I wished to. As a matter of fact the coffee came at that very moment and it was not till I'd finished the first small cup that I lighted a cigarette. She said she smoked only rarely.

"No headache this morning?"

"No," she said. "As soon as I gave you that card yesterday morning, everything was suddenly different."

"I'm glad," I said. "But before you tell me all about things, let me assure you that everything will be in the strictest confidence.

I won't dot the i's and cross the t's but just leave it at that. In other words, you can trust me."

She gave me a quick, almost startled look.

"How did you know that it was something that would—well—involve trust?"

"Because it's my job," I said. "And didn't your invitation mention confidence?"

"I'd forgotten," she said. "I was so flurried at the time."

"But you're not now?"

She smiled.

"Perhaps I'm even more so. I hate to guess what you'll think of me when you've heard what I'm going to tell you."

An elderly couple had come in, but even if we'd talked fairly loudly, they wouldn't have heard us from where they sat. That lounge was almost as big as a tennis court.

Maybe I haven't sufficiently impressed upon you that she was an extraordinary woman. I'd made a few more enquiries during the hours that had elapsed since I'd last seen her, and had learned a lot more about her business capabilities. Penford had achieved a considerable understatement when he had called her the power behind the throne. It was she, I was assured, who'd been the driving force in their earlier years, even if now she was content to sit back and leave him largely to hold the reins. And yet she didn't look that kind of woman. There was nothing hard about her. As far as I was concerned she was just a charming person: one with an attractive personality and an admirable taste.

"I don't think my opinion about you will change, whatever you tell me," I said.

"You're being too kind." The smile was still a bit nervous. "But I'd better begin before I lose what courage I have. What do you think about blackmail?"

It was just as sudden as that. It was a moment or two before I could look up.

"It's a horrible crime," I said. "The law looks at it that way too."

"I'm being blackmailed," she told me calmly. "This is the second time. The first time was just a part of it. There are two of us concerned, but I'm not able at the moment to mention the other one's name."

She must have caught something in my look.

"No," she said. "It's nothing to do with any affair with another man. Believe me or not, I was a virgin when Martin married me and I've never looked at another man since. And even though I was said to be very good-looking when I was young."

"I'm sure you were," I said. "But tell me all about it. Start at the very beginning. Let me have the whole background, and everything."

"I'm glad you said that," she told me. "It makes it easier and it's what I want to do. I was born in Balham. My father and mother were music-hall artists; used to do a singing and dancing act together. My mother was consumptive and she died when I was ten and my brother was eight. My father had always been a heavy drinker and he literally died of it a few years later, and it was up to me to keep things together. Long before he died I'd got a job in a London store. Even at fourteen I looked very much older and I was easily taken for sixteen or seventeen. We had a couple of rooms above a shop and one way and another I did keep things going, but all the time I wanted to do more. The stage was in my blood and I wanted to be a dancer. I was very lucky. The proprietress of a well-known dancing school happened to be talking to me at the store and she gave me an audition, as they call it now, and after that I used to go to her classes in the evenings. My brother wasn't very brainy but he had a good mechanical sense and as soon as he left school he got a job in a local garage."

She paused to smile.

"We thought we were on top of the world in those days. Even more so when I got a job in the chorus. My singing voice wasn't too good, though, and I made up my mind to have lessons, and at a dramatic school as well, but that needed money and I couldn't see where it was coming from. And that's where someone came in. I'll allude to him as Painter because he was an artist. He was struggling to make his way, too, and I actually met him through the proprietress of the dancing school. He was looking for a special kind of model for a very special job."

Her face had suddenly flushed and I wondered why.

"There was nothing reprehensible about it—just posing in various attitudes in the nude while he made sketches. He also had a male model—not while I was there, of course—and later he fused the various sketches into a series in which there were both of us. I don't know how he got the commission but they were for a wealthy Greek who wanted a series of panels in a special room on his yacht. They were pornographic: beastly, horrible things. I never actually saw them, of course, till a month or two ago. He—Painter, I mean—had given me a hint about them at the time but I wanted the money and he wanted the money and he said as far as he was concerned it was just a form of art and"—she shrugged her shoulders—"well, there it was. A year or two and I'd forgotten all about it, if you know what I mean. And then, a month or two ago, Painter rang me and asked to see me privately. I suppose you can guess what had happened?"

"Someone had acquired the yacht and the panels and had somehow traced them back to Painter?"

"Not so involved as that," she said. "Painter had kept the sketches: not the originals of me and the other model but far worse than that. The final sketches he had to submit to the Greek. The ones from which he painted the actual panels."

"But how did the blackmailer acquire them?"

"They must have been stolen at some time or other. Artists are just like other people. They hate parting with things, and in spite of how horrible they are they're still works of art according to Painter, and that's why, as he moved up in the world and acquired new studios, he took everything with him. The sketches were together in a large portfolio."

"When did he last see them?"

"He says he hasn't any idea."

There'd been a peculiar emphasis on that word *says*.

"But don't you believe him?"

She gave me a quick look.

"Well—no," she said. "He *must* have an idea who took them. There were other portfolios of purely artistic work and only that special one that was taken. And another thing: Why was *I* included in the blackmail? The likeness was magnificent at the time but I'm positive that no one who saw the sketches now could possibly imagine they were me—as I am now."

"Exactly! Painter, it seems to me, must have done some loose talking. And he probably showed the sketches to friends of his— say at a stag party. But tell me about the blackmailer's approach. When you first heard about it, and so on."

"It was actually at the very beginning of March," she said. "What happened, according to Painter, is that he was rung up by someone who sounded like an educated man who said he had the sketches and wanted a thousand pounds for them, if not he was going to send photographs to the Press and the selection committee of the Academy. Then he mentioned my name and said Painter had better get into touch with me because he wanted a thousand from me too: if not, photographs were going to the Press and to my husband."

"I see. And just one question, and please don't be annoyed about it. Did your brother know about your posing for Painter?"

"He didn't," she said. "He didn't even know Painter. And he was killed at Dunkirk."

I couldn't say anything. I think I grunted and that was all. "We—Painter and I—decided we'd better pay," she was going on. "We neither of us dared risk going to the police, especially as we'd been warned of the consequences. The instructions were to go to a certain room at a certain hotel at a certain time, so Painter went. The door was ajar and on the bed was the portfolio. He checked it and left the money as directed. It was a room with a private bathroom so the blackmailer was almost certainly in there out of sight."

I was shaking my head. I wanted to tell her it was the coward's way out, but somehow I hadn't the heart.

"But am I right in thinking it didn't end there?"

"It didn't," she said. "The day before yesterday Painter was rung again by the same man. He said he'd forgotten that photographs had already been made of all the sketches in case Painter made trouble and we didn't pay. All the photographs and the original plates would be handed over for another two thousand pounds. Detailed instructions would be sent later in the week—this week."

I gave another grunt—a big one: a Whartonian one.

"And that's how it'll go on," I said. "You'll pay and then he'll remember that there were some more photographs he'd forgotten all about. Why in God's name didn't you both go to the police? Or to a reputable investigator?"

"I know," she said. "Or rather, I don't know. I still don't know. But now I've come to you. Painter doesn't know it, by the way. But what can you do?"

"Maybe nothing—maybe quite a lot. But I'd have to see Painter and get some correct answers. Unless he was frank I wouldn't even dream of looking at the Case."

"And if he is frank?"

"Then I might get your blackmailer for you. It's the kind of thing we've handled before. But Painter's got to be frank. The least idea that he's holding something back and I'll refuse to handle it. You've got to make that absolutely clear."

"I will," she said. "And perhaps I may be able to ring you. Where should it be?"

I gave her an Agency card and wrote my private telephone number on the back. She put it carefully in her handbag and eased herself forward from the deep chair.

"I'm more than grateful to you. You wouldn't believe how much you've set my mind at rest."

"That's fine," I said. "I only hope we'll be allowed to finish the job."

"Perhaps I'd better go first," she told me. "But don't be anxious if I don't ring. It may take some time."

Her head was high as she walked with that sure poise across the room to the foyer. As soon as she was out of sight I followed. I hurriedly collected my hat from the cloakroom, and as I came to the main swing doors I saw a commissionaire ushering her into a taxi. As it moved off I came out. I was amazingly lucky. Another taxi was just decanting a fare and I hopped in at once.

"See that taxi ahead, the last on the left in the queue at the traffic lights? Keep just behind it. Wherever it goes, you go too."

Two other cars passed us as we moved off. The traffic lights had changed but we had our taxi always in view. At the next traffic lights we actually eased up with only one car between us. And that was how we kept till the fork at Knightsbridge. There we went left towards South Kensington and the car in front of us went right. Another three minutes and the taxi in front of us turned left into Wensum Road, one of those high-class residential oases that are a persistence rather than a survival. Then the front taxi began to slow. The driver's hand went out for a right turn. I tapped on the window and indicated that we, too, were to slow. We'd been about fifty yards behind and as the driver of that front taxi opened the door to let Rose Penford out, I got the number of the house.

We went slowly on. I glanced back and the other taxi had moved round and was cruising back. That was when I saw the postman emptying the pillar-box.

"Just a minute," I told the driver when I got out.

I crossed the road to the postman.

"Excuse me, but is Sir James Wood still living at Number 47?"

"Number 47," he said reflectively. He shook his head and smiled. "No one of that name there, sir—not unless he's only staying there. A Mr. Sigott's living there, and has done the last few years."

"Sigott?" I said. "I wonder if I know him."

"He's a painter, sir. A very famous one, so they say. A Royal Academician or whatever they call it."

"I see. Which means I was mistaken about Sir James living there."

I pulled out some loose change and gave him half-a-crown. He protested it wasn't necessary, but took it. I thanked him again, went back to my taxi and told the driver to take me to my club.

The club was a much better headquarters for the job in hand than the Agency. I rang Norris and warned him about a possible telephone call for me and then I rang my wife in case Rose Penford should decide to call my private number. After that, on the strength of Penford's handsome cheque, I took a gin and tonic to the library and started in on the reference books.

I learned quite a lot about Brian Sigott, A.R.A. His training had been at the South London School of Art and from there he'd won a scholarship that took him to the Atelier Rambaud in Paris. His age was now fifty-two. He was also now a portrait painter and there was quite an imposing list of those who had sat to him. He also occasionally painted *genre* and conversation pieces. His "Saloon Bar" was in a famous American collection and his "Mannequin" had been acquired by Melbourne. That last seemed to strike a sort of bell and I began looking up the volumes of *The Royal Academy, Illustrated*.

There that picture was, and the year 1953. It was one of the years when I'd visited the Academy and I remembered that picture well. From the monochrome of the reproduction I could even recall the colouring of the original. The central figure was the mannequin, dressed in a costume that had looked to me more Spanish than English. She was a red-haired, beautifully complexioned woman in the ripe and luscious twenties. The hair I remembered especially well: it was a dark red, the colour of Spanish mahogany. On the handsome face was a flaunting of amused indifference and a curious suggestion of sex. That touch of satire was repeated in the looks, frankly lascivious, of the men in the background and, even more ironically, in the blank faces of the women who were trying themselves to be indifferent. And I remembered that there was something about the face and posture of the mannequin that recalled a picture I had seen elsewhere. A few days later I had stumbled across it in the National Gallery: "Dona Isabel Cobos de Porcel," by Goya.

Lunch had been on for some time but I managed to get a seat. Just as I was coming up to the dessert course, I caught sight of Charles Muhler, the seascape painter, and he was just about to leave the table.

I knew him as well as I knew most members of long standing, so I abandoned the rest of my meal and managed to be at his heels as he was making for the lounge.

"Haven't seen you for quite a time," I said at his ear.

He looked round, blinked a bit, and then smiled.

"How are you, Travers? You're a bit of a stranger, too."

I asked him if he'd take port with me and we settled down in a couple of corner seats. Five minutes or so and I was able to get in my question.

"Lucky for me I ran across you," I said. "I've been rather worried."

"Nothing serious, I trust?"

"Not perhaps serious but perhaps a bit worrying. I wonder if I might put something up to you in confidence?"

"My dear fellow—do."

"It's like this," I said, voice lowered. "A certain society with whom I'm connected wishes to make a presentation portrait. Money, by the way, is no great object. One of the donors suggested Brian Sigott and I'm supposed to submit a confidential report."

"Sigott's a good man," Muhler told me. "You couldn't do better. But I ought to warn you that he does have that rather malicious streak about him. What I'm getting at is that unless he finds the subject sympathetic your society might find itself landed with something highly unacademic."

"Thanks for the tip," I said. "I'll bear it in mind."

"By the way, I can pass on a bit of fairly confidential information about Sigott," he went on. "He's likely to be commissioned to do a portrait of a most important personage which is intended for one of the Commonwealth Parliament Houses. I'm open to bet he won't try any monkey tricks with that."

"What's he like in himself?"

"A queer sort of devil; like a good many more on what I'd call the genius fringe. Very good-looking in a florid way. An excellent bedside manner, and he can be perfectly charming." He leaned sideways, hand side-cupping his mouth. "A great one, so they tell me, for the ladies."

I nodded knowingly. And then a mutual acquaintance came up and no more was said about Brian Sigott. Not that I needed any more. The blackmailer, it seemed to me, had chosen two excellent victims: one with a husband who was going to be knighted and the other who was going to paint a royal portrait. The slightest breath of scandal about either and a couple of geese would be cooked. And in that same context it also struck me that if—a very big if—I were called in on the Case, then I already had some capital clues that could lead to the identity of the actual blackmailer.

At half-past two I was back at Broad Street and I hadn't been there ten minutes before there was a private call for me.

"Mr. Travers?"

"Speaking."

"How are you, Mr. Travers? I'm Brian Sigott. A mutual friend has mentioned that you may be able to help us in rather a tricky matter. You catch the allusion?"

"Perfectly," I said. The approach was as suave as his voice.

"Good," he said. "I think you were also given a hint that the matter was urgent and I'm wondering when you could come along here and see me."

"When do you suggest?"

"Well—" he paused for a slight, apologetic cough, "what about at once? I happen to be free."

"I don't see why not," I told him. "Say in half an hour's time."

"Capital, capital!"

In the same hearty tone he gave me the address and told me how to get to it. Just as he was about to ring off, I had a question for him.

"Just one last thing, Mr. Sigott. Did our mutual friend tell you the conditions upon which I'd take the case?"

That seemed to nonplus him for a moment. Then he cleared his throat. The tone was only a trifle less hearty.

"Indeed, yes."

"That's fine then," I said. "Just as well to have a perfectly clear understanding before we begin to discuss things."

There wasn't a lot of time to spare but I managed to grab a taxi at the end of the street, and at once I began jotting down a few leading questions. You can learn quite a lot from a voice over the telephone when you've been in the game as long as I have, and my idea was that Brian Sigott would turn out to be a highly plausible customer. Even Rose Penford, in a calculated understatement, had said he'd known more than he'd been prepared to divulge, even to herself.

The notes so preoccupied me that I was quite surprised when the taxi came to a halt. I glanced at my watch and it was almost to the minute of that half-hour I'd suggested to Sigott. As for the half-hour or so that was to follow, I wondered just what sort of a half-hour it'd be. In fact, I was quite anticipating it all as I walked up the three wide stone steps and rang the bell.

# 3

## LOST CLIENT

GORGEOUS is an extremely overworked word as applied to blondes but I can think of no epithet more embracing for the one who opened the door and ushered me into Sigott's drawing-room. Perhaps, too, I ought to beg his pardon about that room: he probably regarded it as a *salon*.

"Mr. Travers?" she said.

"Er—yes."

"Mr. Sigott is expecting you," she told me, and as if she'd expected to be politely stared at. "Will you leave your hat and coat here?"

Everything—or almost everything—was just right about her: height, figure, face and walk. It was the voice that didn't score full marks. I think sultry is the usual term for it. Her own idea was probably that it had a kind of seduction.

"Do make yourself at home," she told me. "Mr. Sigott will be here in a moment. The cigarettes are in that box."

I wondered what her status was in that house: secretary, receptionist, model, or all three? Or was she just a niece? A second wife? His first wife, according to the reference books, had died in 1952. But she surely couldn't be a wife or she'd have spoken of Sigott as "my husband".

I looked round the room and I knew it was one of the most charming I had ever seen. Sigott, I was sure, must have made the devil of a lot of money in his time, but I hadn't guessed that he'd spent some of it so wisely. Everything about it was good, from the Goyer Louis XV clock to the William and Mary secretaire. The Chinese carpet was that rare apricot with a single black spray. The water-colours were eighteenth- or early nineteenth-century English, and the one above the Adam mantelpiece was a David Cox. A pair of Colebrookdale figures that flanked the clock had their bocage absolutely unchipped, and I was having a covetous look at them when Sigott suddenly came into the room.

"Afraid you caught me in the act," I said. "Another minute and I'd probably have pocketed these and made my getaway."

He chuckled throatily as he held out his hand.

"Quite charming, aren't they? You a collector?"

"In a modest way. I couldn't begin to cope with a room like this."

That pleased him but I hoped he didn't think it had been offered by way of flattery. I wondered what he'd say if I ventured to express the personal opinion that the room, for all its superbly managed charm, was—like himself—just a little too much on the handsome side. He and that room certainly went well together. He too had an air of distinction. He was tallish, with a profile that was Greek—or perhaps Greco-Semitic. His lips were full and sensual. His hair, nicely greying at the temples, had just the right length and backward sweep, and the little side-whiskers that ran alongside the ears lent another touch of the romantico-artistic. His voice, expanding now, as it were, about that room, had just a little more of the unctuous bonhomie that had reached me over the telephone.

We all have our sudden allergies, and Sigott was one of mine. I didn't like him and, what was more important, I doubted if I'd trust him. And something was all at once telling me to make a new kind of approach. I hoped my smile was faun-like rather than a leer.

"By the way, you have a nice taste in secretaries."

He gave me a quick look. He decided that I, too, was a man of the world.

"It doesn't cost any more to have them decorative, you know."

"Give me the tip if she leaves you," I said. "I could do with a bit of decoration round my own office."

He laughed.

"You sounded a pretty grim sort of cuss on the telephone, but, do you know, I think we're going to understand each other. About this business of mine, for instance."

"If you mean the circumstances under which you did that series of panels, then I certainly understand," I told him. "I don't say a lot of people wouldn't."

"You'd like to see the drawings? They might have some influence on your ideas."

So there I was, hoist with my own petard. Heaven knows I have plenty of vices but a taste in pornography isn't one of them.

"A quick look might help," I said, and he merely went across the room, lifted a cushion from an easy chair and there was the portfolio beneath it. He drew up a low table between us and he slowly showed me the drawings, turning each over after a moment or two of inspection. I tried to let myself see them and yet not see them, though even like that they were to be a dirty smear across my inward eye for many days to come. They were colour-washed and the sheer bravura took one's breath away. I could understand why he'd never had the heart to destroy them. All the same, I thought he'd been a fool to sign them.

"What mastery of drawing!" I said. "Refreshing in these days when to draw is to be artistically damned."

We talked art for a minute or two and I was thinking that Rose Penford had been right when she said that the model for those drawings would never be recognised as her present self.

"But about this problem," I said. "I'd like you to ignore the fact that I've seen our mutual friend and tell me the whole thing from the very beginning. Every single detail about it from the word go."

His account varied in no important particular from that which I'd heard from Rose Penford. He gave the same reasons—or almost—for not having gone to the police.

"If it had been a question of myself only, I might have done," he said. "But there was our friend. That complicated everything. And that's the reason why you've been called in now, as it were. There just mustn't be any risk."

I explained most patiently about the attitude of the police towards blackmail, and that their secrecy, like my own, would be that of the confessional. He and our friend would not even have to appear in court.

"Believe me, I'm giving you the best advice," I said. "The fact that that advice would rob me of a client ought to convince you of my sincerity."

"No," he said abruptly. "I'm not having the police brought into it. I respect your views but you've also got to respect mine."

"Right," I said. "Let's get down to the question of who stole these drawings. What ideas have you?"

When I say that I knew at once that he was lying, please take the assertion in the right way. George Wharton boasts that he can smell a liar a mile off: a pretty broad claim but with quite a lot of truth. Most of his life, like my own, has been taken up with the observation and questioning of our fellow men.

"The whole thing's a mystery," he said. "How they got into the wrong hands, God alone knows."

"Then let's get down to brass tacks," I said. "We'll begin by calling our mutual friend by her name, and I'm dead certain that no one would ever recognise the woman of those drawings as Mrs. Penford." There was something he wanted to say but I stopped him dead. "Let me finish. Until only a very few years ago, she was a nonentity, living in the Midlands. Even now she's a nonentity by a good many standards. She never has her picture in the glossy illustrateds. Her portrait hasn't been the picture of the year. She's just a woman—a charming woman, admittedly—of humble origins who's the wife of a successful business man of almost similar origins. Then who could possibly have known that she was the model for those drawings?"

He clicked his tongue impatiently.

"My dear fellow, haven't I told you, the whole thing's a mystery?"

"Very well: let's try to arrive at some facts. The drawings were stolen. When did you last see them? When, in other words, was the last moment you knew they were in your possession?"

He assumed a pose of thought. That was stupid. The question was so obvious that long ago he must have done all the thinking and known the answer.

"I can't rightly say," he told me at last. "I know they were here and intact when I came here. That was eleven years ago. I seem vaguely to remember noticing them again just before my wife died. That was just over three years ago."

"A blunt question. Had your wife seen them?"

He drew himself up in the chair.

"Good God, Travers! What sort of a swine do you think I am?"

"Then your wife's eliminated," I told him imperturbably. "Who were the members of your household since, say, just before her death, when you last knew the drawings were here?"

There was the same pause: the same pose of thought: the same wonder how to conceal.

"No one who isn't beyond suspicion," he said. "My house-keeper is still with us. There've been changes—not many—of daily women but they were never allowed in the studio."

"Models?"

"Just the one." He said it as if he wished I hadn't put the question. "Margaret. She was also my receptionist. She was the model for one of my things you may or may not have seen—'The Mannequin'."

"I did see it," I said. "A superb bit of work. But surely she could have taken the drawings? Why, for instance, did she leave you?"

"She married," he said. "I'll own up frankly that she let me badly down. She sprang this marriage suddenly on me. Simply brought the man here one afternoon: introduced him as her husband and announced they were sailing the following day for Australia where he had an uncle." He shook his head in a sad sort of way. "I was furious at the time. But I ought to have known. She'd been acting in a most peculiar way for some time—not turning up and so on."

"You've heard from her from Australia?"

"Hardly time yet, also I'm not likely to. I told you we didn't part on very pleasant terms. She left me with a half-finished oils on my hands with only the actual figure to complete."

"She knew about the drawings?"

He looked so horrified that I hastily begged the question. "But of course she wouldn't. Would you mind showing me the studio and where they were when you saw them last?" The airy, spacious studio was built out at the back of the actual house. It was little different from others I'd seen: the same tools of the trade and the same stacked canvases round the walls. There was a fireplace with cupboards at each side that ran up to the ceiling. Sigott went straight to the farther cupboard and opened the door of the lower half. It was cluttered up with portfolios and loose drawings.

"This is where the missing portfolio was," he said. "On that shelf, under a couple of other portfolios."

Curious, wasn't it? A few minutes before he couldn't tell me when he'd last seen the portfolio. He'd had to arrive at it like a man emerging from a mist. And now he knew just where the portfolio had been.

"If Margaret, the model, is really in Australia, then it's obvious she can't be the blackmailer," was what I said. "How long ago was this marriage?"

"Last February."

"What was her name?"

"Mann. Margaret Mann."

"And her husband's name?"

That sad shake of the head came again.

"Believe it or not, I don't know. I was so furious that I didn't ask her. I believe she called him Jack. A tall, showy-looking character. Looked as though he played in a dance band."

"Was she the kind of person who *could* have taken that portfolio?"

There was again that irritating pose of thought. He was of the opinion—his exact words—that she might possibly have taken something of value in a moment of temptation or covetousness, just as anyone might. But even if she had rummaged among those shelves and come across the portfolio, she couldn't possibly have thought it valuable.

"It would have disgusted her," he said. "The first sight of those drawings and she'd have blushed to the roots of her hair and shoved the portfolio back."

"Another blunt question," I said. "Did you ever sleep with her?"

A sudden red ran across his pink cheeks.

"Is that sort of question necessary?"

"We're both human," I told him. "What's so queer about a widower, and one so presentable as yourself—"

"It's objectionable," he said. "I can be blunt, too."

"Fine," I said. "So let's say that Margaret didn't take the portfolio. What about your present—whatever she is."

"Unthinkable."

"And no workmen in at any time? No one but yourself and sitters and your housekeeper, if it was she who did the necessary cleaning?"

"No workmen. And my housekeeper is absolutely reliable."

"Looks as if we're faced with what you called a mystery," I told him. "But I have to go on being blunt. Just between ourselves, did you ever show those drawings to any close friends?"

"Never." He made it emphatic but that didn't make it the easier to believe.

"Well, that's that then. And I don't have to ask you if you ever mentioned Mrs. Penford's name. That's the really fantastic thing about this business, don't you agree? There are the drawings out of sight for years and then suddenly someone gets hold of them and knows at once that the woman model is now Mrs. Penford."

"I know," he said. "It's as you say—fantastic."

"You kept in touch with her over the years?"

"Heavens, no!" he said. "I knew she'd married and I actually sent a present. That was ages ago, and since then there've been no contacts."

I thought things over for a minute or two and his eyes hardly ever left my face.

"This late model of yours," I said at last. "I can't help thinking she's somehow concerned. She left you suddenly last February and she hadn't been gone long before you were being black-mailed. Where did she live?"

"Well, here for the last two years. She was more than a model, you know. My housekeeper was quite an efficient chap-eron—if one was necessary."

I could have said, "Chaperon, my foot!" What I did do was to ask him to tell me all he knew about her. He said it'd be a waste of time. He was positive she'd had no hand in the affair. But since I was insisting, all he could tell me was that he'd run across her, as one does, and had been struck by the looks of her, and that was that. She'd also shown herself sensible and level-headed and he'd been delighted to employ her as receptionist and occasional model.

To my mind it was obvious that he was covering up. I decided to apply the acid test.

"Would you allow me to have a few minutes' private talk with your housekeeper?"

That tied him in a knot. You could almost see his brain tick-ing over as he hunted for the right answer.

"But why?" he said. "It's lunacy to think she had anything to do with it."

"I'll take your word for it," I said. "I wanted to talk to her about Margaret. Women are the ones to question about women."

He'd known from the beginning what I'd meant.

"Believe me, it's quite unnecessary," he said. "It's preposterous to think of Margaret being concerned in anything like that. Besides, she's now in Australia."

"And you've no further clues? No hints, no nothing?"

"Nothing. I've told you all I know."

"The devil you have!" I thought to myself. But we'd been moving towards the studio door and now we went along the short corridor to the hall. He opened the drawing-room door to usher me in again, but I stayed where I was.

"Will it suit you if I ring you a little later and give you our decision about taking the Case?"

He looked quite startled.

"But what is there to decide? You've heard everything. And seen everything."

"Just our way of doing business," I said. "After all, we might be too busy. And there's always the question of what it might cost you."

"Money's no real object," he assured me. "It'll be set against a possible saving of a couple of thousand pounds."

"Then we'll leave it like that," I said. "I'll give you a ring before six o'clock after I've talked things over with my manager." I had to pick up a quick hand. "Nothing to worry about there. He's implicitly reliable and he'll be given no names."

There was a sound of a door opening. The blonde appeared.

"It's all right, Laura," Sigott told her impatiently, and she disappeared. He helped me on with my overcoat and saw me to the door.

I didn't look back when I'd gone down the steps to the street. I didn't even look for a taxi but walked slowly towards Knightsbridge where I found a tea-shop. I was there for about twenty minutes and then I did take a taxi, back to Bond Street. Long before I got there I knew that I wouldn't handle that Sigott business whatever I was paid. In my considered judgment he was practically sure who the blackmailer was. I was almost as sure that calling me in was merely his way of placating Rose Penford. I was even prepared to believe that in the matter of that first bit of blackmail, the *total* demand had been a thousand pounds and that she had therefore paid it all. The second demand might be the same, or even bogus. And the last thing of which I was sure was that the one thing he didn't want was for the blackmailer to be found.

So as soon as I'd settled one or two other items of business I went home and rang Sigott from there. I said that owing to pressure of business we were regretfully unable to handle so complicated a Case. He tried to be most indignant. He even rang off in the middle of my repeated advice to consult the police.

There must have been a hurried conference the following morning between Sigott and Rose Penford because she rang me at about eleven o'clock at the office and suggested a meeting. I said that was impossible for the moment and asked her to speak as freely as she could.

"I'll come straight to the point," she said. "You've turned down Mr. Sigott, but will you undertake it for me?"

"Frankly—no," I said, "and for this reason: When you hinted that he wasn't being frank even with you, you were right. He was an enormous way from being frank with me, and that's putting it generously. And if I worked for you, then I'd still have to go to him for information. He's the only one who has any. In other words, I'd still really be working for him."

"Yes," she said heavily, "I see that. But this morning he was rung again by You-Know-Who and the money has to be paid to-morrow."

"Listen," I said. "I never gave more serious advice in my life. And it's this: tell your husband everything. Ask him to go with you to the police. Go straight to Scotland Yard. I'll give you the name of a certain Chief-Inspector."

"I can't," she said. "I know you're right, but I just can't. But thank you. Thank you very much. . . ."

There was a kind of trailing off of the voice as she hung up, and I guessed she'd been pretty near to tears. But what else could I have done? It was one of those moments when I wished that I too had been free to turn the whole thing over to the police.

I heard nothing else from her or Sigott, and during the next few weeks I remembered that rather distressing business only at rare intervals. Then something brought it back to my mind.

An old friend from the country was spending a long week-end with us, and on the Saturday afternoon we three went to the summer exhibition at Burlington House. It was a thundery day at the end of June and I remember that we had to take a taxi there because of a storm that suddenly broke. I'd thought of the Sigott affair when Bernice had first broached the idea of spending the afternoon at the Academy, and as soon as we got there I was consulting my catalogue for Sigott's pictures. He had three portraits, each of distinguished people—a bishop, a Colonial Governor and a famous composer. That Royal portrait wasn't there. What was also there, in the place of honour in another room, was a picture of a woman, half-asleep, half-awake, on a chaise longue. It was called "Laura Resting". It was a magnificent piece of work, pure Sigott and yet hauntingly reminiscent of Renoir.

What intrigued me most about it, of course, was that in spite of the pose and the lighting, I recognised the Laura at once. I'd stood so long looking at it that my wife, who had moved on to another room, came back to look for me, and I rejoined her before she could ask awkward questions. Among other things that I'd been thinking was that Sigott hadn't lost any time. The model, Margaret, had left him in February and Laura couldn't have taken her place before the end of that month or the beginning of March. And yet, in spite of other commissions, he'd been able to send that picture in at the appointed time.

I'd also felt a vague something else. A model is a model, if you know what I mean. Sigott could have painted her in any pose whatever, clothed or in the nude, and yet there seemed something elusive about that picture: something I ought to be gathering from it: some private information it had to give. But I didn't know what. On the face of it, it was just a magnificently designed and superbly executed painting of a blonde in a diaphanous kind of deshabille that let the flesh tones come subtly through. One bare arm was carelessly behind the head so that the breast beneath it was revealed. But there was nothing sensual about it. As far as I was concerned it was scarcely sensuous. It was the sheer bravura of the thing that carried one away.

For some weeks after that I again forgot the Sigott affair. There was just one faint reverberation towards the end of July. I'd been out on a job of work and the taxi had dropped me in Oxford Street. I was meeting my wife in a certain store there and as I went through the swing doors I came practically face to face with Rose Penford. Her face gave a violent flush but she looked clean through me, and a second or two later she was out on the pavement. She had seen me—there wasn't a doubt of that—but the last thing she had wanted was to speak to me.

If that told me anything it was that she hadn't taken my advice and gone with her husband to the police. And so, thanks to that moral cowardice, and maybe also the trickery of Sigott, some scoundrel was the richer by another couple of thousand pounds.

# THEME II
# LARCENY

## 4
## ALYSIA RIMMELL

ONE evening towards the end of July I was rung up by John Hill of United Assurance.

"Can you possibly see me here in the morning at about ten?"

United Assurance is our most valuable retainer. I said I'd be there.

"Alone, or shall I bring Hallows?"

Hallows is our best man. Hill knew him well.

"It'd do no harm," he said. "It isn't an arson case, by the way. Just a matter of theft or burglary. Several queer points about it."

In the morning Hallows and I turned up on time at Lombard Street. We were virtually three old friends, so coffee was brought in and cigarettes were alight before he'd began telling us about the Case. He knew the way I liked to have a Case outlined and he made a good job of presenting the facts.

"The scene's Hanway Gardens, S.W.," he said. "Do you happen to know it?"

"Yes, sir," Hallows said. "A block of flats just back of The Mall."

"That's right. About thirty years old but fine-quality flats. The client has one of the very best—Number Three, which, of course, is on the ground floor. Her husband had a considerable financial interest in the flats, which was why, when he died at their house in Effingham Square, she was able to move in at Hanway Gardens. His name, by the way, was Major-General Rimmell, and the widow is Alysia Rimmell. She's now an old lady of eighty-six. You're going to see her: appointment's at eleven o'clock, and I warn you that she'll surprise you. She's as spry as few women are at seventy. A little woman but very much of an old war-horse.

"The first peculiar thing about the affair is this: the policy was taken out some thirty years ago by the husband. There was a list of jewellery which is unimportant, comparatively, since the value isn't a great deal. With one exception—what I'll call a Russian Cross. It was a cross of some five inches by three given to a great-great-grandparent by the then Czar of Russia: solid gold and set with five very large diamonds in the main stem and one each side on the cross stem, making seven in all. When I tell you that each is approximately four carats, you have some idea of their present-day value. Not that that affects us since we pay on the terms of the original policy. And that, believe me, isn't anything to be laughed at.

"I'm not going to tell you too much because I want you to approach this case with an absolutely open mind. All the same there are a few facts you ought to know beforehand."

He glanced at his notes.

"The first is that all we have is a list as drawn up for the purposes of the policy thirty years ago by our appraiser. He's been dead some ten years now and he's the only one who saw the cross. The General saw it, but he's dead. Mrs. Rimmell didn't see it at the time. She can't remember when it was that she did see it last. Make a note to ask her about that.

"The next thing is that she's that rare bird, a woman who isn't interested in jewellery. All she wears is utilitarian stuff of what one might call the usual kind. There was a safe at the house in Effingham Square and all the valuable stuff was kept in it and, believe it or not, not in cases but wrapped up as one wraps up silver, in green baize. The cross was kept separate and it was also wrapped in baize and tied with tape. When Mrs. Rimmell was leaving the house after her husband's death she didn't remove any of the wrappings but simply transferred the whole lot to the bottom of a trunk, which went into the bedroom at the flat. I should explain that that flat was unfurnished and she transferred to it a lot of her furniture and pictures and so on and sold the rest. There was a policy on that which was adjusted at the time. Not that it's at all important. In fact it's of no importance at all."

He consulted his notes again.

"Oh, yes—something that *is* important. You'll get the family history from Mrs. Rimmell but what you should know is that she has a grandson, a Herbert Rimmell, who's a Canadian. He came over here to see her and she wanted him to see the jewellery. He was thinking of getting married and she wondered if she should give some or all of it to his wife. When she rummaged at the bottom of the trunk among a whole lot of other things she didn't want but kept, she discovered the jewellery wasn't there. In other words she hasn't the faintest idea when it was stolen. That was two days ago. I saw her yesterday and got the facts which I've given you. You and Hallows are seeing her at eleven this morning, as I said."

"And that's all?"

He gave a curious kind of smile.

"Oh, no. I've left out the biggest mystery of all. It's something I'd like you to discover for yourselves, then you'll approach it with open minds."

"You're not giving us even a hint?"

"You won't need one," he said. "Ask everything you can think of about that cross and the mystery'll hit you clean in the eye."

"I wonder," I said to Hallows. "Strikes me this chap's toying with the idea of getting rid of the B.S.D.A. and hiring another firm. He wants us to fall down on this puzzle of his so that he'll have a good excuse. We allowed to put any questions here and now, John?"

"Depends what they are."

"Then who had access to the flat?"

"They're service flats," he said. "The staff are above suspicion."

"Friends and callers?"

"A woman of that age hasn't many surviving friends," he told us dryly.

"Which leaves us with only the grandson. Had she mentioned the jewellery to him?"

"No. You can take that as an undeniable fact. It was to be a surprise."

"The trunk was locked?"

"Yes."

I grunted.

"Like getting blood out of a stone," I told him, and got to my feet. "Maybe the old lady'll be more communicative."

He gave me that wry smile again.

"Your problem'll be to stop her, not to start her. And I hope that cheers you."

He walked with us to the lift. He held it for a minute for a final word.

"You'll spot the real problem all right. Just give me a ring when you're sure."

Hill had been pretty accurate in his description of Alysia Rimmell. As far as my experience went she was unique. She was about five feet tall and I think I could have lifted her with a hand, but her back was straight and she was as perky as a humming-bird. Her skin had the patina of age, but the shrewd black eyes missed never a thing, and while she prattled away in that old world, musical-box treble of hers, the thin wrinkled hands were all the while making little gestures. Eighty-six she might be, but if ever a woman looked a certainty for the balance of fourteen more, it was she.

She was wearing a plain grey dress with a stiff sort of collar that practically touched her chin, and I noticed at once that she was wearing no jewellery except a wedding ring and an old, but far from valuable, cameo brooch. But the room in which we sat hadn't that restraint: one could only call it a riot. No Victorian drawing-room of my youth was so cluttered up and crowded and, as I'd made my way to the chair she'd indicated, I'd kept my arms tight for fear of sweeping some portrait or knicknack or other off the series of spindly tables and what-nots.

And Hill had also been right about her volubility. I suppose it was a kind of garrulity of age: in any case if I reproduced each word we heard in the long hour we spent in that flat, it would run to a couple more chapters.

"Such a nice man, Mr. Hill," she told us. "And you are insurance agents? Or are you the police again? But no: the police were here the day before yesterday."

There was no real snobbery about her. It was just that she'd never really got beyond the dim, Victorian days when people like police and insurance agents came in by the kitchen door. I didn't bother to create any particular status for Hallows and myself: I merely said we'd come to hear all about the robbery and try to assess the value of what was missing.

"The police found signs of a forcible entry, Mrs. Rimmell?"

"There wasn't any," she said. "And what you must remember, young man, is that no one knew when the robbery took place. It might have been at any time after I arrived here."

"Exactly," I said. "That's an excellent point."

"There's no need to be condescending about it," she told me archly. "People of my generation were taught to use our eyes and ears. Now my father. . . ."

"Can we see the actual chest in which the jewellery was kept?" I managed to ask her at last.

There were two bedrooms, and, of course, she had to show us the spare one first.

"My grandson, Herbert—he's named after *my* father—sometimes uses this room," she said. "He calls himself a Canadian but of course he's English. You can't change your nationality by simply going to another country."

"Your only grandson?"

As soon as I said it I thought what a fool I was to give her so good an excuse to wander from the point. As a matter of fact I was lucky. The family history she gave us was to be mighty important.

She'd married Cuthbert Rimmell in 1890 when she was twenty-one, and her only son—named Cuthbert after his father— married in 1926 when he was thirty-four, and his only son was born the following year. Cuthbert had been killed during the retreat at Dunkirk and within a year his widow had married a Canadian and had gone at once to Canada with him, taking the fourteen-year-old boy with her.

"A most unfortunate marriage, my son's," she told us. "An impossible woman of very questionable class. Indeed, if poor Cuthbert had not been killed, my husband would have given him grounds for divorce. She was that kind of woman, you know. Actually carrying on—you'll excuse the phrase—with a Canadian even while Cuthbert was still out there serving his country. We had definite information to that effect. An abominable woman!

"But of course we missed the boy when they went to Canada. In a way. He was just about to leave prep. school—not the kind of school we'd have picked for him, I may say—but I was going to insist that he went to Wellington. All the Rimmells went to Wellington. She was spoiling him, too, and sometimes he could be very unpleasant. But that's all different now. He's broken away from her and standing on his own feet. He insisted on coming over here to see me and he broke with his mother because of it. Don't you think that was very brave of him? Not that the Rimmells ever lacked courage."

She might have been talking about a boy instead of a grown man. I asked if he were still in England.

"He just came over last year for a week or two but now he's here again," she told us. "A wonderful change in him, too, and looking just like his father. He's quite an important figure in the fur trade, so he spends quite a lot of time in Manchester, but he's in town at the moment. And he's going to marry a very charming Canadian girl when he goes home. From one of the oldest Canadian families. Remind me to show you her photograph."

We managed to see the other bedroom. It, too, was pretty well cluttered up. Over her bed was a large oils of her late husband in full war-paint, and we had to hear all about him. As for his death, it had followed a stroke, from which he'd never fully recovered.

"Such a mercy," she told us. "He lingered on for almost two months but never really regained consciousness. I don't know what I'd have done if it hadn't been for the nurse we had. Dr. Kossack—he was a neighbour of ours in Effingham Square—recommended her to me and she was quite a godsend. She even helped me with all the tiresome work of moving my belongings here. A real treasure of a woman. I do wish I hadn't lost sight of her."

And so at last to the travelling trunk which looked to me to be as old as its owner. It was a huge affair; stout leather with the bottom and semi-circular top reinforced with wooden slats. There was a strong leather handle at each end and it was fastened with two locks at the front.

"I always keep the key here," she said, and produced it from the drawer of a small, Victorian bureau. "Perhaps you'll open it for me. It sometimes goes a bit stiff."

It went fairly smoothly for me. When I lifted the lid I saw it was absolutely crammed with a host of things: curtains, lengths of material, linen sheets, embroidered pillow cases, various furs and heaven knew what else.

"And where was the jewellery actually kept?"

"Here," she said. "In the very bottom. In this corner. I remember distinctly that's where we put it. Later on, when I was settled, I repacked and I put it back in exactly the same place."

"And when you opened the chest last and discovered the jewellery had gone, did you notice whether things were disturbed?"

She'd noticed nothing. In any case the discovery of the loss had been a great shock to her. What a lucky thing it was, she said, that she hadn't mentioned the jewellery to her grandson. Think of his disappointment if he'd known beforehand that she was intending to give the jewellery, on his marriage, to his wife.

"The Russian Cross," I said. "Will you describe it to me?"

She said she hadn't actually seen it for a good many years. It was far too ugly to wear and was regarded only as an heirloom.

"You've never actually worn it?"

"Only once," she said. "My husband and I were going to a fancy-dress ball: he as a Russian general and I as his wife. It was—let me see—in 1893, just after Cuthbert was born."

The beady black eyes suddenly opened wide.

"What was your name again? Curious, isn't it, how one forgets names."

"My name's Travers."

"Travers. Of course. You're the one Mr. Hill said I was to give the photograph to."

"Photograph?"

"Yes, the one that was taken the day after that ball." She gave a little tinkly laugh. "Apparently there's some mystery about it. Mr. Hill seemed quite puzzled. He said it didn't show the actual diamonds."

The photograph, faded with age, was handy enough in another drawer of the same bureau. It was what used to be called—and for all I know maybe still is—a cabinet, half-length. I put my glass over it, then passed photograph and glass to Hallows. There wasn't a doubt about it. That cross that hung by a thin chain from the neck of the very lovely young woman was without the seven diamonds that should have been inset in the gold. All one could see were the sockets that had once held them.

"Amazing!" I said. "You wore the cross yourself when the photograph was taken. Didn't you notice the absence of the diamonds?"

"I'm sure they were there!"

What could I do but shrug my shoulders? What could I say? Photographs don't lie and so there was a fact staring me in the face. There'd been no diamonds when the photograph was taken, and yet she insisted that there were. Was hers just some naïve denial of some kind of fraud?

"I expect we'll get to the bottom of it," I told her, and slipped the photograph into my breast pocket.

"There was another photograph," she said. "My husband put it with the cross. He was very methodical, you know. It was there when I put the cross in the trunk because I could feel the shape of it through the wrappings." Her look was almost pathetically apologetic. "I told all that to Mr. Hill."

"Please don't worry," I told her. "We'll try to straighten it all out. But tell me something: why was the cross, and the jewellery, more or less hidden away?"

The explanation was simple. Most of her husband's service had been abroad and the family silver and valuables were kept in the safe of an English bank. When he finally retired and took the house in Effingham Square, he got them out of the bank and kept them in his own safe. He handled all that himself.

"And when you were moving to this flat your woman's curiosity didn't make you want to have a look, after all those years, at the jewellery?"

"Young man," she told me severely, "I'm not so young as I was. After my husband's death I had far too much to do to spend my time looking at jewellery."

I allowed myself to be crushed. We went back to the crowded drawing-room but I didn't take a seat.

"I don't think we need worry you any more, Mrs. Rimmell," I said. "Perhaps I might see you again in a day or two if we've managed to clear this mystery up. Is that a photograph of your grandson?"

It was one of four photographs in silver frames that stood among the bric-à-brac on a side table. I'd happened to see on it the word Montreal. She sprang up—believe me that's the right word—and handed me the photograph. I had to do some adroit lying, for the face of the young man of that photograph looked pretty weak.

"And he's staying in London?" I said.

"At the Court Hotel. That's in Lonsdale Street, you know. We always used it and I recommended it myself."

"Lovely for you to have him here again," I said, as I replaced the photograph. "I suppose few of your friends are left now?"

"None," she said. "But it's no use making one's self miserable about it. One ought to be only too thankful to be alive."

"That Dr. Kossack who was a friend of yours in Effingham Square—is he still alive?"

"I wouldn't call him a friend," she told me primly. "He was very handy to call in when my husband had one of his unpleasant turns." She let out a sigh. "Poor man, he was killed last year in a car accident. He always did drive very fast. His widow, I believe, is still there. A most disagreeable woman."

That was about all, so I thanked her and said we'd be going. "I shall tell Mr. Hill what agreeable people you were," she told us graciously. "I always think it does no harm to let employers know about their employees."

I said that was very kind of her. We bowed to each other, and Hallows and I went silently along the short corridor and out through the swing doors to the road. Everything was so quiet and impeccably discreet that it was almost like leaving a church.

Half an hour later we were back in John Hill's room in the Lombard Street office. Hallows and I had talked over the extraordinary affair of that Russian Cross and, if we hadn't arrived at anything positive, at least we had our own ideas as to how an enquiry could be made. And that wasn't so easy or so obvious. There was doubtless no survivor, other than Mrs. Rimmell, of that fancy-dress ball at which the cross had been worn. As for the photograph, the firm that had taken it had long since gone and even the premises they'd occupied had been pulled down. Sixty years is the very dickens of a lot of time.

"I knew you'd spot the mystery," was almost the first thing Hill told us. "When I was confronted with it and tried to find a solution—well, I was flabbergasted. Even possible solutions were things that couldn't have happened. I told myself, for instance, that her memory was wrong and that she didn't wear the cross, and then I had to put against that the fact that the photograph said she did, and that she said she did. Still, let's hear what you've got to suggest."

I said that Hallows and myself were of the opinion that Alysia Rimmell herself was the problem. Was she, for instance, capable of being a party to a fraud? I thought she wasn't. She hadn't done a lot of protesting when told the diamonds were missing: she'd simply reminded us that she'd been wearing the cross and that the diamonds had then been in their settings.

"Were the Rimmells always well off?" Hallows wanted to know.

"Oh, yes," Hill said. "Plenty of money. After payment of death duties the general's estate was about eighty thousand pounds. There was never any conceivable reason to commit a fraud. Besides, where *is* the fraud?"

He was right, of course. There'd never been at any time an attempt to swindle an insurance company. Even now it wasn't a vital point that there was a possibility that the cross had lost its diamonds.

"We're prepared to pay the valuation accepted in the policy," Hill said. "All the same, if the diamonds had been extracted and sold, then there'd be fraud and, if we could prove it, then we shouldn't pay."

"What makes things all the more mysterious is this," I said. "That photograph was taken in 1893, and it shows the diamonds were missing. But when your appraiser saw the cross thirty years later, the diamonds were back in their settings. That means they were taken out temporarily for some special reason. And if so, why have a photograph taken when that photograph would prove the diamonds weren't there? And why keep that damning photograph? The general even wrapped another copy of the photograph with the cross."

"I know," Hill said. "I thought of most of that myself and that's why I wanted you and Hallows to see everything at first hand. I hoped you'd drop on some perfectly simple solution that hadn't dawned on me."

"Sorry we disappointed you," I said. "But our idea is this: there are certain things we have to accept: that both the late General Rimmell and his wife were incapable of fraud and that therefore the cross, and not, say, a dummy package, was in that trunk when Mrs. Rimmell moved to the flat. So let's disregard the mystery of the missing diamonds and concentrate on the theft. Should we discover who committed the theft, who knows but what we might find tied up with it the answer to the diamond mystery. You agree?"

"Most certainly. The theft was always the main problem. We stand to pay out quite a large sum of money. To put it bluntly, we're paying you to recover the jewellery, including the cross. If it's an impossible task, then we'll be satisfied as always that you've done your best." He peered at me over his pince-nez. "The police, of course, are doing the same thing, except that their primary job is catching the thief. You don't mind my suggesting that a little surreptitious collaboration might be useful."

"We'll bear it in mind," I told him dryly. "We do have ideas of our own, you know."

"Such as?"

"Well, there were various people who had the comparative freedom of the flat. There was that nurse—"

"The treasure," he said, and chuckled.

"Exactly. Mrs. Rimmell's exact words were *we put the jewellery in the trunk*, the operative word being *we*. Unfortunately, Mrs. Rimmell has lost track of the nurse, which might mean that the nurse took good care to lose track of *her*. Then there's this grandson who even occasionally has slept in the flat. There's also a Doctor Kossack, now unfortunately dead, who might have known something. But his wife is still alive."

"Capital, capital!" Hill told us benignly. "Get on with the good work, and the very best of luck."

All I could tell him was that I had an idea that we were going to need it.

# 5
## FINDING A THIEF

IT WAS just the wrong time for a call at Effingham Square and in any case Hallows and I had had no lunch, so it wasn't till after two o'clock that I rang Mrs. Kossack to make sure she was in. A woman's voice, just a bit quavering but perfectly audible, told me she was resting, so I thought I'd better give my name and say I'd be along in half an hour to see Mrs. Kossack on urgent, private business.

When we got to the house, the door was opened by the old retainer who'd answered my telephone call. She took the special card that named me as an official investigator for United Assurance, and was back almost at once and showing us into what she called the sitting-room. A smell of cooking mixed with a general stuffiness permeated the house, so I wasn't surprised when the room itself had a frowstiness, too. It was like the lounge of a third-class provincial hotel.

Mrs. Kossack was seated in an old-fashioned stuffed chair, a tea-tray on a bamboo table not far from her elbow. She reminded me somehow of a full-blown Caroline Testout rose. In a fluffy kind of way she must have been quite pretty when she was young. Now, at what I guessed was well on the way to fifty, she had run to too much fat, and she was probably past caring. There was something cheap and vaguely unpleasant about her, and her look and her tone were peevish. As she looked again at that special card, for instance, she said she didn't see why she should be worried about insurance after she'd paid her solicitors to handle everything. But when I told her why we were there, she was suddenly another woman. She scented scandal. A theft in connection with the Rimmells was really something. We were asked to sit down.

"What a wonderful old lady Mrs. Rimmell is," she said. "She used to walk miles in a day: seeing the shops and everything. Not that I've seen her since she moved." She couldn't keep back a little sniff. "After all, Effingham Square is nothing to be ashamed of. At least we don't have thieves here."

"You knew the husband, Mrs. Kossack?"

"Oh yes," she said. "An extraordinary old man, even older than she was. Quite a character, as they say." Her voice lowered. "Between ourselves, I had the idea he was slightly mental but my husband—my late husband, that is—wouldn't hear of it. Just eccentric, he called him."

"I believe Dr. Kossack attended him in his last illness."

"Yes," she said. "Charles—that's my husband—was killed in an accident only a year ago and I was sure the Rimmells used to make a convenience of him. His surgery, of course, was in Harley Street but they were always ringing him up here or sending someone round when anything was wrong with the general. And trying to make out it was purely neighbourly: his visits, I mean. I had to put my foot down before he would send in a proper bill."

I nodded sympathetically. And as soon as I mentioned a highly confidential question, she was leaning forward, all agog again.

"Of course you can rely on me. I'd never dream of saying a word."

"It's about the nurse," I said. "The one who attended the general in his last illness. I believe your husband recommended her."

Her lips had clamped together and she was looking positively vicious.

"I know," she said. "The Lister woman. Elizabeth Lister. A hussy if ever there was one."

"In what way?"

She gave me a quick look. She moistened her lips.

"I can't tell you that. You'll have to take my word for it."

"But what's being said is in absolute secrecy," I pointed out. "If I didn't regard you as being utterly discreet I wouldn't have told you what I have."

"Well then, I think—in fact I know—she'd been carrying on with my husband."

"Really?" I looked suitably shocked. "You mean they were actually having an affair?"

"Well, that's what it amounts to. After all he's dead now and it can't do any harm to speak the truth." The voice sank again. "It was while she was still attending the general that a lot more came out. My sister begged me to have him watched so I could get a divorce. But as I told her, that would have played right into her hands."

"What happened about the affair?"

"It stopped," she said. "Not that he didn't have other women. He was very good-looking, you know—and a bit younger than me. It was my money that got him where he was."

"But how do you know it had stopped?"

"Because I challenged him with it and he swore he hadn't seen her for months. Said she'd been married for some time. You could always tell when he was telling a lie."

"This Nurse Lister was good-looking?"

She sniffed.

"In her hussy-like way, if you know what I mean. And she could be all mealy-mouthed and pious looking." She sniffed again. "Sex written all over her. I wouldn't have trusted her an inch, not in anything. In my opinion you needn't look much farther if you want to find out who took that jewellery."

"Perhaps you're right," I said. "But could you describe her to us? Age and appearance and so on?"

"She'd be getting on for thirty—well, very much over twenty. She was dark and with one of those swarthy complexions as if she never really washed properly. Looked more like an actress than a nurse."

"Do you know in what hospital she had her training?"

"I'm pretty sure she was at the Metropolitan once," she said. "I always thought that was where my husband met her. But she wasn't there when she came to look after the general. She came from Nursing Services Limited. My husband was always recommending people from there. Nurses who'd given up hospital work for private work instead. It pays better, you know. And trust her to look after number one."

"I suppose you've never clapped eyes on her since?"

"Never," she said. "Nor heard of her. Not that I wanted to."

"Well, we're very grateful to you, Mrs. Kossack," I told her, "and we'll take up no more of your time. It's been a great pleasure meeting you, and what you've told us will be a tremendous help."

That pleased her. She asked if we'd let her know what happened.

"Only too pleased to," I told her. "Especially if the lady turns out to be the one we want."

"She's the one. You mark my words."

We were at the door as she told us that, but even when we were out in the square again I could still somehow see the look, part sneer, part triumph, that had been on her face.

What we had to do was separate spite from fact, though it seemed to me that when spite was discounted, we hadn't done too badly in that last half-hour.

We walked through to Piccadilly where I rang the Court Hotel. After a time I was put through to Herbert Rimmell. His voice sounded a bit thick to me.

"Travers?" he said. "I don't know anyone named Travers. What is it you want?"

"Your grandmother has mentioned a certain theft to you?"

"Ah, yes," he said.

"I'm the representative of the insurance company. I thought perhaps you might help us."

He thought that over.

"Better give me half an hour," he said. "I had rather a heavy night and I'm not feeling so good."

I got his room number and said I'd be seeing him in half an hour's time.

Hallows was going to the office of Nursing Services Limited. He'd found the address in the telephone directory. Then he was to go to the Metropolitan Hospital to try to unearth anything else that might be interesting about Nurse Lister, and, if there was a chance, about the late Dr. Kossack. It might be a pretty protracted business so he'd better report to my flat.

Hallows, if you haven't met him before, is one of those quietly spoken, unobtrusive people who, unlike myself, can merge into any background. I—six-feet three, lamp-post lean and blind as a bat without my hornrims—am the kind it's impossible to miss or forget. Hallows can be practically anybody: professional man or manual worker. He's probably the best-paid operative in town, and he's worth it. That afternoon, for instance, I didn't need to give him any detailed briefing. He knew the kind of thing I hoped he'd unearth, and I knew that if anyone could unearth it, it was he.

He took a bus at Piccadilly: I, with time to spare, walked to the Court Hotel. It was some years since I'd been in it and as soon as I was through the swing doors I saw it looking as exclusive as ever. Nobody challenged me so I walked up the heavily carpeted stairs to the first floor and found Rimmell's room. I had to knock twice before it was opened. Rimmell had got as far as his trousers. He was holding them up with his left hand while his right drew back the door to let me in.

"Mr. Travers?" he said off-handedly. "Take a seat. I'll be with you in a minute."

It was a large, well-lighted room with a private bathroom. Rimmell was large too: tallish and extremely thick-set. But for the rather weak mouth and chin, his short-cropped hair would have given him the look of a bruiser. Except for the dark beneath his eyes and a slight sallowness about his skin there was no sign of that heavy night he had mentioned over the telephone. His voice was a bit drawling, with the accent noticeable and no more. The whole man was rather a puzzle, at least till I realised that when his grandmother had said he'd been at an English prep. school just before he was taken to Canada, the age he then was made it impossible for him to have retained much more than memories. At any rate there was not much of the heir of all the Rimmells about the man of twenty-eight who was finishing his dressing in that private bathroom.

When he reappeared he was putting on his coat. He stopped at the dressing-table mirror, adjusted his tie and generally preened himself before he looked my way.

"Aren't you the one who called on Mrs. Rimmell this morning?" he asked me, just a trifle belligerently.

"Yes," I said.

"She rang me just after you did and I asked her about that theft you mentioned. That's how I came to know. She was pretty cagey. What's it all about?"

"Nothing of any seriousness," I said. "Just the theft of some not too valuable jewellery. And an old Russian cross."

He looked puzzled and I was sure he wasn't acting.

"An old gold cross, just a small thing, given to one of your ancestors. Just worth its actual gold value now, so we think."

"Yes, but where do I come in? Why come and see me?"

"That's confidential," I said, "and I'd rather you didn't mention it to Mrs. Rimmell. We're of the opinion that the nurse who attended your grandfather in his last illness might have had something to do with the theft, but the trouble is that Mrs. Rimmell thought the world of her and it might have been awkward to have made the suggestion. What I wondered was if she'd ever mentioned the nurse to you?"

"I think she did," he said. "She didn't sound to me like anyone who'd be mixed up with theft."

"Glad to hear it," I said. "That's someone then we can waste no more time over."

There was a fireplace with an electric stove in the room and he'd been leaning against the mantelpiece. Now he brought out a gold cigarette case.

"Cigarette?"

He lighted it and his own with a gold lighter and resumed that negligent, cocksure pose again.

"You insurance people are going to pay, aren't you?"

"Most decidedly."

"Doesn't look like it to me," he said. "The way I'm beginning to figure it, you're looking for reasons not to pay. I'm a business man myself, you know, and I guess it's up to me to look after Mrs. Rimmell's interests."

"There'll be no need," I told him a bit sharply. "A company of our standing always pays. But that isn't to say we're not in order in making an attempt to recover the proceeds of a theft. We have an enormous regard for your grandmother. What a wonderful old lady she is, by the way."

"Yes," he said, and smiled. "She's sure some gal."

"And she thinks a lot of you."

"You think so?"

"I'm sure of it. I think she idolises you."

He gave a self-satisfied nod.

"Well, that's good hearing. But hey there: what about a drink? Scotch, gin—what'll you have?"

"Good of you, Mr. Rimmell, but it's a bit too early for me. Thanks all the same."

"Mind if I have one myself? Hair of the dog that bit you, as they say."

He produced a bottle from the chest in the far corner and poured himself a stiff whisky. He took a good pull at it and let out an appreciative breath.

"You sure have some good whisky over here, if you know where to buy it. But about Gran, as I call her. I think a lot of her, too. I don't mind telling you that she and my mother didn't get along. You know how it is. When grandfather died I reckoned we ought to have come over. No use keeping up these old quarrels. But would she hear of it? Not on your life. Then I thought things over and told myself I ought to make a stand. That's why I came over last fall." His lip drooped. "Now me and my mother aren't on speaking terms. Not that that worries me a lot now I've heard both sides. I reckon Gran has been mighty shabbily treated."

I wondered why he was forcing all those family affairs on me. And I couldn't get away from the idea that he was putting on an act and I thought I'd like to hear a bit more.

"Let me see. Didn't your mother go to Canada when you were quite a boy?"

"That's so," he said, and took a seat on the bed. "Dad—that's what I always called him—was a big shot in the Alaska Trading Corporation—the company I'm in myself. The Canadian Government sent him over here when war broke out. He died a year or two back."

"And you're still with the company?"

"Yes," he said. "I suppose I'm a bit young but I'm holding down a mighty important job. Keeps me pretty busy over here. Even so, I always find time for Gran."

Every word and gesture was intended to impress. I was beginning to feel sorry that he could be in no way connected with that missing jewellery.

"By the way," he said, "she had her portrait painted specially for me. I reckon it'll be a kind of heirloom. It was this way. Last fall I asked for a special photograph and she reckoned she'd have something for me when I was back, and sure enough, there it was. I've just managed to get it shipped back home."

"I'd have liked to see it," I said.

"Wait a minute. I've got a photograph right here."

It was in a drawer of the dressing-table: a glossy print that gave no idea of the colouring of the original. But that original must have been a fine piece of work. The old lady was throned in a high-backed Spanish chair, looking like a wee and almost malicious empress. On her face was a look of faint amusement as if she was enjoying to the full the irony of the pose. As a portrait it was life-like.

"The original must have been magnificent," I said. "Do you know who painted it?"

"It's written on the back. One of your Academicians. Must have cost her a packet, as they say."

I suppose I looked at the back of that photograph for quite a minute. Not because it was Sigott's name that was on it but because my thoughts had at once gone back to that blackmail case of a few months before.

"A good man, Sigott," I said. "One of our very best. That portrait will be something to be proud of."

"It's Gran," he said. "It'll be good to look at her when I'm back home."

That was about all. He again offered me a drink. He asked me if I played poker. A few Canadian friends occasionally fore-gathered, and it was a pity I didn't play for they had pretty wonderful sessions. After that we shook hands and he gave me a patronising pat on the shoulder as he opened the door.

I walked towards Oxford Street and a bus, and I couldn't help feeling that somewhere something was radically wrong. The man with whom I'd spent that last half-hour had been vastly different from what I'd expected to see. And then again, I didn't know. After all, Herbert Rimmell had been taken to Canada at the age of fourteen. An impressionable age, and it wouldn't have taken long for him to have forgotten the earlier boyhood and to have acquired a wholly new environment and new values.

But that didn't alter the fact that he'd been putting on an act. Maybe he thought I'd be seeing his grandmother again and would speak of his devotion to her in the words he had used with me. But there'd also been a discrepancy or two.

At one moment he'd been the important executive who had to make frugal use of his time in order to spare for her an intimate hour or two. Maybe he'd forgotten about that when he'd mentioned those poker sessions. As for the position he claimed to be holding down, even if it had been his by right of inheritance from his step-father, surely there'd never been an important executive so self-inflated and so brash.

Still, all that was no business of mine: it wasn't, so to speak, within my terms of reference. Herbert Rimmell, I was quite convinced, had been in no way concerned with the theft of that jewellery and cross. It also struck me that he'd have been several kinds of a fool if he had. After all, he was the last of the Rimmells and, almost certainly, now his grandmother's heir. But something was also telling me that I might do worse than keep on good terms with both Rimmell and his grandmother. That was why I rang her as soon as I got to the flat.

"Travers, here, Mrs. Rimmell—the insurance investigator."

"And you're a very naughty man," she told me archly. "I spoke to Mr. Hill about you on the telephone as I said I would and he told me you were not what I thought you were, not that I didn't notice at once that you were a gentleman."

I felt a bit of a fool, elevated though I'd been to the stratum that included the Rimmells.

"Very nice of you to say so," I said. "But I've just had the pleasure of meeting your grandson."

"How *was* the dear boy?"

"Very well," I said. "And, if you don't already know it, he's remarkably fond of you."

"I know he is."

"Well, I was most discreet. I just mentioned that loss of yours as something trivial. I thought you'd like it that way, and so that he wouldn't know you'd been looking forward to giving the jewellery to his wife."

"Now I call that most charming of you."

"Not at all, Mrs. Rimmell. I also asked him about that nurse of whom you were so fond. That was very wrong of me. He didn't know anything about her and also I'm convinced she couldn't possibly have had anything to do with the theft."

"You should have taken my word," she told me severely. "But when am I seeing you again?"

I said as soon as there was anything whatever to report, and that was that. I didn't trust Rimmell not to tell her that I'd mentioned that nurse, and I was telling myself that I'd forestalled any possible breach of faith. My wife was out for the evening but I was on quite good terms with myself as I made a pot of tea and then settled down to wait for Hallows.

At six o'clock he rang: he was on to something and had to wait till the pubs opened. He hoped to be along before eight o'clock. It was nearer half-past when he actually arrived. I rang down for another service dinner and fetched some beer from the refrigerator. He talked while he ate.

He'd gone first to that nursing association and had worked the old line of looking for a beneficiary under a will. Elizabeth Lister, he learned, had had just one job after leaving Mrs. Rimmell. When he told me what it was, I could hardly believe my ears.

"She went to a painter," he told me, consulting his notes. "A man named Sigott. His wife was very ill. She died later and shortly afterwards Lister wrote to the association asking for her name to be struck off the books. Said she was getting married. Her original address was 24 Mallow Grove, Hendon. Where she is now, no one knows."

I didn't comment.

"Next call was at the Metropolitan. I saw various people there, and worked the same lost heiress stunt. Got some very interesting material. Lister did her training there and later was dismissed for carrying on with a patient. Just the matter of a private room and her being found there in a highly compromising situation when she ought to have been elsewhere.

"What worried me was how she could have got on the books of that nursing association and the answer seemed to be that she'd only to give a regular practitioner as a reference. No need to mention the hospital. The doctor would fill in the necessary form. Her guarantor was Kossack."

"Good work," I said. "It's fitting in well."

"Wait for the rest," he said. "Kossack was a much younger man than his wife. Very brilliant, I was told. Throat and ear specialist. And he had a narrow squeak a few years back. Up before the Council on a charge of intimacy with a patient. Let off with a caution, if that's what they do. It never became public because it was during the war: at least that's the explanation I was given. After that he must have picked out his women pretty carefully. Couldn't get any more details though.

"But about Lister. I got her address for when she was at the hospital. Ramley Green, that's just in Hertfordshire. Handy for further enquiries. Then I got into touch with an attendant at the hospital who'd known her well: well enough to wink when I mentioned her name. He was on duty but we agreed to meet at the Blue Boar in Harris Street as soon as he was off duty. I'd also asked him to try and get me a photograph. And he did. Says we have to get it back in case it's missed."

He undid the small package he'd brought in with him and handed me the photograph. It was of the nursing staff of what was called Block IV. He pointed out a figure in the middle row. I fetched my glass.

I didn't gather a lot. The then Nurse Lister was a remarkably pretty young woman, dark-haired, rather taller than most of her colleagues and with a serious expression that very much ran counter to what I'd just heard of her. Maybe that was because of the presence of the matron as the centre-piece of the front row. I fetched a stronger glass and had another look.

"I can't help thinking I've seen her before," I said. "I'm almost certainly wrong. Perhaps it's a weakness of my old age. I always think I recognise people. Maybe it's because I've seen so many in my time."

"They're all alike these days," Hallows said. "But what about the photograph. Like me to get an enlargement of her before I take it back? I know a man who'll do a rush job to-night. It may cost a bit."

"Hill's paying," I said. "Any other news?"

"Don't know that there was," he said. "Nobody has the faintest idea where she is at the moment. Someone, according to that attendant, said she had a sister in the millinery line. Still, I might pick up some more about that at this Ramley Green place. Someone may even know where she is."

He had finished his hasty meal and there was no reason to keep him. And except for congratulating him again, I didn't tell him what I was thinking. He was off, in any case, to get that photographic enlargement. In the morning he'd be seeing what he could unearth at Ramley Green.

# 6
## DEAD END

THE next morning I wasn't at the office at the usual time. I wanted to ring Sigott and, as he might be a late riser, I left him in peace till after nine o'clock.

At the very first sound of the woman's voice at the other end of the line I guessed I was going to talk to the blonde, Laura. A couple of words and I knew I was wrong. This was an older voice, pleasant and assured: the voice of someone who wouldn't be easily flurried.

"May I have your name, sir?"

I gave the name. And I guessed she was the housekeeper.

"I believe Mr. Sigott's in the studio, sir. Would you mind waiting?"

It was a couple of minutes before I heard the rattle of the lifted receiver. Sigott began clearing his voice. I spoke first.

"Travers here, Sigott—"

"How are you?" he cut in austerely.

"Keeping pretty well," I said. "And you?"

"About my usual. You wanted me about something?"

He didn't sound as if he'd be very co-operative.

"I want you to do me a favour," I said. "I've a case on hand which makes it essential for me to get into touch with a certain Elizabeth Lister. She was on the books of a nursing association and I understand she attended your wife during her fatal illness."

There was no sound from Sigott.

"Are you there?"

"Yes," he said. "But what is it you want me to do?"

"Well, do you know what happened to her after she left you?"

"Sorry, no. I hardly knew the woman. She was paid and she left."

"And you've never heard of her since?"

"Never. *Should* I have heard?"

"Not necessarily," I said. "She can't be traced after she left you and I was hoping against hope that you might be able to help."

"Is it in order to ask what you want her for?"

"Quite in order. Just the matter of a legacy."

He gave a little grunt.

"Sorry. Afraid I can't help."

"Well, thanks for letting me take up your time," I said. "Oh, by the way, I met a Mrs. Rimmell the other day. I believe she sat for a portrait recently."

"Why, yes," he said, and there was an extraordinary change in his voice. "The most interesting subject I've had for years."

"Marvellous, isn't she? Eighty-six and gadding about like a debutante. Did you go to her or did she come to the studio?"

He actually chuckled.

"Here, my dear fellow. Three sittings. And in that horrible weather we had early in February." He chuckled again. "If you see her, give her my love."

"I'll be delighted to. And thanks again, Sigott. Be seeing you some time."

I hung up. Mind you, I'd been drawing a bow very much at a venture. That's how it has to be in my kind of game, and especially when you're wondering if you've come to a dead end. You hunt around and you question and you hope, and all the time you know there isn't much point to it. My hope had been that since Sigott had an eye for a pretty woman, and since also what I knew about Nurse Lister had cried aloud that an affair would be very much in her line, the two might have kept, shall we say, in touch, and that with a little careful mendacity he might have thought it safe to give me a hint as to her whereabouts.

I sat down, lighted my pipe, and began to think it over. That curtness on Sigott's part, I decided, was a kind of defence. He was warning me in his own way not to mention that blackmail business. As for that change of tone when I'd mentioned Alysia Rimmell, that was partly relief that I had *not* mentioned the blackmail affair, but chiefly a really delighted remembering of a very pleasant professional episode. As for Nurse Lister, I still couldn't help but wonder, even if normally I haven't a particularly salacious mind. In fact, I told myself that the odds rather were that a man like Sigott would have been very much aware of a woman like Lister in his house, especially as his wife was on a sick bed. And if that were so, and he did, in spite of protestations, know her whereabouts, then that mention of a legacy might help enormously. He might get into touch with her, and then, of course, sheer cupidity would make her get in touch with myself.

It was about ten o'clock when I got to Broad Street, and I hadn't been there five minutes before there was a personal call for me. I guessed it was Hallows. It wasn't. It was Alysia Rimmell.

"Will you have lunch with me?" she asked straight away.

"Nothing I'd like better," I said. "How are you, by the way? Not that I need ask. You sound as gay as ever."

"Flatterer!" she told me archly. "Will to-morrow suit you? One o'clock here. They serve the most admirable food in the restaurant."

"Delighted!" I said. "Life begins anew at one o'clock to-morrow."

She was chuckling to herself as she rang off. I was smiling, too, and then I settled down to work. Later I went out to lunch. There was nothing much left for me to do and at about three o'clock I was thinking of going back to the flat when Hallows rang. He said he was piling up a whole lot of information which might be important or might not, and he didn't think he could get back till the early evening. I told him to take his time and report at the flat.

It was even later than the previous night—nine o'clock—when he turned up. Bernice and I were having a domestic evening. Hallows had had a meal, so we left Bernice and adjourned to my little study. I fetched some beer.

"Been a scorcher to-day," he said when he'd ruined the first glass. "What kept me so late was having to see my friend at the Metropolitan again. I gave him back that photograph this morning and he said he'd scout round and might get some more news for me. This is the enlargement, by the way. The best that could be made of it."

It wasn't good. There hadn't been enough for the photographer to work on. I tried the big glass on it and the effect was merely to detract from her looks. Hallows was opening his notebook.

"I've got some dates for you. Lister is about twenty-nine. She began her training in 1945, when she was eighteen. They were badly short of staff then and she got in a bit early. She was dismissed in 1950: attended General Rimmell the next year and must have gone practically straight from there to that painter, Sigott."

"Any other news from the hospital?"

"Only that she had a couple of boy friends during the last part of the time she was there. One seems to have been a regular and she let fall that his Christian name was Reg. More about him later. Then there was an older man: described by my friend as a posh sort of gent. He only turned up at intervals and seems to have been a bit hush-hush. He came by taxi and waited for her. And that's about all from the hospital."

At Ramley Green it hadn't been as easy as he'd hoped to get details of the Listers, but he'd finally run down a woman who'd been their nearest neighbour. There were two girls, Doreen and Elizabeth. They'd been evacuated from London at the outbreak of war and their parents had been killed in a bomb attack in 1941, and then they'd come to live with their aunt at Ramley Green. She was a rather superior woman who owned a small cottage just outside the village: a spinster who's been a nurse in her time. Probably that was why Elizabeth wanted also to be a nurse. Doreen, the older by two years, wanted to be a milliner.

"That's just the wheat separated from the chaff," Hallows said. "I could have filled a couple of notebooks with what I had to listen to, so we'll move on to Abbots Bulford, the market town about six miles north. The two girls went to the grammar school there and then Doreen went into the millinery department of the one big store. When Elizabeth left school later, she also went there but just as a time-filler till she could be old enough to be taken on at a hospital. And now to something which might be a lead.

"The two girls were very different. Doreen was said to be a sharp and calculating one, always on the make, but she hadn't any time for boys. Elizabeth did. She had a boy friend named Reginald Wakes. Remember the Reg. of the hospital? He was a good bit older than she was: about twenty-five to her seven-teen as far as I could make out, and he had a little photographer's shop he'd inherited from an uncle."

He consulted his notes again.

"This is the important thing. The year before Elizabeth went to London, Reggie got himself in trouble. He'd gone in for the pornographic photograph business—dirty postcards and that sort of thing—and he'd had the bad luck to try to sell some to the wrong man. Why they let him off with a fine beats me, but that's how it was, and he disappeared. We know he went to London. He was a good-looking sort of chap in a showy way, so the repor-ter on the local weekly told me. Used to dress showily and had one of those streaks of moustaches. The next thing is that when Elizabeth had been only about a year in London, her aunt died. It made me a lot of work trying to figure out what the estate was, and the nearest I can get at is a couple of thousand pounds. After that everything is just gossip and it'd take another visit—two probably—to get nearer the facts. My guess, though, is this: Doreen certainly went to London and joined her sister. She'd boasted she was going to open a shop of her own, and I think Elizabeth lent her her share of the money."

He pushed his notebook aside, poured himself another beer, and sat back.

"And that's all. Doesn't seem a lot for a long day, but there it is. I might add that, as far as I could make out, not a soul in Ramley Green or Abbots Bulford has heard a word from or about the sisters since. Looks as if they shook the dust off their feet."

"We might do worse than try the telephone directories," I said.

We looked through them. No trade address for a Reginald Wakes. No trade address for a Doreen Lister.

"Neither name is very attractive," Hallows told me. "What they probably did was use some swanky trade name. I suppose in time we could run them both down and so get a line on Elizabeth."

Then suddenly he was giving me a queer, inquisitive look.

"Do you mind telling me something, sir? Just suppose we did run down this Nurse Lister. What would you do then?"

"I haven't thought it out," I said. "But now you ask me, I think I'd interview her and remind her of how she'd helped Mrs. Rimmell put away the jewellery. I'd probably work along the lines that Mrs. Rimmell's memory hadn't been all that good, and she might have imagined the whole thing: anything to keep Lister from thinking she herself was under any suspicion. And all the time, of course, I'd try to gather from her reactions whether or not she'd been implicated in the theft. If I really thought she had, then I might pass the tip to the police."

"Yes," he said. "That'd be the way to handle it." Then he smiled ruefully. "Except, of course, that it might take weeks to run her down."

He got to his feet.

"I'll write a full report and perhaps you'll be able to see something I've missed."

"Good," I said. "Take a day off to-morrow. I'm having lunch with Mrs. Rimmell and I might see Hill later on. Perhaps you could drop in at the office about four."

I had an excellent lunch with Alysia Rimmell. There was, as they say, never a dull moment. I asked her where she got her amazing energy from.

"Oh, I rest," she said. "It's a legacy, I suppose, from India, but every afternoon at two o'clock precisely, I take what is really a siesta. My late husband used to do the same. Not that you must hurry over your meal. This is an occasion, you know."

She had coffee brought to the flat and it was almost half-past two when I left, and I honestly think she was talking most of that time. After she'd made some blunt enquiries about myself—chiefly in the social line—I merely directed the course of the stream. I heard all about life in India. I also heard about Japan where her husband had been for some years. What I heard about the business that had made me accept her invitation could be written on one manuscript sheet of paper. I was like a man struggling to get through a densely packed crowd. I'd see a slight gap and dart through, only to be practically at once hemmed in again. Perhaps what I did gather from her had better be given in the form of extracts.

(a) How was I progressing? That was easy, since it was almost the first thing she asked. I said I expected the insurance company would be paying almost at once.

(b) Did Nurse Lister know what was in the two wrapped packages at the bottom of the trunk? It took some manoeuvring to get that question in. Nurse Lister did know.

(c) Information about her grandson, largely unsolicited and some a repetition. He might be in England for quite a few weeks. The Corporation was thinking of opening agencies over here and he was in charge of things. His home was in Montreal. He was now living apart from his mother. "And all on account of me. Don't you think that was very brave of him? But of course I am making it up to him."

It was clear that she still absolutely loathed the mother. And so to what struck me as a most amusing statement, made by her with never a qualm. When Herbert was married and settled down, she was proposing to pay a visit to him in Canada. Not bad for eighty-six?

(d) The Russian Cross. How could she remember in every detail what had happened sixty years ago? She'd had many photographs taken and, though she couldn't swear to it, she was positive that the diamonds had been in the cross when that one photograph was taken. And—with a charming bit of feminine illogic—what did it matter in any case?

I suppose that on the whole I ought to have been quite pleased with the information I did manage to unearth. I know that she seemed quite sorry when I said I had to go, and she seemed also to have quite forgotten about the siesta. And I left with a souvenir. I'd been admiring some of her porcelain, and the contents of yet another trunk—chiefly Indian and Japanese work—and she insisted on giving me the loveliest green jade figure of a horse. It was so lovely and obviously so valuable that it embarrassed me, but she only laughed at my protestations and said I could get over my scruples by giving it to my wife. And I must bring my wife to see her. She liked meeting people.

And so much for a really delightful hour and a half. I thought I'd walk back to Broad Street by way of the Embankment and it was after three o'clock when I got there. To my surprise Hallows was waiting for me.

"I thought you were taking things easy," I said.

"You know me," he said. "I just have to keep on the go. And I thought you might like to look at that full report."

I went through it very carefully and he looked pleased when I told him he'd already separated the wheat from the chaff. After that we adjourned to a tea-shop to talk over what ought to be done next. We decided it all depended on what Hill was prepared to spend. We both doubted very much if he'd stand for a protracted search for Nurse Lister, particularly in view of the fact that she might have been wholly unconcerned with the theft.

"I think we'll leave it like this," I said. "All the reports can be summarised and collected. I'll get hold of Hill and tell him they'll reach him in the morning and then, if he thinks fit, he can see us later in the day."

That was how we left it. I helped Bertha Munney lick the reports into shape and then I added suggestions for proceeding with the case. By ten the next morning the whole thing was in Hill's hands. He rang after lunch and asked if we could see him at three o'clock.

We were there on time. Harry Levine, the chief gem appraiser, was there. Hallows and I had met him before, so it meant only an extra minute or two of chit-chat before we got down to business.

"You people have certainly been diving and mining," Hill said. "Would you mind telling me, though, why this Nurse Lister is so important?"

"Because she's a logical suspect," I said. "She's the only one besides Mrs. Rimmell who knew exactly where that jewellery was, and what it was, and almost certainly where the key of the chest was kept. Then, when she was helping Mrs. Rimmell move to the flat she had every opportunity to get a key made. Also she's not a person of what you might call the highest character."

Harry gave a laugh that might have meant anything.

"From your report she merely sounds a bit over-sexed. Otherwise she might have a heart of gold."

"Exactly," Hill said. And then a bit placatingly, "Not that you weren't right to try to investigate her. But what struck me was this. If she had that key back in 1951, why are you so sure she didn't commit the robbery then?"

"Let me think this out," I said. "You two seem to be ganging up on us. Why didn't she commit the robbery then? Well, the answer is that she did commit the robbery then."

"Why?" from Hill.

"How d'you know?" from Levine.

"It's all in the report," I told them blandly. "Nurse Lister went straight from Mrs. Rimmell to Sigott. She attended Sigott's wife and when the wife died, she left. She just disappeared. She didn't commit the robbery before she went to Sigott, and for the reason that if she'd taken the jewellery she wouldn't have had any need to work. But why did she disappear? And particularly with never a word to Mrs. Rimmell? I say because she took the jewellery immediately she left Sigott and that was in the January of 1952."

"Yes," Hill said reluctantly. "That sounds logical. She had a key, she knew Mrs. Rimmell's habits, so she simply let herself in and took the jewellery. It was bad luck for us, in a way, that Mrs. Rimmell only just discovered the loss. Nearly four years is a big gap to pick up a trail. In fact, we've decided not to proceed."

"You're probably right," I told him. "As I told you frankly in that report there, it might be a very expensive business running the woman down. And even then not being able to pin the robbery on her."

"Yes," he said. "We've decided to pay. Between ourselves we've been uncommonly lucky. Had that policy been renewed and the stuff re-appraised at General Rimmell's death, we'd now be standing to lose many times what we're paying."

I told him I thought he was wise. Then Levine cut in. He'd been bursting to say something and I'd wondered what it was.

"That Russian Cross business," he said. "It's got me beat. I've only just come into the affair but would you mind giving me your own ideas?"

"I haven't any," I said. "And Hallows hasn't any. All we know for a certainty is that sixty years ago Mrs. Rimmell had a one and only photograph taken in which she was wearing that cross. You have the photograph there. I'd like it back when I leave, by the way. It shows the stones had been removed. Mrs. Rimmell says with a look of the frankest innocence that the stones *were* there when the photograph was taken. That statement is reinforced in a way because United Assurance had the cross valued thirty years ago and the stones were back in place. No mention is made of their having been removed and re-set."

"That's how I see it," he said, and clicked his tongue in annoyance. "And the devil of it is, no one's alive who ever saw the cross—except Mrs. Rimmell. We've nothing but the description of thirty years ago to go on, and this photograph. But why *should* the stones have been removed sixty years ago! Even more exasperating is why they were afterwards replaced. And we know they weren't sold."

"They might have had to be given as a pledge for something," Hill said, but he didn't sound too serious.

"But the Rimmells were wealthy people!"

"Sorry I can't help you," I told Levine. "It's puzzled me from the start, and I'm afraid it's going to go on puzzling me."

Hill stood up.

"Well, there we are. Maybe we'll know the answer one day. Thank you for what you've done, Ludo. And you too, Mr. Hallows. Let us have your account when you feel like it." We sent in the account at the end of the month and it was paid without question. And that was virtually the end of the matter. It was the end if you omit that a day or two after we'd seen Hill and Levine, Alysia Rimmell rang me. She was all cock-a-hoop. Everything was settled, she said, and the company had paid in full.

"I'm sure that you've helped," she told me, "and I feel I ought to do something to show my gratitude."

"Young lady, I did nothing," I said, and caught her little titter at that gross flattery. "In any case you've paid a hundred times over. Which reminds me, my wife was delighted with that jade horse. She'll be ringing you at once to thank you personally."

Bernice did ring. The two fixed up lunch together, and after it Bernice could talk of nothing else for days. And that happened to be the last that either of us actually saw of Alysia Rimmell—alive.

# THEME III
# MURDER

## 7
## JAMES HOVER

IT WAS the morning of November the first—a Tuesday. The time was just after half-past eleven when Bertha put a call through to Norris. "City Detection for you," she'd said.

I wasn't paying much attention since I was busy over an income-tax query. I did hear Norris say, "Morning, Bill. How are you?" and after that the talk between Bill Fraser of City Detection Ltd. and Norris was merely a faint sound in the background.

It stopped. Norris cleared his throat. I looked up.

"A client on the way," he said. "Not much of a job but cash down, Bill says. He can't handle it so he passed it on. A Danish lady—well, she was Danish. Married an Englishman who's dead. Wants a man picked up at Brixton Jail—one of the inmates who's leaving. That's all. Wants to know where he goes to for the night. Will you see to her?"

He had some prints he wanted to have checked at the Yard, and in a few minutes he left. The bottom had gone out of the job I was doing, so I put the papers away and waited for the client. Five minutes later Bertha announced her arrival. The name was North. I told Bertha to show her in.

Lilli North was a Scandinavian blonde, her hair so fair that it was almost white. She had a thin, acidulous look: hair drawn tightly back from the forehead, lips without rouge and wearing thick-lensed glasses. Her age might have been anything from thirty-five to forty. She wore no jewellery except a platinum wedding ring. She was well but plainly dressed.

I placed a seat for her and offered the cigarette box. She said she didn't smoke. I wondered what she did do. She looked to me to be a woman wasted. Put her in the hands of a first-class coiffeur and then a beauty specialist, and she might have been quite a good-looking woman. Her figure was excellent, even if she didn't carry herself too well.

She apologised for her English, but it wasn't bad at all. She spoke her words carefully and the intonations were often wrong, but I'd have liked to speak Danish half as well. I've been over there several times and my vocabulary in its entirety could still be written on a postage stamp.

I make no attempt to reproduce her English as it was spoken. And there wasn't all that much said. From first to last she wasn't in the office much more than ten minutes. Her story was as follows.

Her late husband had had an interest in a porcelain factory in Denmark and also a business of his own in Birmingham. He'd been dead just over a year and just before his death he'd been swindled out of quite a large sum of money. She hadn't let the matter drop. Her solicitors had got on the track of the man, only to find he'd been jailed for another fraud. Their opinion was that he was without funds and it would be merely vindictive to bring another charge. Far better hold the charge over him and try to make him pay up at least something. So that was what she was going to do. A good friend of her husband would see the man as soon as he came out of jail.

I asked what the swindler's name was and she said he'd had several names. She looked at a paper in her handbag. Several names, she said again, but the name under which he'd been convicted was James Hover—that surname by the way, rhymed with Rover.

She said in that rather staccato, colourless voice of hers that details didn't matter. What mattered was that Hover was being released from Brixton Jail on the morning of November the fourth. All she wanted us to do was pick him up and find out the hotel or lodging to which he went. She gave me a Regent telephone number.

"I think we can do that for you, Mrs. North," I said. "I'll get a contract drawn up."

"How much will it cost?"

I thought it out.

"It's difficult to say. Hover might take quite a time before he decides on a hotel. Shall we say ten pounds? We'll take a chance on how long the job takes."

She produced the money from her bag and counted the notes carefully out. She said the Mr. Fraser at the other detective agency had said we could be trusted, so a contract was unnecessary.

"Nice of them to say so, Mrs. North, but I insist on giving you a receipt."

She put the receipt in her bag and rose from the chair.

"I've been to Denmark several times," I said. "Where did you live yourself?"

"Odense."

"Ah! Hans Andersen's birthplace."

She was moving towards the door and gossip didn't seem in her line. I saw her through and Bertha took her over. There wasn't a taxi outside. I went through to the operatives' room. French was there, playing patience.

"Quick!" I said. "A woman's just gone out. Blonde hair. In a dark costume. Let me know where she goes."

He was off like a shot. I went back to the office. After the first few moments I'd known there was something phoney about that woman. If she were really an educated Dane, then the English I'd heard her speak wasn't that which was spoken by educated Danes. Their English is practically perfect. Hers had been the kind of English spoken by any other kind of foreigner—especially French. It was the kind of thing one hears on the wireless. And when she'd told me that her home had been Odense, she'd given herself away. Have you ever heard a Dane pronounce that word? I have, dozens of times, but my rendering of it has never been the real thing. Neither had hers. Only a Dane can get that curious catch in the throat when pronouncing those d's as in Odense.

I rang the Yard. Norris was still in the finger-print bureau. He was once a chief-inspector himself and he takes his time when he runs across a contemporary.

"Arising out of that client sent us by Bill Fraser," I said. "Find out all you can on a man named James Hover—swindler or con man, now in Brixton. He's being turned loose next Friday."

I took out those income-tax papers again, but in ten minutes French was back. He said ruefully that his taxi had lost hers at the traffic lights in the neighbourhood of Marlbury Street. I asked him to start from the beginning.

"Well, I caught her up just round the corner in Wallace Street," he said. "That's where she'd parked the taxi she came in. I've got the number. A tallish man with a sprained ankle or something was standing on one leg by the taxi and leaning on a stick. He got back in as soon as he saw her. I was lucky to get a taxi myself. Quite easy following it up. Straight through to Piccadilly and then we lost it."

"No bones broken," I told him. "You've got the number. Find out where the taxi dropped her."

Another half-hour and Norris was back.

"Found out about your man," he said. "James Hover, with a string of aliases as long as your arm. In the 'con' game and everything else that's going. Someone tipped off the police at Hurst Park last February and they got him red-handed with a packet he'd been entrusted with by a hopeful backer. He's coming out on Friday after doing a twelver—with deductions. But what's it all about as far as we're concerned?"

I told him the whole thing.

"Uh-huh," he said. "Fishy, as you say. And we've taken her money. What do you think's the idea?"

"Don't know," I said, "but I can make a guess. She may be Mrs. Hover. She may also be the one who tipped off the police and now she's scared stiff."

"Then what should we do?"

"Nothing we can do," I said. "It's a perfectly right and properly professional job for us to pick up Hover and report where he looks like going to roost on Friday night, so we just do the job. The only thing we may have to blush for is that it ought to be an easy ten pounds."

During the afternoon French reported again. He'd located the taxi-driver. Mrs. North and the man with the sprained ankle had been dropped half way down Marlbury Street, almost opposite Smith's Hotel. The taxi-driver had asked the fare about that ankle while they were waiting for Mrs. North to come back from our office. French gave us a description of the fare: tall, thinnish, well-dressed, but age difficult to assess since he'd worn a neat spade beard, rather like Mr. Dunhill's advertisement. The taxi-driver and French between them put him in the late thirties.

On the Thursday afternoon Norris reminded me about Hover. There was nothing much doing at the time so once more we talked the whole thing over. We agreed that it looked remarkably as if the bearded man in the taxi would have picked up Hover outside Brixton Jail himself if it hadn't been for that sprained ankle. Who he was we couldn't even begin to guess, though there might have been something of truth in what the woman had told me about a firm of solicitors.

"Something tells me we oughtn't to put just anybody on to-morrow's job," Norris told me. "White lies are nothing new to us here and generally they don't matter: not when you spot them and know just what they are. But I don't like this job, somehow. Why should she pretend to be a Dane when she was nothing of the sort?"

"Maybe she's got Danish friends," I said. "But why should we worry? It's a perfectly simple job—or should be. It might mean just an hour's work."

"Well, I think I'll put Hallows on it," he said. "It's his free day but he won't mind. And he can have French with him. Must have a couple on the job. No telling how Hover'll get to where he's going. Might be by taxi, bus, Underground or anything."

That was how it was left. I wasn't too early at Broad Street the next morning and Norris told me that our men were already on the job, with Hallows using his own car. French was a good driver and they'd worked together before. I didn't think any more about it. As Norris had said, we were used to subterfuges from clients and, provided they weren't too serious, we could always skirt round them and handle a job in our own way. And if our Mrs. North was really Hover's wife then she might have had every reason to pretend to be what she wasn't. Admittedly her act had been a mixture of subtlety and crudity but, to quote the universal excuse, it takes all sorts to make a world.

Friday is Norris's busy day and I helped him out with time sheets and reports, and I was amazed when I realised it was well after twelve o'clock.

"Thought we'd have heard from Hallows by now," Norris said. "There might be something from him while I'm out."

He went off to his usual haunt for lunch and he hadn't been gone ten minutes before there was a call. French was on the line.

"That you, sir? . . . Thought I'd let you know we were still on the job. Been half over London already."

"Where're you speaking from?"

"Hendon," he said. "Picked him up all right but he's been leading us a dance. Not trying to ditch us: just going places. Hallows said to tell you we'd report back as soon as we can."

I told him to carry on. Norris came back and he didn't look too happy about what I had to tell him.

"Looks as if we're going to be losers over the job," he said. "Two men best part of a day and heaven knows what in expenses."

"One has to take the rough with the smooth," I said. "No blame attached to you. I was the one who worked out costs. Not that ten pounds either way will make us or break us."

It was two o'clock when I got back. Norris had an appointment in Regent Street at three and there was still no sign of our two operatives. Bertha brought me a cup of tea just before four, and it was while I was drinking it that Hallows arrived.

"Hope you weren't worrying about us," he told me in his mild way. "Never had such a run around in all my life. Still, it's all over now. Hover's booked a room at the Ferney Hotel in Bever Street and I rang the client: at least I suppose it was the client. She said it would be all right."

I buzzed through for Bertha to bring another cup of tea. Hallows had his notebook open.

"One or two surprises for you, sir," he said, and gave me a dry smile. "Like to hear them first, or from the beginning?"

"Everything from the beginning," I said. "What was Hover like, by the way?"

"A man of about fifty. Dark hair just greying, about my own height and build and quite distinguished looking in a way. Walks like a Guards' officer: back straight and as if he owned the town. No trouble about picking him up, he walked through to Milroy Street and took a bus for the City. French got on the bus too and I tracked them with the car. When Hover got off he went direct to the Cheapside branch of Barclays Bank and he was there for a good quarter of an hour. He patted his breast pocket when he came out, so probably he'd had an account there and had been replenishing his funds. At any rate, the next thing he did was take a taxi.

"We managed to keep on his tail right through Leicester Square and round into Wardour Street where he stopped at Number 275, a music shop. His taxi waited and he was inside the shop for about ten minutes. He didn't look too pleased with himself when he came out and then his taxi went up to Oxford Street and into the Edgware Road and right through to Hendon. It turned left and into a Mallow Grove, Number 24. That's an old-fashioned block of flats."

He looked up from his notes.

"Does that strike a bell?"

"No-o," I said. "Should it?"

"Think again, sir," he said. "Number 24, Mallow Grove, Hendon."

"Yes," I said after a minute. "It does strike some sort of bell. But it must be a pretty distant one."

"Enquiries at that nursing supply place."

Then I remembered.

"Good Lord! That was where that Nurse Lister lived while she was working!"

"That's it," he said. "I told you you'd have a surprise or two. But there wasn't one there. He went into the flats and he wasn't there ten minutes. I was too far away to see his face but his taxi reversed and went back down the Edgware Road again. When it was about three quarters of the way down it began to slow. Then it drew up outside the Golden Lion. Hover got out, paid off the driver and went inside. I went in, too, and that's about the time French rang the office here.

"They do lunches there and he walked through to the dining-room as if he knew the place well. He had lunch and a pint of bitter with it. I had a table in the far corner where t could watch him in the mirror. After the meal he treated himself to a cigar and when it was well alight he went out to the street and began walking towards Marble Arch. I'd lost him for a moment but it turned out he'd gone into a garage. The Upton Garage it calls itself: in Rensham Street, just about fifty yards down.

"I got out this time and had a look at what was in the window and I thought Hover was never coming out. When he did come out, a garage man was with him. What I heard him say was this: 'That's all right, Colonel. You can have her on Monday.' Hover said something, and then the other chap said something about the battery. Then Hover gave him a tip: a pretty good one I'd say by how it was taken. And what I'd guess about that was that Hover had had a car garaged there when he was nabbed, and under the name of a Colonel Someone. I couldn't find out, of course, because he was walking back to the Edgware Road.

There he managed to pick up a taxi and off we went on the old Cook's tour."

He looked up from his notes again.

"If you want a bet, sir, I'll lay you fifty to one in shillings you won't guess where he went to, not in three tries."

"I won't try it," I said. "Where *did* he go to?"

"To 47, Wensum Street, Kensington."

It took me a moment or two before I could speak.

"But that's fantastic! It's Sigott's studio!"

"Well, that's where he went," he said. "It was a bit tricky for us as we had to keep a fair distance away. But I got the glasses on him. A middle-aged woman in black opened the door and they had a few words and then he went in. He was there for exactly four minutes. He turned in the doorway and spoke to someone inside and then got in the taxi. It circled round and back to Hyde Park Corner and through to Marble Arch again and just round to the back of Oxford Street.

"The taxi was going pretty slow as if they were looking for something, and at last it stopped at a shop where they sell travelling trunks and so on. He paid off the taxi, waited till it had gone and then crossed over to the shop. When he came out it was with a very nice bag, all dolled up with labels. You could tell it was empty by the way he carried it. Then he landed up on Oxford Street again and took another bus. French followed inside. He got off at Piccadilly and walked along to Shaftesbury Avenue, and there he went into a man's shop and bought himself quite an assortment of clothes, including a new hat and a swanky grey overcoat. The bag looked pretty heavy when he came out. He was on the right side for a taxi and he managed to get one. I nearly lost him then but we picked him up at the traffic lights turning into Regent Street. He went about three-quarters of the way along it and turned into Bever Street. He got out at the Ferney Hotel and the driver carried his bag to the door where a commissionaire took over. I slipped on a different coat and hat and generally messed about with myself and then went in too. Hover's bag was just being taken to the lifts and he must have gone ahead. I asked about a fictitious arrival and managed to get a look at the register. This time Hover's name was Colonel Despard of Nairobi. His room number was 105. After that I stopped at Piccadilly Underground and rang the client and then came straight here."

"The devil of a day," I said. "But about ringing the client: just what happened?"

"Well, I got through to the number and a woman's voice answered—"

"What sort of a voice?"

"Well, a rather common voice, now you speak of it. I asked if she was Mrs. North and she said no but she was to take a message, so I simply said that a certain man was where he was and then made her repeat. I asked if she was sure Mrs. North would get the message and she said it would be absolutely all right."

"If it isn't, we'll be hearing from the client herself in double-quick time," I said, and brought out my pipe. "But the whole thing's past believing."

"One thing stands out a mile," he said, and lighted a cigarette. "Mind you, I didn't give French even a hint about this, but it looks to me dead certain that Hover was hunting for that Nurse Lister."

"Yes," I said. "And, by the way, Mr. Norris knows nothing about that Lister business except what he may have read in the reports, so let's keep this strictly between ourselves for a bit. As for a report on this morning's job, I doubt if either the Hendon address or the Wensum Road one will convey anything to him at all. But what's behind it all? Let's say everything's above board as far as Mrs. North is concerned, but where can she come in as between Lister and Hover—if Hover really was looking for Lister."

"There's no other answer," he said. "He *was* looking for her. And he didn't find her for the simple reason she was at neither of the places where he looked for her."

"Hover's a crook," I said. "That makes it even more possible that Lister was a crook and that she lifted that jewellery and the Russian Cross. All that's been disposed of long ago—melted down and so on—but it'd be a feather in our caps if we could go to Hill one day and prove we weren't such fools after all. You got any more ideas?"

"Yes," he said, and then smiled wryly. "For what they're worth. Hover evidently didn't know that Lister had left Sigott long ago, and that she'd left Hendon. That looks to me as if he'd either been out of England for the necessary time or else in stir. It might be a good idea to get hold of his record."

"We'll do that," I said. "I'll handle that myself. Anything else?"

"Only why it was that practically the first thing Hover did to-day was start looking for Lister. What's the connection between them? You don't think they're married?"

"Easy enough to find out," I said. "It's too late now but first thing in the morning go to Somerset House and see what you can unearth. I won't be here to-morrow, so you'd better report to the flat."

Then I remembered something.

"It's a free day for you to-morrow, making up for to-day, so we'll call that Somerset House job just something between you and me. Go straight there and if there's nothing doing, give me a ring. If there is, report to the flat."

I left Bertha to hold the fort and went home. I didn't ring the friend at the Yard who'd been asked about Hover before as he might wonder just what our interest was. The one I rang was Chief-Detective-Inspector Jewle with whom I'd more than once worked.

"You'd like a complete history," he asked, "or just the main facts?"

"Just the main facts. Previous convictions, if any, will be enough."

"That shouldn't take long," he said. "Like it sent round or will the morning post do? Purely unofficially."

I laughed. It was pretty clear what that last bit meant.

"I get you," I said. "Which reminds me. How's our good friend Forlin?"

"Him!" He gave a grunt and left it at that. "Hope to see you sometime for a chat."

What I'd asked for arrived by the first morning post, in a plain envelope with a covering note, initialed but unsigned.

> Con men, as you know, usually stick to their trade. J.H. seems to have had a crack at everything. That Norwich job was following up with blackmail after defrauding a widow of quite a good sum, most of which was later recovered. America seems to have got too hot though nothing actually pinned on him. Description, if you don't know it: five-ten, military carriage, dark hair grey at temples, brown eyes, can pose as either English, American or Australian.

I had a look at the extracts from Records. Hover had had quite a busy life:

JAMES HOBART HOVER alias Blackburn alias Colonel Johns, alias Hon. George Mitchell, etc.

Born Brisbane 1905. Father architect. Believed to have defrauded father's firm but affair hushed up.

*Convictions:*

> Sydney, 1930—2 yrs. fraud.
> Melbourne, 1932—5 yrs. fraud.

Joined Royal Australian Forces 1939 under name James Blackburn. Rose to Warrant Rank—Quartermaster. 1 yr. 1945—wrongfully disposing of stores. To America where believed implicated among other things in a bank robbery. England in 1950.

> Norwich Assizes, 1951—4 yrs.
> Central C.C., 1955—1 yr. attempted fraud.

As soon as I'd had breakfast I took that record to my room, switched on the electric fire, lighted my pipe and settled down to fitting in the facts. By the time Hallows arrived, which was just after eleven, I thought I had Hover snugly fitted in. But there were two gaps in the puzzle, or two pieces that just wouldn't fit.

And then, when Hallows did arrive, I knew I had an answer to one of them. It was even possible that I had an answer to both.

# 8

# BOMBSHELL

HALLOWS was looking pleased with himself.

"Guessed right for once," he said. "That is if James Prestwich is the man we think he is. The marriage was on May 10th, 1951."

The relevant details were that Elizabeth Lister, spinster, of 24 Mallow Grove, Hendon, had been married to James Prestwich, Colonel retired, Royal Australian Forces, at Holborn Register Office.

"Have a look at these records," I said, "while I get some coffee."

Bernice was out so I had some sent up, and some biscuits.

"Just ready for this," Hallows said. "And Prestwich is our man. A million to one."

The pair of us settled down to fitting things in. Elizabeth Lister, it was practically certain, had had two strings to her bow while she was at the hospital—her old flame Reginald Wakes and an unknown man whose description fitted that of Hover. When she was dismissed from the hospital and had had to think about making a living, she decided to marry Hover. Against the glib tongue of a professional con man Wakes would have had little chance.

It looked, too, as if the pair had lived at Mallow Grove with Doreen but then there'd been disaster, and only a few months after the marriage. That Norwich job had put Hover away for four years. Elizabeth had to make her own living again and this time she got into touch with yet another old flame, Dr. Kossack. Hence the nursing jobs: the Rimmells at the end of 1951 and then the Sigotts. But then came, for us, the first snag. *Where did she go when she left Sigott early in 1952?*

We could only guess. Kossack might have fitted her up with a flat somewhere, or she might have worked in the shop of Doreen, her sister, to whom we thought she'd lent the money inherited from her aunt. But on the whole it seemed to us that these missing years didn't matter. The important thing was to move on to the time when Hover left Norwich Jail, and that would be at the very end of 1954. What happened then?

It was surmise, of course, but we worked it out like this. Elizabeth took Hover back but there was bad blood between them for obvious reasons. She wouldn't have been scrupulous about the way he made his money, but there he was—and for all his big ideas—with hardly a cent. And during his stay in jail she'd consoled herself with Wakes. She might even have been living with him.

Get back to Hover's reappearance at Mallow Grove and the quarrels that must have followed. Maybe Hover taunted her with being unable to make any real money without himself, and maybe she said she could always go back to Sigott—the emphasis on the *famous* Sigott—whom she'd mentioned in her letters. *And that surmise had to be right.* It was the only way of explaining why Hover had gone to Sigott's studio for news of his wife—if she was his wife. Marriage under a false name was almost certainly an invalidation.

And then Hover had a scheme. He would have to be living at an expensive hotel for it to work, and it did work. He reported exultantly that he'd found a victim and that—in his pose of racing owner—that victim and he were going to Hurst Park where the said victim would entrust a pretty big sum to be put on a stone certainty. And that was the chance of Elizabeth and Wakes. The police were tipped off and Hover was in again, this time for only a year. Doubtless they'd expected more. And before Hover came out they'd have to cover their tracks. He'd guess who'd shopped him and he'd be out for revenge.

But the birds had flown. There was no Elizabeth, and almost certainly no Doreen, at Mallow Grove, and no Elizabeth at Sigott's place.

"I'll bet that first place he went to—what's now a music shop—in Wardour Street, was Wakes's place," Hallows said. "So he'd changed his quarters too."

"We may have to check up on that," I said. "But we've got right back home. Who was the Mrs. North who wanted to know where Hover spent last night?"

"Quite possibly another wife."

"Yes," I said. "But why not Doreen?"

"That's it," he said. "That's it for a fiver."

"What about the hair?"

"Just a minute," he said, and began thinking. "Elizabeth's hair was jet black. . . . Yes, now I remember. Doreen's was dark brown. Easy enough to bleach. And, come to think of it, she'd have to bleach it or do something to disguise herself so that Hover wouldn't be likely to spot her when he came out. It was Doreen Lister you saw here. Wakes couldn't pick up Hover at Brixton himself because of that sprained ankle, so she came to us. All three wanted to keep tabs on him because he'd be looking for them."

"You're right," I said. "And I'll bet they had something else on him and were going to put the police wise and get him tucked away for another year or two or else deported."

"That's it for a fiver."

Then he was giving me one of his quiet, quizzical looks. "Just where do we come in on all this?"

"In a roundabout way through that stuff that was lifted from Mrs. Rimmell," I told him. "Let's suppose something. Suppose we track Elizabeth down. We put pressure on her by threatening—or say hinting—that we'll give her away to Hover and make her tell us who lifted that jewellery and the Russian Cross from Mrs. Rimmell. A million to one it's too late to recover either but it'll put us in well with John Hill."

"Sounds good," he said. "But I've thought of something. What we've guessed is that yesterday Hover was looking for both Wakes and Elizabeth but the birds had flown. But why wasn't he looking for Doreen?"

"Yes," I said. "I'd forgotten that. But maybe he was a bit tired of hunting out the others and thought he'd get himself fixed up at an hotel first. What about going there and seeing if you can trace his movements? I don't think he'd stay in that hotel without going somewhere."

He got up at once. He said he'd give me a ring.

Bernice came back and we had a service lunch in the flat. She said it had been very cold in town and I could believe her. I hadn't stirred out but I could see the little wisps of fog from the window and the way people walked as if leaning into a cold wind.

"Guy Fawkes Day," she said, and smiled. "What a pity it is one seldom sees guys being carried round by small boys. They were quite common when I was a girl."

I said one could probably still see them in the suburbs but the police'd be up against that sort of thing in the heart of town. She said I was a coward and hated to face up to a lost youth. I asked indignantly who'd lost what youth, and then the telephone went.

"Hallows here, sir. Trying to follow up something so thought I'd let you know I mightn't be seeing you for an hour or so."

I went back to the fire and a crossword. Bernice was knitting and reading at the same time. I guessed the knitting was for my Christmas pullover but I didn't say so. It was quite a domestic afternoon but it brought no Hallows. Four o'clock came and Bernice brought in a pot of tea and cake. That was when Hallows arrived. We adjourned to my room with the tray and Bernice said she'd make another pot for herself.

Everything had gone swimmingly for Hallows. He'd taken a chance at the Ferney Hotel by asking the commissionaire if Colonel Despard had gone out the previous afternoon. When the commissionaire had been given a description of the Colonel he had plenty of information. He'd taken a taxi outside the door at about four o'clock.

Hallows went through the motions of going to the desk to make enquiries. He came back to the commissionaire.

"The Colonel isn't in," he said. "You don't happen to know where he went yesterday afternoon? He might have gone to my place."

"Can't say, sir." The hand of the commissionaire closed over a half-crown. "I can tell you the taxi-driver, though, sir. He's Shorty Green. Try the stand in Somers Street."

Hallows had to wait almost an hour before Shorty came in. Almost at once he was off again, taking Hallows to where he had taken Colonel Despard, and that was to a woman's shop, as Hallows called it, just off Sloane Square. The name was Helen Blair.

"I went in and saw this Helen Blair," Hallows said. "Just a trade name. She was a dumpy woman: quite friendly though. She'd bought the whole caboodle from Doreen last April. The shop used to be called 'Doreen'. Doreen had told her she was giving up business and going abroad. All this came out, of course, when I asked about Colonel Despard and what he'd talked about. I tried the old trick of flashing the Agency card at her and hoping she'd take it for a warrant card, and it worked. All the Colonel wanted to find out was the whereabouts of Doreen, and he didn't get any help. The lady hadn't the least idea where she was. All I got from her was the name of the estate agents who'd managed the property. They're a Hammersmith firm. I guessed they'd be closed on a Saturday afternoon, so I gave them a ring. No one answered but I thought I'd better run out there and make sure. Nothing doing."

"Plenty of time for them, if we need them," I said. "The great thing is that we know now that Hover completed his enquiries. The thing is, what's he going to do next?"

Hallows gave his dry smile.

"Or what's our friend Mrs. North going to do next. She knows where he is, and so does Wakes, if it was Wakes who was in that taxi that waited for her while she was seeing you. Don't forget, sir, that she didn't ask us to keep tabs on Hover. She, or someone else, is taking that over."

"Yes," I said slowly. "And our chief problem is what we're going to do with all the information you've unearthed. Call it no business of ours? Or follow it up?"

"It'd be nice, as you said, to show Mr. Hill we've got our wits about us."

I thought it would, provided we didn't do any trumpet-blowing. Once we had what we wanted—if we had it—our best approach to Hill would be of the casual kind, arising out of something more important.

"Do you still happen to be interested in that Rimmell business? It's a funny thing but we happened to stumble on something the other day that looked as if it might be tied up with it and, just out of curiosity, we followed it up."

The client is always right but that sort of thing, we thought, should do the trick.

"How we're going to get the full information is another matter," I told Hallows. "What do you say to taking a weekend to think things over? We mightn't even think it worth while to do anything at all."

He said it sounded a good idea, and that's how we left it.

Sunday's not a somnolent day at the flat: the Travers couple sleep no longer and they eat no more. It's what I'd call a nice, peaceful sort of day. Bernice goes to church, catches up with her correspondence and generally takes things easily. I do the three crosswords in my two papers, though the hardest one sometimes straggles over till a day or two later. I catch up with reading and I potter around, and Sunday night is always my best for sleep.

That Sunday morning I had a quick look through both papers as usual before settling down to a crossword. There didn't seem any news except the optimistic prophecies about the Russian New Look and the Geneva Conference. I'm no Delphian Oracle and no Cassandra, but I told myself that I wouldn't wager a bad penny on an amenable Molotov—but I'm prejudiced. Newspaper prophets can get away with anything, including murder.

And the really strange thing was that just as I had that thought in my mind I actually saw the word MURDER. My papers are not the sensational kind and there weren't anything like banner headlines, but there the word was.

### BODY FOUND IN BONFIRE
### POLICE SUSPECT MURDER.

I read the account in one paper and then found it in the other. There was hardly a word different, so what had been printed was obviously a police communiqué. But it was a highly interesting story for all that.

Bromford, one of those suburbs on the outer fringe and lying just off the main by-pass, had arranged for a special bonfire with the usual firework display on Guy Fawkes Night, and there was also to be a procession with decorated cars and fancy dress and a collection on behalf of the Cancer Campaign. It was a fine night with only here and there a patch of fog and, after the procession was over, the bonfire was lighted.

The by-pass just skirts the village and that bonfire had been piled on a meadow between by-pass and village. It went off to a roaring start, thanks to a plentiful use of tar. What little wind there was lay to the north-west. That was the side where the fire was lighted and it was naturally that part of the bonfire that burnt clear first. And just when some feet of it were receding in a roar and sparkle, someone noticed legs sticking out clear of the fierce on-rush of heat. At first it was thought that someone had stuck in an extra guy, but by then the shoes had burnt away, and a couple of constables who were on duty didn't like the look of things.

At any rate, they advanced with a rake and behind a tarpaulin held as protection against the heat, and tried to draw the body out. They couldn't make much of a hand of it. Meanwhile a knowing villager had brought a long ladder and, with it as a kind of battering ram or bulldozer, the fire was pushed away from the body. But that had been done too late. When the fire had died down sufficiently for inspection, what was seen was merely the charred mass of what had once been a human being.

Later that night it was established that the charred body was that of a man. That he should have been a tramp or down-and-out who'd intended to doss for the night in the bonfire material was out of the question. The police, the account concluded, were working on the assumption that it was murder.

Every man, they say, to his trade, and, looking at things with a professional eye, I had the feeling that that bonfire case might be a tough nut to crack. If that body had been burnt to a cinder, then the police would have nothing to go on, except possibly the teeth. What struck me, in fact, was that it was just the kind of murder that George Wharton would take over, and, had it taken place a year ago, there'd have been the possibility of my being called in too. Not that I was in any way jealous or disgruntled, I told myself. I'd long since forgotten about Forlin. Or had I? Hadn't I mentioned him to Jewle only the previous afternoon? But that was just an episode. I'd probably be interested in how that bonfire case developed—no use denying that—but my eye would be the eye of detachment. And in any case I had more than enough to do as it was.

To show that independence of spirit I set about a crossword. It was one of the easier ones and somehow it didn't hold me, so I began tackling the really tough nut. I made heavier going of that too, and I wasn't sorry when Bernice came in from church.

And so to a quiet afternoon and a peaceful evening. I read and Bernice performed her usual feat of reading and knitting at the same time. We had supper a bit late and it was just as we settled down for a last half-hour before the fire that the telephone went. It wasn't Norris and it wasn't Hallows. It was, of all people at that time of night, Chief-Inspector Jewle.

"Hallo, Mr. Travers," he said. "Sorry to disturb you on a Sunday night but are you likely to be still in, say, in half an hour's time?"

"I certainly shall be," I said, "and glad to see you."

"Thanks," he said. "Shan't keep you long. Just a little matter of business."

Human nature, we're told, is a queer thing: just as queer is the enormous capacity for self-deception. As I hung up I couldn't help feeling a bit complacent.

"That was Jewle," I told Bernice. "I wouldn't be surprised if he's coming to talk over that murder. The one in the papers to-day. The bonfire one."

I had to do all that repeating because it takes her a moment or two to get disentangled mentally when she's doing the two jobs at a time.

"That horrible affair," she said, and then gave me a look. "But I thought you'd finished that sort of work."

"So I have," I said piously. "But Jewle isn't Forlin. If Jewle has the idea I can help him in any way, then I'm only too glad to try."

A few minutes later she said she'd go to bed. The lazier the day, the sleepier one got. And she hadn't been out of the room five minutes when Jewle arrived. I noticed he wasn't wearing any go-to-meeting clothes.

"Made it a bit earlier than I thought," he said, as I took his hat and overcoat.

"Beer? Coffee? What'll you have?"

"Nothing, thanks." He warmed his hands at the electric fire. "To tell the truth I've just had my first meal since breakfast. Matthews and I are handling the bonfire case. I expect you saw it in the papers."

"Yes," I said. "And it looked to me as if it might be a pretty tough nut to crack."

"It might have been—if we hadn't had a lot of luck."

I stared.

"Don't say you've solved it already!"

Jewle is one of those big men with a quiet way. When he smiles, as he did then, he looks one of the nicest fellows in the world, and the easiest to work with.

"Wouldn't go so far as that," he said. "But whoever put that body in the bonfire was dead sure there'd be nothing much left when the show was all over. Thanks to those two coppers who had more sense than most, there was something left to go on. Mind if I smoke?"

I apologised for forgetting the cigarettes. He pulled out his pipe and I passed my pouch.

"Thanks," he said, and grinned. "Nice to smoke real toff's tobacco for once. But about what we found. One arm happened to be tucked under the body. There wasn't a lot left of that but the hand wasn't too bad. We managed to get a set of prints."

"Fine!" I said. "And you found he'd got a record?"

"Quite a nice record."

He gave a puff or two at the pipe, saw that it was going nicely and then swivelled round in the chair and faced me. There was a quizzical sort of look on his face.

"You ought to know what it was. I put it in the post for you myself on Friday night."

I gaped. The balloon was suddenly deflated.

"You don't mean . . ."

"Yes," he said. "It was Hover. The one you wanted details about. So I thought I'd hear just what you'd got to tell me."

There was just a slight grimness in his tone. But that was nothing. Wharton would have been blustering or hectoring.

"Better let me sort out my ideas."

"Look, sir," he said. "We're dealing with a murder. That body wouldn't have been dumped just there if Hover'd died naturally. In other words, I'd like all your cards on the table."

I'd been like a boxer who'd taken a nasty one clean on the chin and who'd been hanging on till he got his wits once more about him. Now I thought I knew what to tell and what it might be safe to keep back.

"Right," he said, when I'd finished. "Hover was picked up at about a quarter past ten. He sort of strolled round the town looking at the sights and then he fixed himself up with a bag and some clothes with the money he got from the bank and then he got himself a room at the Ferney Hotel. You reported that to your client and, as far as you were concerned, that was the end. But would you mind telling me a bit more about the client?"

I told him, but I didn't say I'd been suspicious of her or that she'd been followed.

"Mrs. North," he said. "A Danish woman who'd married an Englishman. And claimed that Hover had swindled her late husband. What was her address?"

"No need for it," I said. "The whole thing was so cut and dried that I saw no reason for it. No, that's not right. I didn't even think about it, but I can give you the telephone number to which we reported. Regent 777. It was easy to remember." He asked for a description of the woman and I gave it. After that he just smoked his pipe for a minute and said nothing. He grunted softly to himself.

"A bit slack, weren't you?"

"Now, now, now," I said. "I'd never heard of Hover in my life. A woman comes into our office, wants the most childish job of shadowing done, gives an excellent reason for it, and pays cash down. Just like that. Where's the slackness?"

"Maybe I was looking at it from our angle," he told me apologetically. "But I take it you're prepared to give us every possible help?"

"You personally, yes," I said. "But I'll not do a damn for Forlin. And I'm going to do more. The Agency looks to me to have got itself well mixed up with murder. It looks, in fact, as if Hover's whereabouts on Friday night were wanted by someone who intended to wipe him out. That Mrs. North must have been some kind of a fake, and that sort of thing might make us some pretty bad publicity."

"We shan't mention the Agency unless we've some very good reasons. You co-operate, sir, and there won't be any reasons."

"We've got our personal pride," I told him. "You won't be tripping over us, but we shall make enquiries of our own."

"And pass on what you happen to find out?"

"If it's worth the passing on."

He knocked out his pipe.

"Well, that sounds fair enough. In any case, it's a free country. There's no law against making enquiries, if, as you say, you don't get under our feet."

I helped him on with his overcoat.

"I'm sorry about this," he said. "It's between ourselves, but I'd have liked you to be in on it officially. There's every reason, seeing how things are, so what about my dropping a hint to Forlin?"

"I'd rather you didn't," I said. "It's good of you but, honestly, I'd rather not. But you're different. Whatever I can do, I will."

I saw him to the lift. When I went back along the corridor my forehead was damp and I wiped it with my handkerchief. I guessed it'd be damp again before the night was out. Skating on thin ice is pretty tough work.

Back in the flat I made straight for the telephone. Hallows was asleep but he has an extension by his bed.

"Travers here," I said. "Jewle has just been in. You'd better take an urgent note of what I'm going to say."

I told him the whole thing; just what he had to remember and what to forget.

"No need to mention French at the moment. Also I'm sure Jewle won't have you out of bed. But don't give him the chance to see you early in the morning. Get here at about eight and we'll talk the whole thing over."

# 9

## SLEIGHT OF HAND

I DIDN'T disturb Norris. Only Hallows and myself knew at the moment that Hover was the man in the bonfire, but in the morning the whole thing would be spread across the front pages and that would be the time to ring.

The man who did worry me was Bill Fraser. He'd sent the client to us and I didn't know how much he'd listened to before he'd regretted he couldn't take her case. But as Norris had reported it, Bill hadn't done much questioning. Not that Bill could be any sort of obstacle across the somewhat tricky path I was proposing to tread.

I was mapping out that path as I lay in bed that night waiting for sleep. I told myself that I'd given my word to Jewle and that I'd play scrupulously fair, but that didn't mean that I was to renounce a heaven-sent chance to prove to Forlin that rigid adherence to rules and regulations was not the best way to solve a murder case. What I'd try to do was to reverse the whole procedure: I would not so much be helping Jewle as he helping me. As soon as I had something to tell, I'd tell it, and get what he knew in exchange. Jewle also would play fair. If and when that case was solved, it'd be the thrill of his life—and, I thought, of George Wharton's—to let Forlin know what might be done when red-tape was thrown out of the window.

I'd set the alarm clock for half-past six and it was one of those nights when you wake up at half-hourly intervals, wondering if you've overslept. When I did get up I felt a bit washed out and it wasn't till I'd had a cold shower and a cup of tea that I could begin thinking things out again. Then I rang Norris. He hadn't yet seen a morning paper so I had the explanations to myself.

"Nothing for us to worry about," I told him. "Jewle came in last night and the whole thing's right and tight. See you in the office later. By the way, I may be a bit late."

Bill Fraser has a flat above his office and I rang him there. As it happened he hadn't known the name of the man whom the client wanted picked up and he was quite pleased to be told about it. I told him I'd reported to the police and he even sounded grateful to us for handling the business and leaving him in the clear.

Next I slipped out and bought another newspaper or two. There were headlines and photographs but little more in the way of news. It also said that Chief-Det.-Inspector Jewle and Det.-Sergeant Matthews of the Yard were in charge of the Case. One crime reporter was of the opinion that as the Bromford Guy Fawkes Night had been publicized in the Press, the one who had put the body in the bonfire had been able to plan ahead and had also probably surveyed the scene beforehand. Overtime must have been worked, for there were biographies of Hover, even if the additional details were of no use to myself.

We had breakfast rather early and then Hallows arrived.

He'd already eaten so we went at once to the den. It was best, I thought, to take him absolutely into my confidence.

"I get you," he said. "It's a wash-out following up things so as to get the Agency well in with Mr. Hill."

"Call it a secondary affair," I said. "If we do have the luck really to help solve the bonfire business, that ought to include what we're afterwards able to tell Hill. But what I'm proposing to do this morning is to start from where you picked Hover up and go everywhere he went to. I'll tell you about that after I've seen Mr. Norris. In the meanwhile you check that telephone number to which you reported. Then wait for me at Broad Street. I'll bring my own car."

Norris seemed quite unperturbed. I doubt if he'd even have mentioned that bonfire business if I hadn't brought it up again.

"I can't help thinking we ought to get ourselves a bit better covered over that Mrs. North business," I said. "Jewle did think we'd been just a bit off-hand. So if you can spare Hallows for a day or two, I'd like to try to make a few enquiries. Charge the whole thing to my personal account."

"But if it's Agency business?"

"It may not altogether turn out to be," I told him cryptically. "Leave it for the moment that I'm paying Hallows's time. Later on we might see."

Of course it would be taking something out of my pocket and later putting most of it back, but things were devious already, as you'll have noted. But I couldn't tell Norris about the suspected connection of Hover and the rest with that jewellery and Russian Cross affair. He didn't know that Hover had married Lister. And he certainly didn't know that Sigott also had a vague connection with everything through having known Lister. I didn't even know if that was just a coincidence or a clue, but I wasn't going to take up the rest of the morning going into everything laboriously with Norris, even if he'd had the time.

Hallows was waiting and we went out to the car.

"Everything fixed up," I said. "You've located that telephone address?"

"Corner of Peddick Road and Radford Road, St. John's Wood," he said. "Don't like the look of it, though. It's a newsagent's. Sounds to me like an accommodation address."

"We'll work our way round to it," I told him. "Jewle's probably been there already. Let's make straight for Hover's bank."

The bank had only just opened and it didn't take more than five minutes from the time we went in till the moment when we walked into the manager's office. He was a middle-aged man, pleasant looking and not too stiffly dressed. He held out his hand.

"Mr. Travers?" He smiled. "I've often passed that Agency of yours but I never thought we should meet."

I introduced Hallows. We sat down.

"Anything I can do for you, gentlemen?"

I didn't smile, even if the look on his face said plainly that his wonder was what we might have come to do for him. I told him why we were there: not in terms of knowing, but suspecting: having reason to believe, as the cliché goes. He wasn't flustered: he wasn't that kind of man.

"Pardon me a moment," he said, "and I'll start some enquiries. You don't know the name under which he banked with me, but he probably cashed a personal cheque on Friday last at about half-past ten. A man of about fifty of military bearing. Might be Australian, English or American."

"Wearing a light-brown suit and a dark-brown overcoat," Hallows added. "A Homburg hat and I think it was fawn."

It was a quarter of an hour before he was back. A messenger had brought coffee and had said we might smoke, so the time didn't drag.

"I think I have the facts," the manager told us. "He opened an account here on the 12th of September, 1951. Seven hundred and fifty dollars which we exchanged. He said he was an American, Horace Walker, of Atlanta, Georgia, over here for what might be a stay of some months. Here's his signature."

The signature was bold. Hallows asked if he might make a rough tracing.

"The account's been very little used," the manager went on. "Those four years in Norwich Jail—about three with remittances—he naturally didn't touch it at all. On Friday last the balance stood at eighty-six-odd pounds. He said he was going back to the States at once and drew out eighty-five pounds. He also said he'd lost or mislaid his cheque-book, and as soon as he found it he'd clear the account."

"Any large sums paid in from time to time?"

"Not large," he said. "In fact only one payment—two hundred and fifty pounds in cash on May 3rd, 1952."

"That'd be after he made a haul of some kind," I said. "But I'd be right in saying that on the whole he simply used his account here as a fund to draw on?"

"Exactly, and, for all we know, he had a similar account or accounts elsewhere. But what do you advise? As far as we're concerned his conduct's been almost irreproachable. There is, of course, the false name."

"There's only one thing you can do," I said as I rose. "Get all your facts in order and a copy of his accounts and then ring Scotland Yard. Ask for Chief-Detective-Inspector Jewle. I'll write it for you."

Five minutes and we were picking up the car again from the bombed site.

"Wonder what he'll think when Jewle tells him his customer was the bonfire body," Hallows said.

"Wonder what Jewle will think when he knows we're already ahead of him."

There was plenty more to wonder as we drove towards Wardour Street: what similar banking accounts Hover had had, and how long it would take Jewle to unearth them: if any of them would show such a largish payment as was to be expected from a realisation of the stolen jewellery and the Russian Cross, and even the wonder if that cross had really had its diamonds intact when it was lifted. Such a payment might determine roughly when the jewellery had been stolen.

"My guess is that it was shortly after his marriage to Lister," Hallows said. "That might be the money she lived on after she left Sigott, while Hover was in Norwich."

It was just after eleven o'clock when we drew up outside that music shop in Wardour Street. The name was the Aeolian Supply Company, Limited. The smallish twin windows had the usual show of hit music, and instruments from piano to harmonicas. This time I went in alone. The only person who seemed to be anywhere about was the manager. I showed him my Agency card. He was a short, middle-aged fellow and you couldn't have found a hair on his head if you'd wandered an inch from his ears.

"Excuse it," he said as he handed back the card, "but you don't look like a detective."

"And you don't look like Heifetz," I said, "but for all I know you might play the violin just as well."

He laughed.

"Like Heifetz, he says. Mister, if I played like him, do you think I'd be here?"

"Who knows?" I said. "They tell me these top virtuosi do all sorts of things. But to get to business. You had a caller last Friday morning—a military-looking man—who was anxious to find out what had become of the man who had this shop before you. I'm looking for that man, too."

He knew nothing, he said, as he spread his palms. He had said the same to the man who'd asked on the Friday. All he did know was that the shop had been a photographer's studio. The name was The Wardour Street Studios. He'd never seen the owner or manager, or whatever he was. His own company— well, it was his son-in-law really—had acquired the lease in the spring and he'd been transferred from the other shop in Willesden to here.

"Do you know who handled the business?"

He didn't, but he gave me the address of the Willesden shop.

"And what's your idea of the sort of business it was when it was a studio? Would it make money?"

"Why not?" he said. "All round are the offices of the film companies. Maybe all the time there are little jobs they want you to do, and once you get in—well, who knows?"

"While you've been here, has anyone asked about that photographer?"

No one, he said, except the gentleman on Friday. A Colonel Someone—he'd forgotten the name. And then he gaped a bit, as if he remembered something.

"Yes?" I said.

He shrugged his shoulders. It was nothing. But that Colonel had mentioned the photographer by name.

"Now what was it?" he was asking himself. "It began with a W—"

"It couldn't have been Wakes?"

"Wakes," he said and stared. "That was it—Wakes!"

"Reginald Wakes?"

"He did not mention the other name."

I took out a pound note and gave it to him. He looked at it and at me.

"There is something you wish to buy?"

"I've bought it," I told him. He stared at me and then again at the note. Maybe he was wondering if I'd made it myself.

I moved the car on at once. A few seconds and I was slowing again. Just on our right were the offices of the Magna Film Company.

I told Hallows what I'd learned. And if Wakes had done any odd jobs for the film companies, then the Magna was the nearest.

"You see what you can pick up. I'll wait here."

I had about twenty minutes' wait. What he'd have to tell me might have made a difference to the rest of the day, so we stayed there.

"I made a contact," he said. "Wakes wasn't doing too badly there, so this chap thinks. He hasn't seen hide or hair of him, though, since he left. In fact he didn't know he'd gone till he saw the place empty."

"Did you get a description?"

"Only the old one: the one with the streaky moustache we got before. By the way, I said I'd been in business with Wakes once myself and I'd just got back from Canada and was trying to locate him. Lucky I did. The contact was a bit nervous and you'll see why. I pretended to be one of the bright boys myself. 'Reg still up to the old postcard game?' He didn't say he had or he hadn't but I'll bet a fiver he knew. 'You mean art studies?' he said, and he laughed and I laughed and that's where I thought I'd better leave it."

"It ties in," I said. "Some time, if we have to, we might see if this pal of yours has any art studies. It might tell us whom Wakes used for a model. But where to now? What about Mallow Grove?"

We went to Mallow Grove and stopped a few yards short of that block of flats known as Number 24.

"You'd better handle it," I said. "I'm a bit too conspicuous." He got out, walked a yard or two and then came back.

"Did you ring the Inspector about Wardour Street or ask that manager to?"

"Neither," I said. "I doubt if Jewle will get on to it. If he does it won't be yet. We'll keep it up our sleeve."

I had a wait of best part of half an hour. When he got back he told me to go on and take the first right, which would bring us to the Edgware Road again. We stopped just short of it.

"Everything turned out well back there," he said. "Just as we worked it out. The two Lister sisters had the flat when Elizabeth came to town. A two-bedroomed flat plus the usual. Elizabeth became Mrs. Prestwich and the Colonel lived there too. Some of his time. From what I could gather he was as much away as there. Probably living at hotels and looking for pigeons. Wakes was an occasional visitor too. But what'll make you laugh is the excuse Elizabeth gave—let's call her Lizzie—what she gave when the Colonel was grabbed for that Norwich job. She said his regiment was ordered to Kenya to fight the Mau Mau."

I did have to laugh.

"Damn funny," Hallows said. "I can see him tackling the Mau Mau. What he'd have done was join them himself and start some sort of racket. But there's a mystery after that. Lizzie wasn't much at the flat, as we know. She was doing the Rimmell and Sigott nursing jobs, but then she dropped out altogether. No one ever saw her at the flat again. Doreen said she'd gone to Kenya to join her husband."

"That gets us back to Kossack," I said. "Looks as if he was keeping her somewhere. All the same, I don't see why she couldn't have come occasionally to the flat."

"Well, she didn't," Hallows said. "Not even when the Colonel came out of jail. He was said to have been invalided home from

Kenya for health reasons. He got back to the old routine. Seen occasionally at the flat and then a week or two away: probably looking for more pigeons. Wakes was in and out as usual, whether the Colonel was there or not."

"A queer mix-up," I said. "Mrs. Kossack said she was sure her husband wasn't having anything to do with Lizzie, and I don't know why Wakes should go to the flat alone if he was keeping her. But she must have been somewhere and the Colonel must have known where. Unless Doreen put him off with lies. But if so why did he hope to get some news about her from Sigott's studio?"

"I know," he said. "It's a fine old muddle. We want some more facts from Mallow Grove. Perhaps I might manage it later if it is wanted."

"You've done marvels as it is," I said. "But what about when the Colonel was jailed a second time?"

"Doreen simply left," he said. "The flat was in their joint names. They didn't leave any forwarding address. It was a yearly rental and only a couple of months or so to expire."

"Well, we're not doing so badly," I told him. "We're tying a few things in. Now what about that pub in the Edgware Road where the Colonel had his lunch?"

We had no luck in the Golden Lion but we had quite a good meal and a drink. The elderly waiter came to our table to ask if we'd take coffee.

"By the way, does my old friend Colonel Prestwich drop in for lunch nowadays?" I said.

He didn't know him. I gave a description.

"Ah, yes," he said. "He was in quite recently, but not at my table, though. I hadn't seen him for quite a long time. I'd even forgotten his name till you mentioned it."

"Did he ever come in with a lady?"

He gave me a quick look. He cocked his head sideways in thought. I had the idea that, in view of his tip, he was trying to guess the answer we wanted. But he knew nothing of a lady, or that's what he said.

We didn't take coffee but went straight to that garage where the Colonel had kept his car. It was just short of two o'clock and only one man was at work. Another came in just behind us.

"The manager about?" Hallows asked the one who was working on an oldish Standard.

"Manager?" he said. "There isn't one."

"The proprietor, then."

"Ah, him," he said. "Mr. Upton. He'll be in at any time now. Been out for his lunch."

"We'll wait," Hallows told him. "By the way, does Colonel Prestwich still have his car here?"

"That's right. He should have collected it to-day. That Austin Twelve, just in front of the Daimler."

We had a look at it. It was in perfect order and looked good as new. A bit démodé, perhaps. The Colonel had probably bought it as soon as he arrived in England from the States. A quiet, competent, unpretentious car: the kind that would give him an air of respectability.

"Interested in the car?"

That was evidently the proprietor—a red-faced man of Hallows's build: fortyish, hook-nosed and wearing a well-worn navy-blue suit. We gave him our cards.

"Uh-huh?" he said. "What's going on?"

"Want to get yourself some nice publicity?" I said.

"I don't get you."

"Let's go to your office, and you will."

I told him about Prestwich. His eyes bulged a bit when he heard about the bonfire body.

"I read about that in the paper this morning. You're sure he's the man?"

"Practically sure. And this isn't some kind of joke. We're a reputable firm."

I gave him my card again and said he could check up.

"I'll take your word for it. But what am I supposed to do now?"

"Get on the phone to Scotland Yard," I said. "Mention my name. Look, I'll write it all down for you."

A minute or two and we were walking back to the car. "And that's Jewle's ration for the day," I told Hallows. "We've got to keep something up our sleeves."

"Yes, but how'll you explain away how you got on to the garage?"

"I shan't. If I have to, there's plenty of time to think things out."

"And where now?"

"St. John's Wood. Jewle's almost certainly been there already, but it'll look good if it does nothing else."

It was a shortish trip. We overshot the newsagent's shop and then came back to it on the side heading for home. It was the usual suburban shop: tobacco, newspapers and periodicals. A bundle of evening papers had just arrived and a thin, mild-looking woman of fifty was sorting them.

"Yes, sir?" She went on with the sorting. I gave her my Agency card.

"Detectives!" she said. "But we've had the police here already. From Scotland Yard."

A woman came in for a magazine. We waited.

"I know," I said, when the shop was clear again. "We're following up on it. Would you mind repeating what you said about the telephone call? This, by the way, is the man you took the message from last Friday afternoon."

Hallows held out a hand.

"Pleased to meet you," she said. "And so you're the one I was talking to."

"That's right. I made you repeat the message and you said it'd be all right."

"I remember your voice now," she said. "But I can't tell you anything. Just a minute."

Another customer, this time a boy for the *Evening Standard*.

"Yes," she said. "The lady came in first thing Friday morning. 'You take letters and messages here?' she asked. 'That's right,' I said. 'What did you want, madam?' She looked a real lady like I said. Then she told me I'd get a telephone message during the day and would I take it and she'd call in later. She asked me what it'd be, so I said a shilling, just on spec., as they say. I'd never had anything like that before. Then I got the message and I had it all writ down for her when she come. She looked ever so grateful."

"A woman of about five-feet seven?" I said. "Very pale blonde hair?"

"That's her," she said. "I could see she was a lady. Oh, and the name was Mrs. North."

"We're very much obliged to you," I told her. "If Scotland Yard should see you again there'll be no harm in telling them we were here."

Out to the car again. We sat talking for a minute or two. I wondered how she'd discovered that shop that took messages.

"You think there's a likelihood that Doreen is living some-where in the neighbourhood?"

"If she is, you can bet your life she won't be seen again within a mile of it," Hallows said. "But if anything had gone wrong, of course, she'd have rung the office."

"I hope I'm not maligning our wives," I said, "but there's something feminine about it. It's too intricate. She'd no need to bring in that shop at all. As you said, she might have arranged to ring the office for Hover's new address."

"Maybe you're right," he said. "But she didn't anticipate any risk. Who was to connect her with the man in the bonfire? It was a million to one chance he'd be a cinder when they found him. And where now, sir?"

I said I thought it was practically all, but it wouldn't be too much out of his way if he saw those agents at Hammersmith and tried to unearth something about Doreen. She'd almost certainly covered her tracks, but you never knew.

I went round by Baker Street and dropped him at the Tube Station. If there was anything to report, he'd give me a ring. If not I'd see him at Broad Street in the morning. I drove on to the office but there wasn't anything doing, so I went home, garaged the car, and looked forward to a restful evening. How restful I didn't know. It might depend on Jewle. I had an idea he'd be ringing me.

# 10

# SPADE WORK

"HAL-*LO*, sir! Jewle here."

It was just after nine o'clock. He sounded quite pleased with himself. My conscience didn't smite me and I didn't blush. I don't think I've blushed since those far-off days when I'd worked only a year or two with George Wharton.

"Hallo, Jewle. Where are you?"

"At the Yard. Just ringing up to thank you for those couple of tips you passed in to-day. They might be very useful. How'd you get on to them, by the way?"

There it was, the big-prize question.

"Hard work and a stroke or two of luck. Can't give away any trade secrets, you know."

He laughed.

"You keep on having the luck, sir, and we won't worry about the secrets."

"It wasn't all luck," I said. "We went to that newsagents in St. John's Wood but your people'd been there before us. Nothing doing. We did have an idea that our Mrs. North might be living somewhere in the neighbourhood."

"That's one thing we did think of," he said. "I'm putting some men on it."

"Lucky you. We've got to grub along with a man or two—if we can spare 'em. You unearthed anything new yourself?"

"Not yet," he said. "It's going to be slow work. But tomorrow we're seeing that widow: the Norwich one that Hover got his four years over. She might give us a lead."

"Good luck to you. And, by the way, we might be on to something ourselves in a day or so—where Hover's actual head-quarters were."

"No!" he said. "How the devil do you expect to get on to that?"

"Ways and means. But just let's suppose something. Suppose we looked back through our books and unearthed a client who'd come to us after being victimised, and—still supposing—we thought we had a tie-up with Hover."

"Yes," he said glumly. "That's where you've got us beat. They never have the nerve to come to us. They don't like us to know they've been made fools of." He gently cleared his throat. "Suppose you couldn't give us the name of this client?"

"Now, now, now. You know you've no right to ask that—even if he—or she—existed."

"Yes," he said. "Still it was worth trying."

"As a matter of fact we'll do better still. I'll slip word to you as soon as we find anything at all."

"That'll be fine," he said. "No idea how long it'll be?"

"Depends on the luck. You might get it as early as to-morrow. But just one thing. Pass the word that if any of your people see ours nosing around, they're not to be brought in."

"I'll do that," he said. "And thanks again. Hope to be hearing from you."

So much for Jewle. Everything had turned out fine. I could tell myself that there'd be no hampering of justice. Jewle, without what he'd learned from us during the day, would have been short of where he stood at the moment. And I was very definitely going to tell him about Mallow Grove. Indeed, when I came to think about it, I knew I daren't delay passing on that tip for more than twenty-four hours. As soon as he had the tip, he'd discover just when Hallows had been there. He'd wonder why he hadn't been notified at once.

Hallows didn't ring me that night, which meant that he'd learned nothing of value about Doreen Lister. In the morning I was at the office rather early but he was already there. What he'd got at Hammersmith was very little. Once more Doreen had sacrificed part of the time still to run on her short lease of the shop.

"When you come to look back at last February," Hallows said, "and just after sentence was passed on Hover, you can see the whole thing. They'd shopped him between them and they knew he'd be out again at the end of the year, so they all ran like a lot of rats. Cleared out of Mallow Grove, and Doreen from that shop of hers and Wakes from Wardour Street and never left a trace behind them—forwarding addresses nor nothing. They must have been scared stiff."

"Yes," I said, and afterwards I was to remember it. "And yet somehow it's not altogether in keeping. Except for that supposed complicity in that American bank job, he never used force. A con-man never does. And he's a game loser. He knows the risks and accepts them. Somehow I can't help thinking they were afraid of something more than having shopped Hover."

"Look at it like this," Hallows said. "They'd given him away and his revenge when he came out might be to give *them* away. All three were probably up to the neck in God-knows-what."

"Let's leave it," I said, and told him about my talk with Jewle.

"Our policy is to keep just that much ahead of the Yard," I said. "We've got a start and we've got to keep it. What I'm proposing is this: there's a clue that ought to be followed up. French is the only one who saw the man we think is Wakes. He later saw the taxi driver and found out that Wakes and Doreen had been dropped in Marlbury Street. That may have been a blind on their part. All they'd have to do was wait and then take another taxi to somewhere else. But we've got to take a chance, so what about putting French on the watch in Marlbury Street somewhere about where they were dropped? That was almost opposite Smith's Hotel."

"Sounds a good idea," he said. "And what's for me?"

I said I had something in mind but he might have a better.

"You're the boss," he said mildly. "I can't think of a thing unless it's Sigott. He's one of Hover's calls we haven't done anything about. But that's more up your alley than mine."

"What about your friend at the Magna Film Company? I'd like to get hold of some of those art studies. Wakes must have had someone to pose. It wouldn't do any harm to know who."

French was on a missing-person case with another operative but I managed to run him to earth. There wasn't a time limit to the job he was doing so I told him to report to me after lunch. When I got back from my own lunch, he was waiting to be briefed. Then Hallows came in.

"Had to go all the way to Denham," he said. "Our man was working at the studios. Almost a wasted morning."

"Why almost?"

"Well, he's still a bit suspicious of me," Hallows said. "Thinks I'm laying some kind of trap. As I kept telling him, there's nothing wrong with buying them—him buying them from Wakes. I told him I was going to work that racket myself and was looking out for a photographer. Gave him an address to drop me a line at if he got wind of one."

"You think he really has some of Wakes' studies?"

"I'm sure of it." He gave a wry smile. "I must be losing my touch. Or else he's waiting for a higher bid."

There seemed nothing at the moment that he could do. I was going to see Sigott, or so I hoped.

"Why not let me fill in with French?" Hallows said. "We can't spare a relief and he'll find it pretty long hours."

He anticipated what I was going to say.

"I know it's a bit of a come-down but this case has got hold of me. I've just got to be in on it. I don't give a damn what I do if it's going to help."

I told him to arrange things with French, and as soon as anything broke that was more in his line I'd bring him in again. By then it was two o'clock, so I rang Sigott.

It was the blonde who answered. She'd forgotten my name but when I described myself she remembered me.

"Could you ring again in half an hour's time?" she said. "Mr. Sigott always has a little sleep after lunch."

"Too urgent for that," I said. "I must see him as soon as he's finished his nap. In half an hour's time."

If I knew anything about London traffic I'd be lucky to get to the studio in half an hour. My bus didn't make bad time but I was five minutes late.

"Mr. Sigott will see you," the blonde said, and as if he was going to step down from a pedestal and let me kiss his hand. "There's no appointment for this afternoon."

He was in the studio preparing a canvas. His manner was a blend of the polite and the wary.

"Afternoon, Travers. What's this urgent business you've come about?"

"As a matter of fact I've come to do you a favour. To be precise, to keep you from being tangled up with the police."

There was a sudden flush of red, and afterwards I was to wonder why. It couldn't have been anger.

"The police? What on earth are you talking about?"

"You've read about the Bonfire Murder?"

"Bonfire Murder?" He was wondering whether to admit anything so bourgeois. "I believe I did see something."

"Well, a man was murdered and his body put in that bonfire with the hope that it'd be charred out of all recognition. Luckily it wasn't, and the police know who the man was. His name was James Hover."

He was listening but the name hadn't rung a bell.

"I'm engaged on that case in a roundabout way, and the police know it. What they don't know is that this man Hover called here last Friday afternoon a few hours before he was killed. He saw and spoke to someone who I think was your housekeeper."

That rang more than a bell. It rang an alarm gong.

"Good God!" he said. "She told me something about a man calling. I was out myself. And you say it was the man who was murdered?"

"I know it was."

"Incredible."

He thought for a moment.

"Would you mind waiting here? I'll get Mrs. Crewe to come in. She's the widow of that poor devil Crewe who killed himself some years ago. He and I were students together."

He went out. Maybe I have too suspicious a mind but I couldn't help wondering a couple of things. Why, with a bell-push almost at his elbow, hadn't he rung for the blonde Laura and asked her to bring the housekeeper in? And why had he given me that potted biography of Mrs. Crewe? Was it because he wanted me to regard what she had to say as even better than gospel truth? And why was he taking so long a time?

It must have been five minutes before he was back.

"Sorry to have kept you waiting. This is Mrs. Crewe. . . . An old friend, Ludovic Travers."

She was a handsome-looking woman in the late forties: as calmly poised as her voice had been on the telephone.

"Ada, perhaps you'll tell Mr. Travers about that caller on Friday afternoon."

"He was a curious sort of man," she said. "A Colonel Something: I've forgotten what. He looked quite a gentleman, but there was something not quite right about his voice. It wasn't in keeping, if you know what I mean. It was rather overdone."

"You mean he was trying to create an impression?"

"That's it," she said. "And that's why I didn't let him get farther than the hall. I was all alone here, you know. He said he was the uncle of a Nurse Lister who'd attended Mrs. Sigott in her fatal illness some years ago, and he wondered if we'd had any news of her. I just told him the truth: that she'd merely come here to nurse Mrs. Sigott and I'd no idea where she was. And that was about all, except that I had quite a job to get rid of him. He kept asking the same thing over again."

"And naturally you'd never seen him before?"

"But of course not!" She smiled. "Didn't I make that clear?"

I smiled, too.

"You did. But I'm just a bit obtuse at times." I looked at Sigott. All the time he'd been motionless and watchful. "I don't think there's anything else."

"Right," he said. "Thank you, Ada."

I nodded my own thanks, and even managed to get ahead of her and open the door to the corridor. She gave me a smile.

"A superior kind of woman," I said to Sigott. "A widow of a friend of yours, you said?"

This time he didn't want to talk about it.

"Yes," he said. "But you really think the police'll be here?"

"Not if I keep my mouth shut about Hover's call here last Friday—and I think I can. But you haven't heard the main point. Hover wasn't your Nurse Lister's uncle. He was her husband."

If ever a man was hit clean in the wind it was Sigott. He literally gaped. He couldn't find any words. He turned away, took a cigarette from the box on the side table and lighted it.

"You rather surprised me for a minute." He forced a smile. "But why shouldn't she have been married to this man Hover?"

"Let's take it slowly," I said, and his eyes were on me again. "Hover was a crook: a con-man and general kind of swindler. At the time Nurse Lister was here he was doing a four-year stretch in Norwich jail."

"But she wasn't married to him then?"

"How do you know?"

He turned away again.

"Dammit, Travers, I'm not in the witness-box. If she'd been married to him she'd have mentioned it."

"Mentioned it? And he in jail?" I grunted. "But let's clear all that up. She *was* married to him when she was here. I have a copy of the marriage certificate. She was married to him about nine months before she came here."

He shrugged his shoulders.

"Even so I don't see how I'm affected."

"We'll say you're not," I told him. "But to rake something else up: something which definitely won't be told to the police. Your Nurse Lister was married to a crook and she must have got into touch with him when he came out of jail. I admit that doesn't make her a crook, but put it with one or two other things we know and there's quite the chance that she might have been pretty shady herself. And so—"

"Just a minute," he said. "What things do you know about her?"

"Why're you interested?"

"God-dammit, man!" He glared at me. "She was in this house, wasn't she? I found her competent and absolutely reliable."

"Glad to hear it," I said. "It saves me from suggesting something—that it might have been she who took those drawings of yours. No, no, no! Just hear me out. I know she didn't take them. If she had, she wouldn't have waited three years before trying to cash in."

I moved towards the door. He was trying to find something to say. When he did speak his tone was exceptionally mild.

"I'm much obliged to you, Travers. Do I take it that this is the last I shall hear of it?"

"Probably yes," I said, and the *probably* was just to leave him with a not too settled mind. "There's no need to mention anything to the police."

He was nodding to himself as he followed me back to the hall. Again there was no sign of the blonde as he helped me on with my coat. At the door his hand-shake almost crushed my fingers.

I followed practically the same routine as on my first visit: walking to that tea-shop, taking twenty minutes or so over a pot of tea and a cake, and then hopping a bus for the City. But this time my thoughts were very different. There were so many of them that I had to write abstracts in my notebook of everything that had been done and said. That pinned them down for dissection but even when I was back in Broad Street I couldn't discern a pattern. What I did see was a kind of governing factor. Behind everything was the undoubted fact that Sigott had had a considerable deal which he was desperately anxious to conceal.

And what I finally did was to put things down in the form of questions. That's how you can sometimes find answers—the right answers—and, if you can't, there're often other questions that arise from them and maybe you'll get the answers just there.

1. Why was Sigott so staggered to learn that L was married?

2. Why fetch the housekeeper himself if not to put evidence into her mouth?

3. Was she under an obligation to him?

4. Why was he so anxious to know what else we might have on L?

5. Why wasn't Laura allowed to show me out, unless it was that he was afraid I should question her?

As I sat looking at those questions I realised that one at least might be answered. I rang Charles Muhler and had the good luck to find him in.

"How are you, Travers?" he said. "I saw you in the club last week but you looked so peaceful I wouldn't disturb you."

"I get like that nowadays," I said. "Second childhood creeping up on me. But tell me something, Charles. Do you know anything about a painter named Crewe? I believe he committed suicide some years ago."

"Ah!" he said. "That'd be Robert Crewe. A brilliant chap but began lifting his elbow. Drugs too, I believe. Finally took an overdose of some kind. A very sad case."

"Did he leave any money?"

"Heavens, no," he said. "Died practically destitute. There was some talk of raising a fund for his wife. As a matter of fact I subscribed to it in my modest way. Don't think it amounted to much, though. Luckily there were no children."

"You know her personally?"

"Well, no," he said. "I seem to remember I met her a couple of times. A remarkably handsome woman, but that was a good few years ago."

"Well, thanks, Charles. A friend was asking about her the other day and I only just had the idea you might know something. You don't know where she is at the moment?"

"Can't say I do. I suppose it's years since I even thought about her."

That was about all but it seemed enough. Ada Crewe looked to be definitely under an obligation to Sigott, and I struck that question out. But it was a kind of dragon's-teeth affair for others at once cropped up. Even the salacious persisted in creeping in. A handsome woman, and still in a way she was. Had she once been more than just Sigott's housekeeper? And had she later been resigned to being supplanted by that red-haired model, Margaret Mann? And was she still keeping a kind of blind eye on anything that might now be going on with the blonde Laura?

And might she have some hold or other on Sigott for which she was being well paid? And might—

But I didn't let that last question peep too far out. George Wharton had twitted me for years with having far too agile and anticipatory a mind. So I let that matter of Mrs. Sigott's death, and the possibility that there had been something fishy about it, remain well in the background. And I'd also remembered that it mightn't be too soon to pass some more information to Jewle.

Jewle wasn't at the Yard, but Matthews was and I was put through to him. I like Matthews. I've known him ever since he was taken off the beat. He's got a sense of humour and he's managed to keep it after years of working with Wharton, and if that doesn't deserve a medal, what does?

"Hal-*lo*, sir! Long time no see."

Matthews, you can gather, reads a lot of crime fiction. He confided to me once that it helped him in his work. I asked how he was and how his wife was and how his boy was, and I was lucky about that last for I'd forgotten whether it was a boy or a girl.

"That garage tip I passed on," I said. "Did you get anything out of it?"

"Not a lot," he said, "except that he didn't use the car very often and when he did he usually came in for it at about half-past one or two. Looks as if he lived somewhere handy."

"Nothing else?"

He didn't speak for a moment. When he did, I could hardly hear him.

"Well, keep this under your hat, sir, because I don't know if I'm doing right to pass it on, but inside the glove compartment on the driver's side there was a special sort of private compartment he'd had rigged up just round the corner, if you know what I mean. It worked with a catch and there was a gun inside. Or rather, there wasn't. One of the mechanics had happened to find that special little compartment and he'd found the gun—a neat little automatic. But Hover had a look at that car on the Friday and made an excuse to send the mechanic somewhere, and when Hover left the gun had gone too."

"Interesting," I said. "You'd hardly have expected it of a con-man. But wait a minute, young fellow. Why not cough up the whole story?"

"The whole story?" he asked, far too blandly. "I don't know what you mean."

"Listen," I said, "I had some more information to pass on but now I'm damned if I'm going to. We'll have a swap instead. I'll know nothing about a gun, but when Jewle comes in you'll be able to stagger him with what I might tell you. What about it?"

"All right, sir, let's swap. You start."

"Oh, no," I said. "A man who's worked as long as you have with Wharton isn't all that reliable. You start."

"And you're really going to pass on something good?"

"Better than good."

"Right," he said. "We haven't passed it out yet but Hover was shot. In the head. The bullet's the kind that might have come out of that kind of gun."

I must have grunted. It looked like being a good swap. "You can tell Jewle I rang up specially to let him know I'd been luckier than I'd hoped about location. Hover's main hide-out. Got a paper handy? . . . Just write this, 'Enquire for a Colonel Prestwich at 24 Mallow Grove, Hendon.' Got it?"

"Yes," he said. "Colonel Prestwich at 24 Mallow Grove, Hendon. Think I'll get out there straight away myself."

## 11

# REGINALD WAKES

I THOUGHT that the morning might bring a call from Jewle but it didn't. He was probably far too busy while we were living on hope. Unless we found Wakes, we'd soon have exhausted the legacy we'd received through that following of Hover on the morning he left jail. We'd have, in fact, nothing more to give. We'd be living on the charity of Jewle.

I couldn't help envying him. If it had been one of his men who'd followed Hover that morning, then by now he'd have found Wakes, and through him both the Lister women. Wakes was a photographer. He might have taken a better-class shop than the one in Wardour Street, or he might have got a job with a film company: in any case all Jewle would have had to do was to put a few dozen men on the job and in less than no time he'd have winkled Wakes out. And the same with Doreen Lister. A thousand to one she now had another and better shop. Very well, then: just give the order to go through every women's shop in the West End and if necessary open out from there to the suburbs. And that, I knew, was what Jewle would now be doing. I'd given him Mallow Grove on a gold platter, and he'd know by now the existence of what seemed the leading actors in the bonfire affair. He'd have their names and descriptions and all he had to do was find them.

I couldn't help but chuckle. When you looked at it, it really was amusing—we, trying to do the same thing as a team of two, with French a temporary addition. I was still thinking about that much later in the morning when Jewle did ring.

"Hal-*lo*, sir: you busy?"

"Far from it," I said. "But why? You got a job for me?"

"Only lunch," he said. "I thought we might have a chat. Can you make Luigi's at half-past twelve?"

I looked at my watch. I could make it comfortably.

He was there first and had booked a table.

"Just a little gesture of thanks for that tip you gave Matthews," he said. "I wouldn't be surprised if we broke that case by the end of the week."

"You found out about the quartet at Mallow Grove?"

"Did we!" he said, and grinned. "The two Lister women and Hover. And we took a chance at Somerset House, and what do you think we found? The younger Lister was Hover's wife. At least, she went through the ceremony of marriage."

I looked suitably surprised. It wasn't easy. That was one of the things I'd had up my sleeve to pass on to him.

"There was another man too," he went on. "A tall chap with one of those wispy moustaches. We haven't got his surname yet but his Christian name was Reg or Reggie. We think he was a photographer of some sort: he was seen once or twice with a camera. Might have been a press photographer. Were just guessing at the moment, but he's the one we want to talk to, and I'll tell you why.

"Remember I was telling you about that Norwich affair that Hover was shopped over? The one with a widow? Well, he had a stooge—the usual con-man's stooge—the one who was brought in to back Hover's bona-fides. The police there didn't get their hands on him but they had a description, and it's identical with the one of the 'Reggie' of Mallow Grove."

"Yes," I said. "He's definitely the one you want to see. And probably the one who tipped off the police about that Hurst Park business. By the way, why did Hover get off with only twelve months when he'd a record as long as your arm?"

"The race-course police stepped in a bit too soon," he said. "They ought to've waited till Hover had actually left the course with the money. But about Mallow Grove: the first thing I thought when we heard about those Lister sisters. Look at it this way. They and Reggie were pretty thick when Hover was doing time, so if one of them shopped him at Hurst Park, you can bet they were all in it together. And the funny thing is Doreen cleared out from Mallow Grove as soon as Hover was in stir again. The other sister had gone long before. In fact, they disappeared into thin air, as the saying is. My guess is as good as yours but I'd say they were taking care Hover didn't find them when he came out of Brixton. And what's that suggest to you?"

"All sorts of things," I said. "One is that the woman who came to us and wanted Hover's address for last Friday night was one of the Listers."

"That's it exactly. But the description you gave us of your Mrs. North doesn't tally. Doreen Lister—she's the elder one— had brownish hair and the other one black hair. Your woman had almost white hair and was much older."

"That's easy," I said. "She could have had her hair bleached, worn it drawn back to make the face look narrower and worn those glasses as well."

"Yes," he said. "And if so it looks as if she was Doreen. She's said to have been a milliner, by the way. The other sister was a nurse. A check of the hospitals ought to tell us something there."

I wasn't happy. I'd been thinking of the poet's tangled web and those who practise to deceive. Only a matter of time—maybe only hours—before he'd discover that someone answering Hover's description had made enquiries at Mallow Grove on the Friday, and what became then of my statement that Hover, before he finally booked in at the Ferney Hotel, had merely been having a look round the town.

Something had to be done. I had to head him off. There'd have to be some more salvaging of valuable material.

"Just a minute," I said. "Did you say the younger sister was a nurse?"

"That's right. At least she was seen in a nurse's uniform and someone at the flats told us it was understood she was a nurse."

"Nurse Lister," I said reflectively. "That's ringing a bell."

A moment or two and I allowed myself to remember.

"Got it!" I said. "But the divisional police who handled the matter might have given a cross reference."

"Reference of what?"

I told him about the Rimmell theft and how a Nurse Lister might possibly have been connected.

"Would you believe it!" he said. "Just shows you you never know what's going to turn up. I'll do a bit of nosing along that trail myself."

We'd been talking and eating and now he snapped his fingers to our waiter.

"Sure you won't let me pay the bill?" I said.

"The tax-payer'll pay," he told me. "You've earned it."

"What about a liqueur with your coffee?"

"Can't stay for coffee. Thanks all the same." He smiled and gave himself a congratulatory nod. "I've got to get the hunt reorganised. The sooner we lay our hands on the Lister women and our friend Reggie, the better I'll like it."

He had his car parked just round the corner. As it drove off I was hoping the reorganisation would lead his pack miles away from Mallow Grove. I was still hot and cold when I thought about Hover's Friday morning visit. And I wasn't any happier when I got back to Broad Street. Hallows was waiting for me. He and French were sharing the day in Marlbury Street and, luckily for them, the weather was amazingly good for the time of year. He had just done the first stretch, from eight in the morning till half-past one. French was carrying on till seven o'clock. Neither of them had seen a sign of Wakes.

"We'll give it another day or two," I told him. "Even perhaps the rest of the week. We've just got to find Wakes before Jewle does."

I told him why.

"We're bankrupt. We've nothing else to trade. And if he does get Wakes, then we'll be out of everything. We can't go touting for information."

"Yes," he said slowly. He picked up his hat. "I think I'll join French for a spell. Two might be better than one."

He wasn't on duty and he wouldn't expect to get paid. That case had certainly got him, and as badly as it had got me.

Hallows had no real part in what was to happen that night but maybe he brought French some luck. I heard about it when Hallows rang me. It was then just after half-past six.

"Luck at last, sir! French spotted Wakes a few minutes ago."

I didn't need to ask him to tell me about it.

"He was standing at the corner of Marlbury Street and Butler Street—French was, I mean—and a posh-looking light-blue Buick was held up a minute as it turned into Marlbury Street, and Wakes was driving it, and he had a couple of women passengers. He only had a glimpse before the Buick slipped into the traffic stream but he swears the man was Wakes. He memorised the number and then he started chasing the car. They got held up by the traffic lights as they turned out of Marlbury Street but he didn't have any luck. Just as he got it in sight again the lights went green."

"It could only have gone one way," I said, "and that's towards Piccadilly Circus. Just a moment. I'll take down the number." As he said, there was no point in hanging about in the neighbourhood. What he'd told French was to do the first shift in the morning. I might check that car number by the morning and orders might have to be changed.

"I'll see what I can do," I told him. "See you at the office at somewhere about half-past eight."

It was grand news and it took some thinking over. I couldn't ring the Yard to have that number checked by some pal or other, or word might get round to Jewle. Then I had a brain-wave. I rang Bill Fraser.

"Will you do something for us officially, Bill? We want a car number checked. Must be done to-night. We'll pay accordingly."

"You're in luck," he said. "One of my men's got some pull. What's the number?"

"A London number—WYX 273. The car's a Buick, light blue, practically new."

"Right," he said. "We'll get to work. Where shall we ring you?"

From where I was speaking, I said, at my private address. After that there was nothing to do but wait: a pleasurable wait like the final traffic hold-up at the end of a long day's driving and you're in sight of the very hotel where you're spending the night. Get Wakes, I told myself, and you get the two women, and Jewle would be welcome to the three of them. And if Wakes was the one he pinned the bonfire murder on, then Forlin might snap his eyes when Jewle's final report was made or evidence was given at the trial. Also Elizabeth Lister ought to be softened up enough to tell the truth about the Rimmell jewellery, and that wouldn't do us any harm with John Hill.

As for letting Jewle know how we had run across Wakes, that could be kept a bit cryptic. Or I could say that we'd been having a general look round for my Mrs. North and we'd had some luck and she'd led us to Wakes. If I said that word *luck* in the right way, Jewle would guess I was being modest and that there'd been a lot of hard work. And then I couldn't help grunting to myself. I was far from the virgin innocent of those far-off days when I'd first begun working with George Wharton.

I hadn't expected Bill to ring much before bed-time, but he actually rang at about nine.

"I think we've got what you want. The car's virtually new. Registered in the name of Raymond Wilson. His address is—you'd better take this down—Woldingham House, St. John's Wood. It's a fairly new block of flats just behind Lord's. The car's down as garaged at Spring's Garage, 31 McCombie Street, St. John's Wood.... Got it? All you want?"

"Perfect," I said. "Good work, Bill. Don't forget to send in an account."

After a few minutes I was too restless to sit. I knew I ought to have a look at Woldingham House and that garage. And yet I couldn't, and once more I was thinking wryly of the mould in which I'd been cast. Doreen Lister—if she'd really been Mrs. North—had seen me, and it might get round to her that some-one of my appearance had been making enquiries. And then I had an idea.

"Like to do something for me?" I said to Bernice. "Just a job of work—pretty important work—and I can't do it myself. We'd have to go out in the car."

"At once?"

"Yes. Better be at once."

She went to her room to put on something warm.

"Your best furs," I called to her. "And earrings. You'll have to create an impression."

An old aunt of hers once told Bernice in my hearing that when she married me she drew a prize. It's been a joke with us ever since. But, strictly between ourselves, I think it was the other way round. As far as concerns my work—at the Agency or the Yard—she's never inquisitive. She just takes it for granted when my hours are erratic or I have to be away from home. She's done many a job for us and she never wants to know what lies behind the instructions.

She did ask where we were going as the car turned into St. Martin's.

"To St. John's Wood," I said. "A block of flats known as Woldingham House."

Traffic's not too bad at night and it was well short of ten when we circled Lord's. I slowed the car to a crawl.

"What name have you picked?"

"My maiden name."

"Right," I said. "We'll go over it once more. You go to the bureau or enquiry desk or whatever it is and you say you're supposed to pick up your niece who's been visiting friends. The niece's name is Joyce Haire but you've forgotten the name of the people. Be a bit helpless about that, but it ought to get you a look at the list of tenants. Remember whom you're looking for?"

"A Raymond Wilson and two women, and one may be named Lister."

"Good. And then the helplessness at the end. You should have met this niece at nine-thirty and you're staggered it's so late. Your watch must have stopped. Better put it back now to about nine-thirty. Sorry you've been troubled, one of your best smiles and that'll be that."

One enquiry found Woldingham House for us. It was quite a handsome block of flats, probably averaging out in the six or seven hundred a-year class. I drew the car round to a few yards from the swing doors. I put on the chauffeur's cap I'd brought with me and held the door for Bernice. I watched her through the swing doors and went back to the driver's seat.

It wouldn't be a long wait if everything went smoothly. Apparently it did. In about five minutes Bernice was at the swing doors again and a bare-headed man was at her heels. I nipped out of the car, stood by the door and whipped my horn-rims into my pocket. I couldn't see a thing but I could hear Bernice's thanks, and her laugh and her goodnight. I hooked the glasses on again and the man had gone.

I drove round the corner and stopped.

"Everything all right?"

"Almost too right," she said. "There was a very charming man at the desk—the one who came out with me. Poor man! I think he guessed I was utterly helpless. Oh, and the people you want are in Flat 12. A Mr. and Mrs. Raymond Wilson and a Miss S. Wilson."

"Wonderful!" I said. "I certainly married a prize."

She laughed.

"I don't know about that but I think I'd make quite a good detective."

"The way you're looking to-night, you'd probably be grabbed by the white slavers," I said. "But remind me to drop a word to the Chief Commissioner some time. And now we've got to find McCombie Street."

"Look," she said. "There's a policeman just up there by that lamp."

I said he was the last person we wanted to speak to, so we sat on for a couple of minutes and then a man hove into sight, leading a dog. He was a sitter for a local resident. A couple of minutes later we were turning into McCombie Street.

"This is a bit trickier," I said. "You can still be a Mrs. Haire but you're thinking of taking a flat near by and the problem is if you can find a handy garage for your car—this car. After that, you don't make it conspicuous but you look round and see if you can spot a big Buick—light blue."

That garage was open till midnight. I'd checked up on that by ringing them while Bernice was getting ready at the flat. I'd reversed the car and was headed for home and I stood by the door, horn-rims ready to slip into my pocket. My Bentley may be oldish but it's still far from a bad-looking car.

It couldn't have been more than three minutes before Bernice was back. I was about twenty yards from the garage entrance. I heard a man say it would be quite all right, and I guessed he'd run a quick eye over the car. Then Bernice came up. I got back to my seat and slipped the horn-rims on. We went round the corner and this time, when I stopped, Bernice took the seat beside me.

"Everything all right?"

"Perfect," she said. "And I saw the Buick."

"Fine," I said. "That means the Wilson family's having a nice quiet evening."

I moved the car on.

"And where're we going now?"

I laughed.

"This is getting into your blood," I said. "Something tells me I'd better stop keeping two homes going, or the next thing I'll know is that you're on my tail."

"Yes, but where *are* we going?"

"Home," I said. And home it was.

I rang Hallows. All I told him was that I'd located Wakes and probably the Lister sisters, and where he garaged the car.

"He's calling himself Raymond Wilson—note the initials— and your friend Lizzie is his wife and Doreen's probably in the spare bedroom. She's calling herself Miss S. Wilson, and what the S is for I don't know. The garage is Spring's Garage in McCombie Street, about a couple of hundred yards from Lord's—the Tavern end. I might be a bit wrong: I only made the trip at night."

"St. John's Wood," he said. "Then it can't be all that way from Peddick Street and that newsagent where Mrs. North had the message sent."

"Oh yes," I said. "It's all tying in. But about the morning. French can stay as agreed. You have your car ready to pick up Wakes at the garage. Be there between half-past eight and nine and let's hope he doesn't go by Underground. The car should be easy to follow. As soon as you find out where he settles down for the morning, check with French and bring him along to the office."

"Check what?" he said.

"Wakes may bring the two women along with him and he might set them down somewhere and French might have seen them."

"Right, sir," he said. "I'll do my best. And I'll be keeping my fingers crossed."

That was another of those nights when I just couldn't sleep. Bernice was sleeping pretty soundly and finally I slipped from my bed in the small hours and mixed myself a stiff whisky and soda and munched some biscuits. When I got back, the bed was so warm in comparison with the living-room that I got to sleep almost at once. I was sleeping so soundly in the morning that Bernice had to wake me. The alarm clock had gone off but I'd actually slept through it.

After breakfast I got to work, trying to anticipate Hallows. I waded through all the R. Wilsons in the telephone directories but there wasn't one that fitted—or an S. Wilson either. Then I drove to Broad Street and of course I was far too early. I had an hour and a half to wait before Hallows arrived, and French with him, and that was soon after ten o'clock. By the look on Hallows's face I knew his news was good.

"Ran him to earth," he said. "A posh place in Daventry Street. Just the word RAYMOND over the door and COURT PHOTOG-RAPHER, one word at each side. And he definitely *is* the man who was with our friend Mrs. North in the taxi that morning."

I asked him to start at the beginning.

"Well," he said, "after you rang me last night I thought I'd better check up so I got the car out and had a look round. Good job I did. That garage isn't much more than a hundred yards from the flats. You just cut down Whitley Street and into McCombie Street and there you are. All the same, I was pretty nearly caught napping this morning. I had the car just beyond the garage and facing towards town and I was reading a newspaper with one eye and watching the mirror with the other and then, at just before nine, Wakes was across the road and a couple of women with him. I just caught sight of them and neither of them had blonde hair. Far as I could see, both were brunettes. Then I saw the Buick come out and it went by me like a bat out of hell. If it hadn't been for its colour, I'd have lost it half a dozen times.

"First stop was Dover Street where the two women got out. I'd had to overshoot him so I didn't see much. Then I followed him to Daventry Street. He parked the car just behind it in one of those narrow, one-way streets. I went straight on, risked leaving my car and watched him go into that studio of his. Then I went to look for French."

"I didn't see a thing," French said. "I might have seen two women, of course, but I wouldn't have known. And you can get anywhere from Dover Street. Round the top into Marlbury Street, for instance. But if so, I don't remember seeing them."

"They must be somewhere near," I said.

"It doesn't follow," Hallows said. "Wakes would have a job getting within half a mile of anywhere from Dover Street, what with one-way traffic and jams and so on. They might be anywhere within walking distance of Dover Street, where they were dropped. But I was forgetting something."

I'd forgotten to ask about it too.

"Hasn't Wakes made a remarkably good recovery from that sprained ankle of his?" he asked me. "Never a sign of it this morning."

"Well over a week since you saw him, French," I said. "A sprained ankle's got to get well some time. But about taking things from here. It's pretty obvious. Perhaps you can wait somewhere near Daventry Street and one of you can let the other know when a car's moved and you can shoot yours in. Then you can go to the pictures or take the day off. All there'll be to do is pick up Wakes to-night. No need to report back unless anything happens. In the morning you'll both be in your car, Hallows, and French'll follow the women after Wakes sets them down. Report here independently."

Hallows grinned. He said he could hardly wait.

## 12

## RUN TO EARTH

REMAINING an onlooker was just too much for me. There was nothing to keep me at the office, so I told myself I'd have lunch at the club and have a look at Daventry Street on the way. I knew it was a dangerous thing to do but I thought that if I kept on the opposite side from Raymond, I could at least get a good view of the studio.

And that's what I did. I came into the west end of Daventry Street via Haldane Street and stopped just short of the studio at a shop whose windows gave not too bad a reflection. That studio was a stylish-looking place: neat and very definitely not gaudy. It had two fairly large windows and the woodwork was painted in turquoise blue and cream. Above the studio were what looked like offices: two storeys of them, with admission by a side door. The door of the studio, exactly between the windows, was imitation Georgian: the fan-light intact but the upper half replaced by glass which was partly concealed from inside by a draped, yellowish curtain.

Photographs were on display in the windows and it was just as I was manoeuvring to get a better view through the mirror-like windows of the shop where I stood that the studio door opened and Wakes came out. I saw the beautifully trimmed dark beard as he turned, and the smartly cut black overcoat and the dark Homburg hat. And he didn't lock the door, which meant that on the premises there would be an assistant or receptionist.

He was making at a fairly smart pace for Piccadilly Circus and I followed him at a distance. When he went down the steps to the Underground, I quickened my pace and took up my stance among the waiting people at the old rendezvous of Swan and Edgar's corner. As far as I knew he might be taking a train to somewhere, but he didn't. In a couple of minutes he had emerged at the north side of Regent Street. I moved parallel along the other side, and then he suddenly turned into the Café Royal.

I waited a good five minutes and then turned back. Wakes, I thought, was doing well for himself: a fine new car, two-thirds at least of the rent of an expensive flat, and now lunching at the Café Royal. A long way from the old Wardour Street days when he'd taken buses and probably lunched at a snack bar and relied on art studies to make a living. With, of course, an occasional job as stooge for Hover.

I stepped out briskly till I came to the studio. In the first window were photographs of weddings that flanked one of a debutante, all signed in the right-hand corner with a flowing *Raymond*. I went quickly by to the other window. That also had two photographs flanking a third: the two of children—a boy and a girl—and the centre-piece of some banquet or other taken by flashlight. Each of the six photographs was uncommonly good: each had that vague thing called style, and a very definite quality. As I walked on towards the club I wondered if Wakes himself had been the actual taker or if he could now afford to employ another man. And I wondered how he got his publicity. And what that studio was costing him. And, above all, where the money had come from. Had he and Hover made a killing which the victim had been afraid to report? Had he handled those jewels of Mrs. Rimmell's, and especially that Russian Cross with the diamonds intact?

It was the question of publicity that intrigued me most at the moment. Daventry Street wasn't too far off the main shopping streets but it was more of a street whose shops were long established. Wakes was a newcomer. But might that not mean that he'd bought the goodwill? I didn't know but I thought it should be easy to find out. So I walked back to the tobacconist's whose windows I'd used as a mirror. I bought fifty cigarettes of the dearer kind.

"It's years since I was this way," I told the man who'd served me. "And I don't seem to recognise some of the landmarks. That photographer's place across the road hasn't been here all that time, has it?"

"Opened last May," he said. "Used to be a men's shop. A chap called Morton had it as long as I can remember, but the lease expired and he wasn't so young as he was. You know how it is."

I said regretfully that we were all getting older and he agreed, and that was that. But when I left the club that afternoon I dropped in at Charing Cross Station and asked a man at the book-stall what photographic weeklies he had. He gave me the *Photographic Weekly* and *The Camera*. When I got back to the flat I had a look at them. Neither carried any publicity for the Studio Raymond. The first seemed to be running a series of first-hand experiences by old-time photographers but I didn't feel like reading and I put the two periodicals away. I think it was through some methodical tidiness that I didn't put them in the waste-paper basket. If I had, there might have been quite a different ending to the Case of the Russian Cross.

Hallows didn't ring till about eight o'clock the next morning.

"We're just off," he said, "but I thought I'd let you know about last night. The two women were waiting just short of St. James's and Wakes halted only to pick them up and then drove straight on. He'd cut back across the Park, the way he came this morning. And one thing I made a mistake about: one of the women is a *blonde*. It was wearing a dark snood that put me off."

I killed time at home and then drove slowly to Broad Street. Hallows was in bright and early—at well before ten. The two women had been dropped this time at the turning just beyond Marlbury Street and French was on their tails. And he'd hardly told me that when there was a call for me. It was French.

"Ringing from Piccadilly Underground, sir. Everything super. They're in a swanky dress-shop. Calls itself 'Simone'. Had 'em right under our noses all the time and didn't know it. It's one of those cut-backs from Marlbury Street, near Smith's, Butler Street."

"That's fine," I said. "You get back on the job and we'll be coming by. You can probably come back with us."

It was incredible, and yet it wasn't. Those cut-backs can take you anywhere: straight on and then round into Regent Street or sharp right and anywhere into Piccadilly. That was why it hadn't mattered much where Wakes dropped the women.

"It's one-way, that cut-back," I said. "We'll sneak in behind it and come out at Marlbury Street. You drive and when we get there, I'll try to get a look from behind a newspaper."

We looked at the large-scale map and decided to come in from Regent Street. November was still uncannily fine, and there wouldn't be any trouble over visibility. What might stop us from getting a good look at that shop would be a stream of traffic behind and in front, and our car always on the move.

We didn't do so badly as far as Regent Street and, once we'd turned off it, we did better still. In five minutes we were approaching Butler Street, the cut-back, as we'd called it. Hallows slowed the car. Two or three cars were behind us and he drew close to the kerb to let them pass. I pulled my hat well down, wrapped the muffler over my mouth and chin, opened the newspaper and we moved on: smartly, this time, with nothing behind us. A gap in the traffic towards Piccadilly let us slip across and there we were at the entrance to Butler Street, and that street was so short that the Marlbury Street traffic didn't seem a stone's throw away. Hallows gave a quick look in the mirror, edged to his off side and let the car sidle very slowly along.

That shop had two quite large windows. In each there were about three costumes or gowns, but I caught them only in the corner of an eye. I was trying to peer through the glass of the entrance and, by a hundred to one chance, I saw a woman clearly as she moved across that narrow field of view. Then a car tooted impatiently behind us and Hallows shot on. We waited for a lull in the traffic and turned into Marlbury Street. A few yards down it Hallows drew in at the kerb. I got out.

"I must have another look," I said. "I don't think there'll be all that risk. Our Mrs. North never saw me with a hat and over-coat on."

It was something I just couldn't trust to a description. I jammed that hat well down again and adjusted the muffler. French met me as I neared Butler Street and I nodded back to the car. I crossed to the other side and, in the windows of an antique shop, did the mirror trick again. That shop, like Wakes's studio, had been redecorated. A long *SIMONE*, in a modern style of script, ran from the centre of one window and above the door to the centre of the other. The window displays had that economy which, so I'm told, always distinguishes the most expensive, if not the very best.

Dresses and gowns convey little to me and I'd easily be fooled by the second-rate, but there were two largish notices in those windows and I wanted to see what they said, so I went to the end of the street and crossed to the other side.

Each notice, as I'd call it, was just a cream-coloured board edged with gold and held in place by a kind of oblong backrest. The lettering, everything, was very chic.

*SIMONE*
(As Advertised)
*HAUTE COUTURE*
at
YOUR Prices

That was one. The other read:

*SIMONE*
(As Advertised)
Display of
WINTER KNITWEAR
Exclusive.

That was all I had time to see, but as I sauntered on I had all at once a queer feeling, exciting and almost exultant. It was the kind of thing you get when you've at last cracked a tough crossword clue. And yet it was more than that. There'd been no great thrill the previous morning at my first sight of Wakes and the windows of his studio. It was as if everything had had a vagueness and unreality, but that quick view I'd had of the woman who'd called herself Mrs. North had changed all that. My head was no longer in the air and my feet were firmly on the ground. That I hadn't seen Elizabeth Lister was no matter. Those three people were now flesh and blood. And what was more, *we had them*. They were ours whenever we cared to put a finger on them. They were neatly tied up in a bundle, ready to hand to Jewle.

Just short of eleven, Hallows and I were at the flat. French had gone to the office to report to Norris. Bernice, who likes Hallows, was preparing coffee.

"Don't go away," I said when she brought the tray to the den. "There's another job of work to do. One of the best you'll have to do. Buying yourself a Christmas present at the firm's expense."

She laughed. She told Hallows there must be a catch some-where.

"Not a bit of it," I said. "Remember the Mr. and Mrs. Wilson and the Miss S. Wilson of the other night? Well, the two women are sisters and they're running a shop off Marlbury Street which calls itself 'Simone'. Very high-class as far as I could see. 'Simone'—as advertised. Have you seen any advertisement?"

She thought for a moment. She just moved an arm and took a newspaper from the top of my desk. She looked at the back page.

"Here it is. It appears about twice a week. Not always the same wording of course."

It was in the Personal Column.

> *SIMONE* of Butler Street, W.l. *Haute Couture* at your prices. Exclusive Winter Knitwear on view.

"That's it," I said. "You free this afternoon?"

"I actually wasn't," she said. "But I can be."

"Good. Then drop in on 'Simone'. It might be best to take a friend with you if you can. Buy something that doesn't ruin us, but, above all, keep an eye on the two who strike you as the owners. One's a blonde with her hair in the old style just flop-ping on her shoulders. What're you laughing at?"

"Just nothing," she said, and gave Hallows a special look.

"Well, that's what her hair looks like to me," I said. "The other will have darkish hair and I don't know just how she'll be wearing it. Listen for names if they address each other. Form general impressions of them. That all right?"

"Now about you," I said to Hallows when Bernice had gone. "Wakes is your pigeon. You've got to have a photograph taken, so let's hatch up a scheme."

It took ten minutes to find what looked like a foolproof one. We looked up Raymond in the directory and Hallows rang. I didn't try to hear what came through from the other end. He said his daughter from the States had been home for a stay and was going back in a few days' time, and she wanted to take with her a really good photograph of her father. She happened to go by the Raymond studio and thought it might be just the place. What were the charges? And could the photographs be ready in a week's time? And, as he was rarely in town, could he possibly have an appointment that afternoon? There was quite a pause after that. Then he said he was very grateful.

"Two-thirty this afternoon as a special favour," he told me. "Sounded like a receptionist speaking. Didn't sound very young. Not less than three photographs and six guineas the three. Choice of one pose out of two. Unmounted but signed. Sounded all very posh."

"Splendid," I said. "You'd better get home and doll yourself up. But about our three friends. Shall we hand them over to Jewle to-morrow, say, or keep them up our sleeves a bit longer?"

"Might talk about it in the morning," he said. "It might depend on what happens this afternoon."

Hallows went off to collect his car. I spent what was left of the morning at the office and came back to the flat soon after three. Bernice wasn't in till after four. She'd gone with a friend to "Simone". The friend, a Mrs. Marlow, had bought a wool jacket with detachable scarf. Quite a bargain, Bernice said, at three and a half guineas. Her own bargain had been a swagger coat with a real beaver collar. Very smart, and only nineteen guineas. She mentioned the price with all the offhandedness in the world. I didn't move a muscle. After all, it's no use trying to hurry a woman when she's talking about clothes.

"And the shop itself?" I managed to get in.

"It's nice," she said, "and they have some very good things. Very nice rooms at the back for trying on and so on. Workrooms upstairs. They make quite a lot of their things. Oh, and the women."

She said that as if it were just an afterthought.

"The blonde spoke with a French accent. Not real, of course. I asked her if she were Simone and she smiled and shrugged her shoulders and said Simone was her sister. I just got a glimpse of Simone: not so good-looking as the blonde, and chestnut-coloured hair cut short and lightly curled."

"You think they're doing pretty well?"

"I should say very well. That sort of place is never crowded but there were two women while we were there. One was spending quite a lot. Oh, and something else. The blonde hair isn't real. It's synthetic."

I didn't tell her that that almost casual afterthought was the most important thing she'd told me. While she was getting tea I thought about it, and somewhere along the line it seemed to me that we'd gone wrong, and badly wrong. From everything Bernice had told me, it wasn't Doreen who'd masqueraded as Mrs. North. Doreen wasn't the good-looking one: Hallows had learnt that long since. And Doreen's hair had always been chestnut. And Doreen was Simone. That made the other sister, the one who had come to us as Mrs. North, into Elizabeth, the ex-nurse. Her hair had originally been black but she'd had it bleached. And my guess was that she'd had it bleached the previous March when the three had been covering their tracks against the coming out of jail of Hover.

During tea we talked about "Simone" again but I learned nothing that looked like making a difference. There was another assistant downstairs—a chic but much older woman—whose name Bernice hadn't heard, and as far as Simone herself was concerned, she seemed to spend most of her time upstairs and only came down when wanted to attend to a customer. When Bernice said that everything was really perfect as to style and cut, I couldn't help wondering if Wakes had a hand in things. It was possible, I thought, that he might have some kind of special, concealed camera with which he could photograph this and that and then Simone's workpeople could reproduce with just sufficient alterations to avoid an action for infringement of copyright, if that's what they call it in the trade.

"Something I forgot to show you," Bernice said when she came back from taking out the tray.

It was a small brochure which announced itself as changed each month—just photographs of dresses and costumes and coats accompanied by all the jargon of the trade. And then I saw something on the glossy back, and my eyes popped a bit. It was an advertisement for the Studio Raymond. I had a good look at it and just as I handed it back, Hallows arrived. He'd had to wait half an hour, he said. The receptionist, a very competent woman of about forty, apologised for an error in the appointment time, but she'd later brought him tea and the waiting-room had been very comfortable. When it was all over he'd had a real tea as he didn't know what time my wife would be back.

"The studio's at the back," he said. "Everything slap up-to-date. Lighting screens and trolley camera and the walls hung with special photographs. Wakes saw to me. A queer chap. Makes you think he's a bit of a pansy. A little bit of a phoney accent, too, and keeps trying to gesture like a Frenchman. His back hair is just a bit long and he's the regular artistic type. High-class Bohemian. Knows his job, though. Oh, and this might interest you. The receptionist handed it to me when I was leaving."

What should it turn out to be but another brochure. This one had specimens of Wakes's work. Two of them were studies that were said to have won gold medals at international exhibitions—one, of an old man, at Madrid and the other, rain falling on a pavement, at Buenos Aires. But on the glossy back of that brochure was an advertisement. Raymond strongly recommended the Maison Simone—as advertised—to women of discerning taste but limited means. I showed Hallows the brochure Bernice had been given *chez* Simone.

"Quite a racket," he said. "Three bugs in a rug. And a nice, cheap way of advertising—straight to the right people."

I asked him if we should take the photographs or cut the deposit he'd paid. He said it had only been a couple of pounds and he'd rather like one at least for a souvenir. Altogether we were feeling pretty cock-a-hoop and we sat on talking about Wakes and the Lister sisters and generally throwing the case around.

"One thing I can't help thinking," I said. "Let's agree that those three between them shopped Hover. What I don't get is why he should have had to be murdered when he came out. Those three had covered their tracks very cleverly. And surely Wakes, if not the others, must have had plenty on Hover to have kept him quiet when he did come out."

Hallows said he saw the point. But Hover had kept a gun in that car locker and that was something Wakes would have known. And what about that other point—Hover having been shot and his gun probably of the same calibre.

"And indoors," I said. "If Wakes shot him, how'd he get the gun? And *where* was Hover shot? Not in the Ferney Hotel. He'd have had to be lured somewhere. And it couldn't have been to their flat. They couldn't have got the body out to take it to the bonfire. It might have been to Wakes's studio or to Maison Simone."

"The way I see it, that doesn't make sense," Hallows said. "Why dodge him and then get in touch with him? What was the point of the dodging?"

He glanced at his watch. It was just after six o'clock and he said he'd be getting home.

"What about the morning?"

"Take an easy," I told him. "Come in after lunch. French is back on the job we took him off but there might be something for us to do."

Then the fact that it was six o'clock gave me an idea. I've said I was feeling on mighty good terms with myself.

"Look. Wakes is now on his way home so he can't be seen till the morning. What about throwing him to Jewle?"

"Mightn't be a bad idea," Hallows said. "It'll keep him happy. And we keep the other two up our sleeves?"

"That wouldn't be more than a very few hours," I said. "As soon as Wakes arrives in the morning he'll be under surveillance. He'll be followed home at night and by the next morning Jewle will have his hands on the women."

So I rang Jewle as soon as Hallows had gone but he wasn't at the Yard, nor was Matthews. I left word that one of them was to ring me as soon as he came in. That turned out to be only half an hour later, with a domestic scene to pass the time. Bernice's coat had arrived and I had to see it on. Still, you can guess the rest.

It was Jewle himself who rang. I asked how things were going.

"Slowly," he said. "Those three certainly covered up their tracks. But we're still hoping."

"Well, I've got something to help you," I said. "We've been slogging away ourselves and we've got Wakes for you."

"You haven't!"

"Yes," I said. "All nicely wrapped up. Just take this down."

I kept to the studio: not a word about the flat.

"How you do it I don't know," he said, "but I can't say how grateful we are."

"Don't try," I said. "You also might know he used to have a little studio at 275 Wardour Street. You might find someone there to identify him."

"You mean there's a chance—"

"Oh no. He's Wakes. No mistake about that. I was thinking you might want to identify him your own way."

"We can do better than that," he said. "There are at least two people in that Norwich case who can identify him. Soon as they do, we'll hold him. Meanwhile we'll be digging down. Suppose, by the way, you've no idea where the Lister sisters are?"

"A hundred to one Wakes'll lead you straight to them."

"Yes," he said grimly. "I'll get busy at once. And thanks a lot. You'd like to be kept informed?"

I said I certainly should.

## THEME IV
## AND FINALE

### 13
### NEW OR OLD

IT WAS about a quarter to one. Norris had long since gone to lunch and I was wondering if it were worth while to go all the way to the club and back. Then Bertha put through a call. "Mrs. Rimmell. For you personally."

I was smiling as I picked up the receiver.

"Hal-*lo* there, young lady!"

"Not so young," she said. "And how's that charming wife of yours? No need to ask how *you* are."

"We're both exceedingly well. And you?"

"I'm very annoyed," she said. "I think I did you an injustice. I didn't say so to that very nice police officer who called . . . What was his name now?"

"Jewle?"

"Yes," she said. "Such a nice man." She gave that tinkley laugh of hers. "Perhaps you'll explain that to him if he's a friend of yours."

"Explain what?"

"What I want to see you about," she told me, and as if I were being rather obtuse. "Could you come at three o'clock?"

"I'll be there," I said, and held on for her to say the last word.

"I knew you would," she said. "And give my love to your wife. We really must arrange another meeting."

She rang off. It must have been quite a few moments before I replaced the receiver. What she'd had in her mind was something altogether beyond me. Something about having misjudged me. Misjudged me about what?

Not that silly business of having taken me, at my first visit with Hallows, for some minor employee of John Hill? But no. That little misunderstanding had been cleared up by Hill himself. Could it be something to do with that Russian Cross? A discovery, or remembering that the diamonds hadn't been in it when that ancient photograph had been taken? But even she, with that delightful hippety-hoppety mind of hers, must know that that was no longer of any importance. And her claim had been paid in full. Why then rake up something which might possibly re-open the whole thing?

An unsolved mystery upsets me. It puts me off my feed and out of my stride. But luckily I remembered what she'd said about Jewle—that she hadn't said anything to him when he'd seen her. I wondered what she *had* said. Jewle would probably be in his room ready to reach out a hand to the telephone and hear what those men of his were doing who were watching Wakes's studio. And that's where he was.

"Travers here, Jewle. Sorry to keep disturbing you."

"You're not disturbing me, sir." I heard his chuckle. "We could do with a whole lot more of your kind of disturbance."

"Nice of you to say so. How're things going?"

"Can't grumble," he said. "We're keeping an eye on that studio and we've got his hang-out from his car number. The two women are there too. This time to-morrow morning we'll have the lot just where we want them."

"Fine!" I said, and told him about that mysterious call from Alysia Rimmell.

"Sorry," he said after a moment, "but I can't explain it. All I was trying to get out of her were details about the Lister woman who attended her husband. And I didn't have any luck. Nor from that cross-reference about the robbery."

"Well, I'm seeing her this afternoon at three, as I told you. If she's remembered anything interesting I'll let you know."

"Good," he said. "I'll be here till at least seven o'clock." He chuckled again, and just in time for me not to have rung off. "Wonderful old lady, isn't she? No bigger than six-penn'orth of coppers and enough energy to drive a steam-engine." He chuckled again. "Well, I'll be hearing from you. And thanks again."

That little chat put me in a more philosophic mood. If only because it would pass the time till three o'clock, I thought I'd lunch at the club after all, so I left a message for Hallows and hopped a bus. And one way and another the time went by. At a quarter to three I was on my way to Hanway Gardens. It was about half a minute to the hour when I pushed the bell of Flat 3.

Nothing happened. I pushed the bell again and let my finger stay there for quite a few seconds. That bell wasn't out of order. Another minute and I was pushing it again and I could hear it ringing. Then I remembered that she always took a nap after her lunch. Maybe she was a heavy sleeper. I gave another ring.

I didn't know what to make of it so I went back to the entrance hall. No one was on duty so I pushed the bell on the enquiry desk. A youngish receptionist appeared. I asked her if she'd seen Mrs. Rimmell go out since lunch. She said she hadn't, but that didn't say she mightn't have gone.

"Shall I ring her for you?"

"I've rung myself, four times," I said.

She smiled.

"Then it looks as if she's out."

I shrugged my shoulders and was turning away when I saw a man come through the swing doors. There was something vaguely familiar about him. Then I knew who he was: Herbert Rimmell. It was the hat and coat that had put me off.

"Afternoon, Mr. Rimmell. Don't tell me you're here to see your grandmother?"

"You're Travers," he said. "I remember you now. Gran said you'd be here at three and I was to come along."

"I can't make her hear," I told him. "Perhaps we might try again."

I had a look or two at him as we walked along the wide carpeted corridor. He looked a bit thinner and the face a bit more sallow. And there was something else different about him, and almost at once I knew what it was. He wasn't playing a part. I was probably seeing for the first time his natural self.

I pushed the bell. He pushed the bell. I pushed the bell again while he listened.

"Wait a minute," I said. "Oughtn't you to have a key?"

"It's back at the hotel. Or I think so."

He felt in various pockets.

"I know I left it at the hotel. No need to carry it when I know she's going to be in."

"Your legs are younger than mine," I said. "Slip along to the desk and get the pass-key. I don't like the look of things."

I pushed the bell a couple of times more. When he came back it was with the receptionist. She slipped in the key, opened the door, and smiled as if it had been all that easy all along. She went off and we stepped in. We listened, but there wasn't a sound.

I made my way across that cluttered room to the door of Alysia Rimmell's bedroom. I rapped and there wasn't another sound. I rapped a second time, listened, then quietly opened the door. I looked round. Alysia Rimmell was lying on the bed. An eiderdown covered her and above it I could just see the top of her dressing-gown.

I held my breath and I watched that eiderdown. There was no slow rise and fall from her breathing. I tip-toed across and watched again. A hand lay by her thin cheek and I lifted it. There was a sound at the door and I let it fall.

"What is it? What goes on?"

"She's dead."

"Dead!" He stared. "You mean she died in her sleep!"

"Better get out of here." I had to lay a hand on his shoulder to turn him back to the door. "You sit somewhere while I ring the police."

"The police! Hadn't you better ring a doctor?"

I'd picked up the receiver and was dialling 1212. I asked to be put through at once to Chief-Inspector Jewle. A matter of extreme urgency. It couldn't have been half a minute before I was hearing his voice.

"Hallo, Travers: what's this matter of urgency?"

"I'm at Mrs. Rimmell's flat," I said. "Just walked in and found her dead. One or two things I don't like. Suggest you come along. And bring the circus."

"My God!" he said. "Like that, is it?"

He let out a breath and said he'd be with me.


"I can't believe it," Rimmell said. "And what was that crack about things you didn't like?"

That was more like the Rimmell of the hotel. Or was it?

"Sorry," I said, "but that's for the police. All you and I do is just sit here till they come."

"But what about a doctor? How do you know she's dead?"

"Because it's part of my job," I said. "And don't worry about a doctor. There'll be one with the police."

He didn't like it. And he didn't like me. He frowned as the thoughts churned round in his mind.

"Care to tell me what your grandmother said to you when she rang you? And when did she ring you?"

"About half-past twelve," he said. "I'd just sat down to lunch. Just got in from Manchester as a matter of fact. I'd had business there."

"And she said?"

"She?" He gave a kind of titter. "Oh, I see what you mean. She didn't say much. Just if I could see her at three about something. She said you were coming."

"See her about what?"

"She wouldn't say. Just said I'd know when I got here. That kind of thing."

Then his eyes narrowed.

"You're doing a lot of questioning? Isn't that a job for the police?"

"It is," I said. "But I'm doing you a favour. They'll ask the same questions. This is a sort of rehearsal. Cigarette?"

"Thanks." He took one from my case, held his gold lighter for me and lighted his own. Some people might have said that merely smoking so close to that bedroom was a disrespect to the dead. We didn't say anything for quite a minute. He, as I knew, would have quite a lot to think about. Was he, for instance, the sole heir? And what could he do with all that money?

Maybe I was doing him an injustice to make such things the first to go through his mind. And maybe I was wrong. What about other things—alibis, for instance? That was what would strike Jewle as soon as he had the main facts—that if anyone had a motive it was Herbert Rimmell.

"I just can't believe it," he suddenly said. "She must have died in her sleep. Good God! look how old she was. When they get that age they just go."

"Well, we'll soon know," I said. "They oughtn't to be long now."

"I've never tangled with the law before. What are your cops like?"

"Nice people," I said. "Jewle, whom I spoke to, is a very nice person. All you'll have to do is answer a few very simple but necessary questions and that'll be all. He'll probably be very grateful to you."

"Is that so?" he smiled. "Guess I was too young when I left here to know much about your police. Guess I was a kind of little Lord Fauntleroy."

"Sounds like the police now," I said, and went to the door.

Jewle was there and old Doc. Anders with him. There was a sergeant from the Finger-Print Bureau, whom I knew, and a photographer and some plain-clothes men.

"Better mind how you move in here," I said. "It's a bit crowded. That's the bedroom. This is Mrs. Rimmell's grand-son—Herbert Rimmell."

They shook hands.

"Be with you in a minute, sir," Jewle told him. "You'd better come in with me, Mr. Travers."

One man stayed with Rimmell, the rest were in the corridor. Jewle, Anders and I went through to the bedroom. Anders went straight to the bed. He gave a little grunt as he looked at the face. He had a long look through his glass at face and neck. He put his hand beneath the eiderdown. He didn't say a word. Corpses to Anders are ten-a-penny, but he didn't make one of his usual cracks. After a minute he shook his head.

"A sweet-looking old lady."

"Yes," Jewle said. "We'll let you write the obituary. But what killed her?"

"Smothered—to put it simply. With this spare pillow prob-ably. There're the bruises. Ten to one we'll find knee marks on the body where she was held down. Not that she'd take a lot of holding down. If she was sleeping at all soundly—and at her age she probably was—a child could have done it."

"How long ago?"

Anders pursed his lips.

"An hour—more or less. If she had her lunch in that restau-rant downstairs we can check it closer."

"Right," Jewle said. "Perhaps you'll see if the ambulance has arrived. Soon as we've got a photograph or two you can take her away."

Anders closed the door quietly behind him.

"A hell of a business," Jewle said to me. "But tell me. Any tying-up, do you think, with that other business?"

"It's all too tricky. If there's a connecting link it's a mighty thin one: just Nurse Lister and that jewel robbery."

"And what about that cove in there?"

"Don't know," I said. "I've met him before when I was investigating for the insurance people. He's a queer character."

"Right," he said. "Let's talk outside."

At the door to the corridor we drew back to let in Anders and the photographer, then squeezed our way out. Jewle looked in again.

"Sorry to keep you hanging about like this, Mr. Rimmell. Just the formalities and then perhaps you'll tell us what you know."

We went a few yards along the corridor.

"Now about Rimmell," Jewle said.

"Just one thing before we begin," I said. "There's something I'd like to make clear. That old lady in there was a friend of mine. I'd got to be quite fond of her and so had Bernice. What I'm getting at is that this is something personal. I'm not touting for official recognition: I wouldn't take it if it was offered me, but I'm very definitely going to do my damnedest to get the one who killed her. Purely unofficially."

"Look, sir," he said. "You and I understand each other. Officially I know nothing, but you carry on. It paid dividends over that bonfire business and I don't see why it shouldn't over this. All I'd like you to do is pass on anything you find out, and I'll tip you the wink whenever I think it's worth it."

"Fair enough," I said. "Where do we begin?"

He wanted me to repeat every word I could remember of that telephone conversation I'd had with Alysia Rimmell. It was as great a mystery to him as to me.

"When you question young Rimmell he'll tell you much the same thing," I said. "She was keeping whatever it was to herself. That was like her, you know."

"I know." He smiled. "I spent a good hour with her. She was hard to tie down and yet you had an idea she was enjoying it. There was something deliberate about it: as if she liked trying to find out about you at the same time. It's hard to explain, but I do see she wouldn't want you to anticipate that visit of yours at three o'clock. And her grandson's. She was keeping everything up her sleeve."

And then he was giving me a quick look.

"Just a minute. Is that why she was killed? To stop her talking?"

"It's an idea," I said. "And it'll need the very devil of a lot of thinking out. Who knew she was going to talk, for instance? And the only one we have at the moment is the grandson. He knew and I knew."

"Yes," he said. "He certainly knew. Like to tell me anything you know about him?"

"Why not do it this way? Let me sit in while you talk to him. He may make a slip or two. Then you and I can have a private talk when he's gone."

We waited till things had settled down. The photographer came out. The stretcher arrived and Anders came out with it. He said he'd had a word with the manager. The procession disappeared at the end of the corridor. The news had got round and there were people taking surreptitious peeps from the hall. Jewle had a word with a plain-clothes man who jotted something down in his notebook and then made for the exit. It was just a little flurry of things happening, and then everything was static again.

Jewle nodded towards the door of Flat 3.

"Might as well hear what Rimmell's got to say."

I followed him into the room. Rimmell got to his feet. I hadn't thought he had that much manners.

Jewle, like myself, had sat at the feet of Gamaliel Wharton, but where Wharton would have been gentle to the point of unctuousness, Jewle was quiet: patently sincere. Even I, who knew him so well, would sometimes wonder if he could really be putting on an act.

The sympathies had been extended. Jewle had heard about the hostility between Rimmell's grandmother and his mother, and how Rimmell had thrown in his lot, so to speak, with the now dead woman. Rimmell must have done a lot of thinking while we were out of the room for he didn't overplay his hand.

"We all liked Mrs. Rimmell," Jewle said. "We couldn't help liking her. That's what makes this business all the more damnable. Which reminds me: is it going to interfere with your plans?"

Jewle had glided subtly into interrogation: so subtly that Rimmell wasn't aware of it.

"I was going back early next week," Rimmell said, "but I guess now I'll have to see to things. The funeral and so on." He smiled faintly. "I don't mean I don't want to do it. It's the least I can do."

"Her lawyers will relieve you of a lot," Jewle said. "Do you know who they are?"

Rimmell didn't. Jewle began looking through the drawers of that small Victorian bureau. I saw him look at something and then slip it into his overcoat pocket. Finally he came back with a letter.

"Here we are," he said. "You'd better have this, Mr. Rimmell. Get into touch with them first thing in the morning. They'll know what to do. I expect you yourself are a very busy man."

I think Rimmell must have looked at me. I didn't know. I was looking across the room. But that half-question of Jewle's must have been a bit of a test of Rimmell's memory. I was listening but still not looking as Rimmell went over the main events of his life—his mother's marriage with Walter Gross of the Alaska Trading Corporation: his own job later with that firm, leading to his present job: his decision to see his grand-mother when he first came back to England: the break with his mother—everything, in fact, I had heard before. But it was told with far less assertion. Every now and again there would be a sad shake of the head or as sad a smile.

"Yes," Jewle said. "These family upsets can be the very devil. I know. But the whole thing does you credit, if I may say so."

He gave a kind of sigh, then his manner was suddenly more brisk.

"Still, there we are. And now a few brief questions, just for the record. This is a queer business, Mr. Rimmell, strictly between ourselves. No forcible entry. Someone just walked in here and into that bedroom and that someone knew she'd be having her after-lunch sleep. You any ideas about that?"

I was watching Rimmell then. He looked uneasy. Jewle's change of mood hadn't been expected. And there was a change in himself, too. I thought he'd been very deliberate and careful over that account of his life and circumstances. Now he seemed merely puzzled.

"Still for the records," Jewle was going on, "but you have a key yourself?"

"Yes," he said. "But I'd left it at the hotel. I told Mr. Travers that. I could come here any time I liked. I slept here occasionally. I was her only member of the family, Gran said. She liked me to be about."

"Yes," Jewle said. "She was very fond of you. We know that. But tell me, did she ever insist on giving you money? You know, just as a grandmother would."

Rimmell stiffened a bit. He played for time.

"I don't understand."

"Well, did she finance this trip of yours in any way?"

"Why should she? I was sent here by my firm."

Jewle took a cheque book from his overcoat pocket. He slowly flipped the stubs.

"Here's her cheque book. Only two unused cheques. Practically the first stub says she signed a cheque almost as soon as you arrived. Made out on the stub to H. That's you? Just a minute. Let me finish. Six weeks ago there's another for five hundred pounds, which makes a thousand in all."

Rimmell laughed.

"Oh, those. Perfectly simple. As I told Mr. Travers, she was coming to Canada in the spring to stay with me and my wife. I'm not married yet but shall be shortly. Then she said she'd like a real Canadian mink coat because I could get it through the firm. The five hundred she insisted on paying on account. The other cheque was for dollars. She paid me the pounds here and I'd give her the right amount of dollars when she came to Canada."

"Good," Jewle said. "I'm glad that's cleared up."

He got to his feet. Rimmell got up too.

"That the lot, sir?"

"At present—yes," Jewle said. "And thanks for being so helpful. I take it I can always get you at your hotel?"

"Thank you, too."

He held out his hand.

"Don't forget the solicitors," Jewle reminded him. "They'll see to practically everything."

Rimmell shook hands with me. He didn't say anything. Probably he thought there was thanks in the smile.

Jewle waited a good minute. He went to the door and looked along the corridor. He shut the door again.

"So much for him, as George Wharton would say. What did you make of him?"

"I hardly know," I said. "He's a good actor, that chap. And he's got a good memory. He hardly varied that tale of his from what he told me at his hotel. Only this time he wasn't throwing his weight about."

"Yes," Jewle said reflectively. "But somehow he's too easy. Not that we don't get the easy ones sometimes. He's the old lady's heir?"

"For my money he is. Anything you like to bet."

"And he had a key. And he knew her habits."

He shook his head.

"Well, we'll know a whole lot more about him in a day or two. Let's leave it at that. Maybe you and I'll be having another confidential chat. Won't keep you any longer now. There's the devil of a lot to do here yet."

"You're testing a possible alibi?"

"A man of mine's on the job already."

I nodded. At the door I heard a sound from him and turned. I thought there might be something he'd remembered.

"Just nothing," he said. "Only I can't help wishing Rimmell didn't look so damned obvious."

# 14

# BACK TO NOWHERE

IT WAS the rush hour and it took me the devil of a time to get to Broad Street. First I looked about for a taxi, then decided to walk to a bus stop. Two full buses went by and I only just managed to get on the third. It was after six o'clock when I walked into the Agency. The night man on the first shift was on duty in Bertha's room and Hallows was with him.

"Sorry about this," I told Hallows, "but something important broke. I'll tell you about it in a minute. You're not in a hurry?"

"You know me, sir," he said. "I never am in a hurry."

"Ready for you almost at once. Ring Mrs. Travers, will you, and say I mayn't be home till very late. And then if you'd like to slip out and get some sandwiches—?"

As I'd stood in that crowded bus I'd had plenty of time to think. The trouble was that the thoughts made no clear pattern: if anything, they contradicted each other. Take, for instance, that last and cryptic remark of Jewle's. I was sure I knew what he meant—and he knew that I knew—when he'd said he wasn't too pleased about having Herbert Rimmell as a first-class suspect. Jewle was like myself. His obsession was that bonfire murder, and he'd wanted the death of Alysia Rimmell to be somehow connected. That's why he'd come hot-foot to her flat. And that's why I'd virtually told him to.

But there was another side, and let's creep up on it like this. There was something bogus about Herbert Rimmell. I'd thought so from the beginning. The wild thought had even gone through my mind that he might be some kind of impostor who'd foisted himself on a grandmother who hadn't seen her grandson since he was a boy. That very distance of time would be ample excuse for his failure to remember this or that. And that afternoon had confirmed in a small way what I'd previously thought.

He'd told me, and his grandmother had told me, that business often took him to Manchester. Set aside the fact that I didn't think Manchester was the centre of the English fur trade or that it would be a suitable place to open an agency for the Alaska Trading Corporation, and the fact remained that Rimmell had made a slip. He'd been talking about just having got back from Manchester—you remember it?—and his grandmother was also in the same context. "And she told you?" I'd said, referring to the grandmother. His thoughts had been somewhere else—*on another she.* And so why shouldn't those Manchester trips be to a lady friend?

There was something else. Alysia Rimmell had asked both her nephew and myself to see her that afternoon at three o'clock. Could it be that she'd discovered something about him and wanted to confront or expose him in my presence? Was that why she had been careful to give neither of us even a hint as to the reason for the visit?

And that again was involved. She *had* given me some sort of a reason. She'd said she'd misjudged me. And she'd virtually hinted that she'd misled Jewle. But I couldn't remember, and neither could he, any way whatever in which she'd given false evidence, shall we say, when we'd seen her officially. So there it was. And what was I, unofficially, to do about it all?

I decided to do the obvious. Implicate Herbert Rimmell or clear him. If he'd had nothing to do with the murder, then we might work on the lines that that murder was tied in with the bonfire affair. After all, there were points of resemblance between Alysia Rimmell's murder and the robbery. In each case someone must have had a key and known her habits. Elizabeth Lister was a good fit for the robbery. How she could possibly be connected with the murder remained to be seen and to be tried out if and when we'd eliminated Rimmell.

So I got to work on those lines. I wrote down succinctly what I knew of Rimmell's history and then asked for a person-to-person call—Ludovic Travers to Bob McGuffie of McGuffie Investigations, New York. Bob acted as our North American agent when we needed one. I'd met him and his wife twice when he'd been over here, and, allowing for the difference in time, I'd good hopes he might be in his office when that call got through. But it might be a long wait.

Hallows came in with sandwiches and a couple of bottles of beer. I told him about the afternoon. It was a shock to him as I'd expected. I told him how things looked from my angle and he was as biased as I was. He wanted that latest murder tied in with the bonfire affair. We talked and talked, and didn't get any further.

"You get home now," I said. "I might have to be here quite a time yet. You've rung your wife?"

"She knows me," he said. "Ours is the sort of house where everything's always being kept hot. But something I'd like to say. I don't care whether I'm paid or not but I'd like to stay somehow on that Wakes and Hover business. Just sort of mooching around. I've got a hunch something'll turn up."

"Not a bad idea," I said. "If Rimmell's in the clear there's nothing to fall back on but that. You carry on in your own way for a day or two but don't forget that Jewle will know all about that Simone establishment early to-morrow morning."

He left, and the empties with him. I sent Cooper, the night man, out for the evening papers but they'd all gone. If I'd had a pack of cards I'd have played patience: as it was I tried composing a crossword. I was still at it at just after nine o'clock when my call came through. Reception was just a bit wobbly.

"Hallo, there, Travers. Bob McGuffie here."

"Travers here, Bob. Got a job for you. Very urgent. Ready to take it down?"

"All set."

"Enquiries at Montreal. Everything on three people. A Walter Gross, now dead, high-up in the Alaska Trading Corporation, his widow, and her son. The son's name is Herbert Rimmell—repeat: Herbert R-i-m-m-e-l-l. Also with the Alaska Trading Corporation and now over here on business for them. That's all."

"Urgent, you said?"

"Very much so. Dig out all you can and get your night man to put through a person-to-person call. Time it any day at five a.m., New York time."

"Right. Hope you'll be hearing from us."

That was all. We'd just made it in the three minutes. I said good-night to Cooper and went out to look for a taxi.

Bernice was placidly knitting and reading when I came in. I'd thought over the question of telling her about Alysia Rimmell. She'd see it in the papers in any case and it seemed better to tell her at once rather than tell her in the morning and make a gloomy day. She was very upset. I didn't feel too good either. I hate to see her cry.

In the morning I didn't feel like hurrying to the office. At breakfast Bernice had something on her mind. I thought she was still thinking about Alysia Rimmell so I didn't say a thing, and then, while I was looking through *The Times*, she did something I'd never known her do before.

"You're not doing anything about poor Mrs. Rimmell?"

The question caught me on the hop. I explained how I stood.

"Look, darling, I don't want to be interfering, but didn't you say you went to the flat because she had something to tell you?"

"That's right," I said. "And she wouldn't give me even a hint as to what she wanted to see me about."

"Then you ought to do something about it," she said. "But that wasn't what I was intending to say. What time was it when she rang you?"

"I told you, my dear. About half-past twelve."

I was watching her. She moistened her lips; she nodded to herself.

"That means she'd just come in," she said. "It was a lovely morning and she always took a walk in the morning."

"Wait a minute," I said. "I think you've got something. Whatever it was that she wanted to tell me had arisen out of something she'd heard or seen yesterday morning. Is that it?"

"But of course," she said. "What else could it be?"

"A lot of things. It might have been something she remembered."

She clicked her tongue. I was being very stupid.

"Yes, but what made her remember it? Something she saw or heard when she was out."

"You may be right," I said. "I think I'll look into it."

You're married? Then you'll know why I didn't want to sit there and have the point laboured. There was a look of resolution on my face as I went out, but it went as soon as I was at the lift. I wondered where to go. I still didn't feel like the office so I walked to the Park and sat for a time in the full sun of an uncannily beautiful November morning. And I was beginning to be of the opinion that Bernice had been right. But perhaps Jewle was already at work on the same lines. If he wasn't, then I could handle the Rimmell murder just like the other: get a fund of ideas and discoveries and hand them out in return for what I'd never otherwise be able to discover for myself.

But almost as soon as that idea came, I knew I could never go through with it. The Hover Gang, as I could think of them, were quite another thing. There was something very different about the wiping out of Hover and the killing of Alysia Rimmell. I couldn't make that murder a bargaining counter. I wanted, even more perhaps than Jewle, to get her killer, and what I knew, Jewle should know.

I don't say that made me feel virtuous: if anything it was the other way about. But it did make me restless, and that's why I went to the club. As I was going into the dining-room I saw Charles Muhler. He had a guest so I didn't do more than wave a hand, but after lunch, when I was still killing time in the library, he came up to me.

"How are you, Travers?"

"Very fit," I said. "No need to ask about you. You get younger every day."

I moved aside on the chesterfield for him to sit beside me, but he said he couldn't stay.

"Something I've been meaning to ask you," he said. "Did that friend of yours go to Sigott after all?"

Liars should have good memories. Use had sharpened mine.

"No," I said. "The arrangements were changed. But how *is* Sigott? Seen him lately?"

"I rarely see him," he said. "You been to the P.P.E?"

"No," I said, and before I knew it was the Portrait Painters' Exhibition he meant.

"He's losing his touch," he said. "I don't mean the royal portrait. That was what you'd expect it to be. Quite good, in fact, but he had a couple of other things." He smiled maliciously. "You have a look yourself. I'd like to hear what you think of them."

I forgot that little conversation almost as soon as Muhler had disappeared through the library door. All I thought was that every painter, every creative artist, in fact, must lose his touch at times: and I also smiled to myself at Muhler's love of scandal and the zest he got out of it. Then I realised it was after three o'clock, so I walked to Charing Cross and caught a bus to Broad Street.

There were one or two little jobs for me but I'd finished them by five o'clock and was thinking of going home when Jewle called me. He couldn't spare long, he said, but could I meet him at the usual tea-shop. He meant an old resort of everyone's— near the Yard and just round the corner from Whitehall. I said I'd try to make it in a quarter of an hour and I nearly did.

"Glad you could come," he said. "Suppose you haven't got anything?"

I had to smile.

"You mustn't think we're magicians," I told him. "I've got an idea if it's any use to you and you haven't thought of it already."

I gave him Bernice's theory and he liked it. As for his own day, it had been a hectic one. Rimmell, he said, had an alibi and hadn't, if I knew what he meant. He'd finished his lunch at half-past one and had gone up to his room. He said he'd had a nap. No one, of course, could prove it.

"One little error in what he told us, though. He was supposed to have got back from Manchester early yesterday, but he didn't. He came back late the previous night. And about ten o'clock yesterday morning he rang his grandmother. Unfortunately the switchboard girl isn't a listener in. I haven't taxed him with it yet. Giving him plenty of rope."

"What time was the actual killing?"

"As near two o'clock as makes no difference. I've seen the lawyers, by the way. Rimmell gets about half the estate. The rest goes partly to some school or other in India that the Rimmells were interested in, and partly to a distant relative of Mrs. Rimmell. Then this afternoon I saw Rimmell again. Got a lot more information about himself. Wharton's just getting into touch with the police at Montreal."

"George is in it, is he?"

"Yes," he said, and smiled wryly. "Funny how he never thinks anyone ever grows up. Still, I suppose it's his job."

"Don't tell me," I said. "I suffered from it for years. But about Rimmell. Does he know he's a suspect?"

Jewle frowned.

"Frankly, I don't think he does. I'm not patting myself on the back, mind you, but I think he's got his nerve back. I've even kidded him into thinking he's helping us. I don't say he was all that keen about giving information about himself but once we'd got over that—well, everything was fine. I only left him just before I rang you. We walked together to the end of the street."

"You're watching him?"

"That's not the policy. The last thing we want is to make him nervy. Soon as we get that information from Montreal things may be different."

"And Wakes's women? You picked them up?"

He told me about "Simone". That was somewhere that *was* being watched, he said. A man at the front and a man at the back.

"The back?" That was a slip but I managed to cover it. "I didn't think there was a back way to Butler Street?"

"Just a drive-in," he told me. "Useful for the shops on the south side."

He was giving me an enquiring sort of look as if asking for comment. It took me a second or two to find it.

"You mean a car—Wakes's for instance—could have driven in there?"

"That's right," he said. "And have taken away a body."

"Yes," I said slowly. "It certainly gives one ideas. And what about Wakes?"

"Wakes is just about ready. He lunches practically every day at the Café Royal and we're counting on his doing so to-morrow. Those people I told you about will be there to have a good look at him. I don't think that beard he's grown will make all that difference. He can't disguise his height and his general look all that much, and he has a trick of fiddling with a handkerchief in his breast pocket. If everything goes right he'll be picked up straight away at the studio and popped into cold storage."

He looked at his watch, gulped down the last half-cup of now tepid tea, and pushed his chair back.

"I'm a bit late. Anything else?"

There was nothing I could think of. As we parted he said he'd send a flash to the office as soon as he hauled Wakes in.

As I walked back along Whitehall towards home I had the feeling that everything was going well, and yet not so well as it might. It was a vague sort of feeling: an impatience, perhaps, and a wish to be doing something personally, and at once: a dislike of living on crumbs from Jewle's table, though that, as I knew at once, savoured more of petulance. But all the same there was a definite frustration, and it was Rimmell who was largely the cause of it. Either he was guilty or he was not: either he could be eliminated or else the Rimmell case would be over, and it was that lack of decision that was holding things back. The wheels of the Yard might grind exceedingly small but I had the idea that at the moment they were grinding annoyingly slow.

It was just after six o'clock when I reached the flat and who should be waiting for me but Hallows. He and Bernice were having a cosy chat when I walked in on them. Bernice left us to ourselves.

"Thought you wouldn't mind me dropping in," Hallows said in his mild way. "I just got on to something and thought you'd like to know. You did give me a description of that young Rimmell who might be mixed up in the murder. Seen this?"

He showed me a photograph of Herbert Rimmell in one of the evening papers. The Hanway Gardens Murder, as the paper called it, was splashed across the front page.

"I bought it to pass the time," Hallows said. "I'd been walking around generally all day—Jewle's men are on the job at 'Simone', by the way—and I thought I'd have another look at Butler Street myself. It was just after five and I saw a man go into 'Simone'. You don't often see men go into a shop like that—not alone—and then something struck me. It was about ten minutes before he came out and then I spotted him. Herbert Rimmell!"

I just couldn't speak. I'd seen it coming and yet it hit me clean in the wind.

"I couldn't be sure, so I followed him," Hallows said. "Lucky for me he didn't take a taxi, but it was him all right. Staying at the Court Hotel in Lonsdale Street."

"But it's incredible! However could he be mixed up with the Wakes crowd!"

"I know," he said. "It's a bit of a facer. That's why I thought I'd better come along straight away."

I was on my feet and prowling about the room.

"It doesn't fit in. You can't make it fit in. He didn't come to England till long after the Lister woman had left Mrs. Rimmell. And Mrs. Rimmell definitely said she'd lost all trace of her at once. Then how the devil could Rimmell have got in touch with her?"

"Yes," Hallows said. "But is that the point? Say he did get into touch with her and what I saw this afternoon looks like it: *why* did he?"

"Wait a minute," I said. "He'd just have left Jewle. Maybe he was reporting something that Jewle had said." I clicked my tongue in annoyance. "But why? He couldn't possibly be a member of that Wakes gang. The only connection between him and them is through Elizabeth Lister. And they didn't come within miles of each other."

Then I thought of something. Those two had something in common. Each had a key to the flat. Was it worth while to ring Jewle about a clue as nebulous as that? I didn't argue the point. I went across to the telephone.

"One thing I forgot to ask you," I said to Jewle as soon as we'd made contact. "Did you collect our friend's key this afternoon?"

"It was collected last night," he said.

"Any other keys, were there?"

"Not to the flat," he said. "Mrs. Rimmell had only the one key cut. A Yale, as you know."

"But didn't the Lister woman have a key?"

"At first—yes. But she handed it in when she finally left. When Mrs. Rimmell gave the grandson a key she distinctly said it was lucky she had one on hand—the one she'd had specially cut for Lister."

"I was just wondering," I said. "Just the wild notion that if Lister had the key still, she might have been the one who did the job at the flat."

So that was that. A second, and I knew it was even worse.

"Elizabeth Lister didn't have a key to the flat," I told Hallows. "She handed it in when she left. And you see what that means? It wasn't she who lifted that jewellery."

"Not necessarily," he said. "She might have had a duplicate cut for herself, just in case."

"No," I said, and very patiently. "Just work it out. If that jewellery was taken, and the cross with the diamonds intact, would those three have gone on living as they did? They'd have been in possession of a young fortune, even working through a fence. But they didn't change their way of life—not until last February when Hover was shopped. And then they all blossomed out: new shops, new flat, new car. And so that's when the jewellery was lifted. And I'm not going to believe that Elizabeth Lister kept a duplicate key all that time—even if she ever had one cut—and didn't make use of it long before last February."

"Yes," he said. "It certainly looks that way. She could have done with the money long before that, and so could the two others."

"So there we are," I said exasperatedly. "We're back to nowhere. If Elizabeth Lister didn't take that jewellery, who did?"

We argued for a bit and then gave it up. Butting a brick wall was nothing to it. Hallows rose to go.

"What about tomorrow?"

"Just go on hanging around," I said. "Maybe you'll have some more luck."

I thought of something as I went with him to the lift.

"With any luck I might get a reply from New York to-morrow. If there is, and there's any discrepancy between it and Rimmell's story, I think I'll see him. I might be able to knock him clean off his perch by asking him about that visit to Simone."

"I've just remembered something myself," he said as he stepped into the lift. "I don't know that I won't try it on."

Before I could ask him what it was, the lift was on its way down.


# 15

## RE-ENTER SIGOTT

PERHAPS it was through thinking I might have that call from McGuffie, but I was at the office early the next morning. A cable was waiting for me—from McGuffie. It had been telephoned in at about midnight and the night man hadn't thought it sufficiently important to be rung through.

> Information almost available. Confidently expect call
> as arranged within thirty-six hours. McGuffie.

That meant I had another twenty-four hours to wait. But, as Jewle had said, Rimmell wasn't going to skip. He had too much at stake for that. All that was needed was a little more patience, even if it was a commodity that, with me at least, had been getting in short supply.

When Norris had finished with the mail I thought I'd let him in on things. He rather looked down his nose. He wanted to know—and it was his job—who was going to pay. I tried to point out the advantages of getting still better in with United Assurance and clinging to good contacts, like Jewle, at the Yard. Then, before I could get more trickily involved, Bertha rang through. Hallows wanted to see me.

"Well, send him through."

"He says he'd like you to see him outside."

I suppose Hallows had good reason, so I put on hat and coat and went out. He was waiting in Bertha's room and we went out to the street together.

"I've got something we've been wanting," he told me. "Those art studies. I had to pay through the nose, though. Five pounds."

He gave me a largish envelope.

"Right," I said. "Let's have some coffee. It oughtn't to be too crowded."

Our usual place wasn't a hundred yards away, and the big downstairs room wasn't crowded at all. We went through to the far end and gave the order on the way.

"Better wait till the coffee comes," I said. "Pretty bad, are they?"

"I wouldn't say so," he said. "They're not filthy. A bit suggestive, of course."

The waitress came, and went. I took the photographs out. There were a dozen glossy, sepia-toned prints, about four and a half inches by seven, and each one different. Each had the same nude, dark-haired model, but when I'd looked at two or three and compared the different lightings, I thought the hair wasn't actually dark: it looked almost fair sometimes where the light flicked it. But Hallows had been right. They *were* art studies—there wasn't a doubt about that. Suggestive? Sensual? Maybe, but sex so superbly presented that one accepted them as what they claimed to be. Enlarge them and you could call them posters for Paphos.

Take the very first one I looked at: the model lying back towards me on a small chesterfield, slim ankles resting on the far end, the head turned, the smile provocative, and a beckoning finger. Beneath, as title, the one word—"Well?" The pose itself, the manipulation of the light and shade, the whole technique, in fact, was masterly. Maybe I'd misjudged Wakes. Maybe he *had* won gold medals. I no longer doubted it. Wakes was a photographic genius.

I looked through the whole dozen and then something made me turn back. I looked at the sixth one again. In it a model stood, nude as always, with hands lightly on hips, the hips provocatively turned. The head was thrown back challengingly and there was the same alluring smile. The title was—"You dare!". But there was something different about that study. Something inherent in the pose, and in the model herself. At the far back of memory I could feel a faint stir. I knew, and I didn't know. And then all at once it broke through, and what I knew was so impossible that it was foolish even to look at that study again. And yet somehow that very doubt made it all the more true.

I looked at Hallows. He was reflectively stirring his coffee.

"Five pounds," I said, and he took me up before I could go on.

"I was afraid you'd think the price was pretty stiff."

"No, no," I said, and began putting the prints into their envelope. "There's one of them that's more than worth the money."

He gave me an interested look.

"Remember that morning when Hover called at the studio of a painter named Sigott? Well, these studies tie Sigott in. I don't know how. Soon as I know I'll tell you some more."

I put the envelope in the inside pocket of my overcoat. Hallows knew when, and when not, to ask questions. As soon as he'd drunk his coffee he said he ought to be getting back to his beat.

"You might be near Wakes's studio from half-past one onwards," I told him. "The tip came through that they're probably taking him in."

And, to get a bit ahead, that's what Hallows did see. I knew about it when Matthews rang me. He wasted no words.

"The Chief says you might like to know that an old friend is booked for a rest cure."

"No bail?"

"No bail."


I had another cup of coffee after Hallows had gone. Then I managed to get a taxi and went to the club. There was nobody in the library at that hour of the morning and I had the room to myself. And in that *Academy Illustrated* I'd consulted months before I found that monotone reproduction of Sigott's "Mannequin". I put that sixth art study alongside it and there wasn't a doubt in my mind. It was Sigott's model, Margaret Mann, who had posed for Wakes. I was right even about the hair. Her hair had been a warm mahogany. In some lights it would appear on a print as black and in others as almost light.

And if that wasn't a facer, what was? How in heaven's name could Wakes have got into touch with Sigott's model-cum-receptionist? And did that make Sigott involved with the Hover Gang? It might be preposterous to have even a suspicion of that when one thought of Sigott's standing, and yet what else could I wonder. It made me think back to what Sigott had told me of her.

If I remembered rightly he'd said that towards the end of her time with him she'd become a bit slack: she'd not been at hand when wanted, which meant she'd been taking a lot of time off. And some of that time might have been spent with Wakes. And that made me aware of something else. It must have been Margaret Mann herself who'd suggested some of those poses to Wakes, especially the one which so closely resembled that of Sigott's "Mannequin". She must have learned a lot, artistically, from Sigott.

But what else had he told me about her? That one afternoon in February she'd turned up with a man whom she announced as her husband. She'd called him Jack, and Sigott hadn't heard his surname. The two, he had said, were sailing almost at once for Australia. He'd added that there hadn't been time as yet to have heard from her.

It didn't help me. I compared the whole dozen prints with that reproduction of Sigott's picture and hoped for inspiration but none came, and I put the book back on the shelf. I lighted my pipe and stretched out my long legs and tried to visualise that model: to see her in colour, as it were, and as flesh and blood. And that was when I thought of something—the hair! Cassis, and the women!

Bernice and I had spent a holiday there and I'd noticed what I hadn't noticed on previous holidays in France: that many women had hair of that mahogany red. I said how attractive it was. Bernice had laughed.

"It isn't the natural colour," she said. "It's just dark hair treated with henna."

"Good lord!" I'd said. "And is it permanent?"

"Of course not," she'd said. "It's like having your hair bleached. If the treatment isn't repeated it'll grow the natural colour again."

So Margaret Mann's hair needn't have been natural. It might have been black. And it might have been Sigott who'd suggested the henna treatment. And then I saw it! At one moment my fingers were instinctively at my glasses and the next moment I could have leapt up from the chair and yelled Eureka! I wanted to yell, but I did something else instead. I pushed the bell and asked for the special Amontillado.

As I sat sipping that sherry I could see the whole thing. Mrs. Sigott had died and there was the remarkably attractive Nurse Lister. Sigott had ideas. He put a proposition up to her and, as soon as she cleared up her affairs at Mallow Grove, she moved in. She'd decided to cut herself off from Wakes and her sister. Hover didn't matter at the moment: he was in jail. And she decided on a more attractive name. And maybe it was she who, after consultation with Sigott, decided on the henna treatment.

That stay with Sigott explained where she had been during what we called the missing period. Kossack hadn't been keeping her and neither had Wakes. But she'd never been the kind to settle down. Sigott, everything at the studio, became boring.

She made Wakes's acquaintance again. And Hover was coming out of jail. And Wakes was the "tallish showy-looking man" whom she'd passed off as her husband. And she'd said she was going to Australia because Sigott wouldn't be able to find her. And he'd certainly be looking for her sooner or later, for it was she who was walking off with that set of pornographic sketches that were going to cost Sigott dear in blackmail.

Beautiful, wasn't it, the snug way it all fitted. Still a few loose ends, of course, but now I could put pressure on Sigott and arrive at the truth at last. And there was no time like the present.

It was Laura who answered me.

"Travers bothering you again," I said. "Is Mr. Sigott in?"

"He has a sitter," she said, "and I daren't disturb him."

"But he's lunching at home?"

"Oh, yes."

"At what time?"

"Mr. Sigott always lunches at one," she told me rather severely.

"Then tell him I'll see him at half-past. Say it's most urgent."

"But you can't do that! Mr. Sigott always has his nap when he's finished his meal."

"What I'm seeing him about will keep him awake," I said. "Tell him so from me."

I had sandwiches and beer at the club and it was half-past one to the minute when Laura drew back to let me step through the door. She was most disapproving as she said Sigott would see me. She didn't ask to take my hat and over-coat: she just showed me into the drawing-room as I was. Maybe it was a hint that I wouldn't be staying long.

Sigott rose from his chair. He looked surly and he didn't hold out his hand.

"You again," he said. "What is it this time?"

"Just another murder. A former client, or patroness of yours: Mrs. Rimmell. You've seen it in your paper."

"Well? And what's it to do with me?"

"That's what the police are going to be very anxious to find out," I said, and helped myself to a chair. "Strictly between ourselves, an old friend of yours is in it up to the neck. An ex-model of yours, Margaret Mann, *alias* Nurse Lister."

His face went so red that I thought he was going to have a stroke. Then the colour went. His hand was so shaking that he could hardly stub out the cigarette. And he couldn't speak.

"You wouldn't know her now, Sigott. She's changed her hair colour again. Blonde, and she wears it long."

"What's it to do with me?" he said, and he wouldn't catch my eye. "As far as I'm concerned she can go to hell."

"But suppose she talks before she does?"

He shrugged his shoulders.

"You're a man of the world, aren't you? What makes you so pure and holy? And where does it concern me?"

"Listen," I said. "I'm not going to bandy words with you. Twice I've come here to keep the police from your doorstep and each time you lied uphill and down. And you induced your housekeeper to lie too. You didn't know anything about Nurse Lister after your wife died. I wonder what the police'll think of that. It was conspiracy to defeat the ends of justice."

"It was true in substance. And what's it got to do with murder?"

"Only this: the Lister woman was a party to Hover's murder. He was her husband, or have you forgotten it? And she's involved in the Rimmell murder." I hoisted myself up from the chair. "Still, there's no use in argument. You won't talk to me so now you can talk to the police. And what about Penford? Forgotten him too? What's he going to do when he learns that you induced his wife to compound with blackmail? And to part with two thousand pounds."

"You can't do this!"

"I not only can but I'm going to," I said. "In a very few minutes I'll be at Scotland Yard. From there I shall go straight to Penford."

"No," he said. "No! We can talk this over."

I laughed.

"Oh no. Twice bitten, thrice shy. I don't like liars, Sigott." He went to the door, looked in the hall, turned a key in the lock and came back.

"What do you want to know? Or what's your price?" What was the point in being indignant? The bluff had worked.

"A cut price," I said. "Dirt cheap. I want the truth. Tell me just one more lie and I walk out of this room."

He sat down and so did I.

"Very well. Ask your questions."

"Oh no," I said. "I'm not being dictated to. You tell me all about that afternoon when the Lister woman left here."

He'd been going out that afternoon to see a man and discuss a picture, he said, and he hadn't expected to be back till well after tea. He'd practically reached his destination when he realised he'd forgotten the preliminary sketches he should have had with him, so he had the taxi turn back. When he got home he saw a taxi at the door and a man bringing some luggage out. Then he saw Lister and wanted to know what was happening. She said she'd a right to leave if she wanted to, and then she introduced the man as her husband.

"I was furious," Sigott said, "and then this husband of hers began striking an attitude. And what could I do?"

"Did you ever offer her marriage?"

He shot a look at me.

"Perhaps I did. But she said she wasn't the marrying kind."

"She wasn't," I said. "As far as she knew, she was married to Hover and he was in jail. I know her record. Pure and holy, to use your own phrase, when she had that nurse's rig-out on. Demure as they make 'em. But she was over-sexed from the word go, and she had the morals of an alley cat. This supposed husband of hers was a man named Wakes. You're going to read quite a lot about him shortly. She'd fooled around with him long before she met you, or Hover. And there'd been a private patient at her hospital, and a doctor. I guess you found out in time about her morals. Was that why you showed her those sketches of yours?"

He didn't answer. He knew there was no need.

"And you had to go and blab about the model who'd sat for them. And you knew all the time that Lister was the only one who could have taken the sketches, and who was working the blackmail racket."

He shrugged his shoulders.

"The second two thousand was paid up," I went on. "And then what happened?"

"I was rung up," he said. "Not for money but to say if I opened my mouth there was another set of photographs."

There was nothing to say. I just gave a grunt. I wouldn't point out all over again what a fool he'd been from the start.

"Well, that's all, Sigott. I'll do my best to keep all this from the police, and from Penford, but there's still one thing you've got to do. Get your housekeeper in here. I want to talk to her."

"You can't do that!"

"Look," I said, "I'm not interested in your love life. I'm helping Scotland Yard—unofficially—to get the truth about a couple of murders. I want to confirm a connecting link between Lister and Mrs. Rimmell."

"But what connection could there be here?"

"Leave that to me," I said. "I can handle this without compromising you. Get your housekeeper in."

He got up reluctantly, gave me another look, made as if to speak and thought better of it. He unlocked the door and pushed a bell. The blonde came in.

"Laura, ask Mrs. Crewe to come in a moment, will you?" He came back to his chair.

"I hope to God you handle this right, Travers."

I didn't speak. Mrs. Crewe was coming in. I got up. "Good afternoon, Mrs. Crewe. You remember me, I expect. Will you sit down?"

She was as self-assured as ever. She thanked me as I moved the chair.

"It's like this," I said. "Oh, and before I begin, Mr. Sigott wishes you to speak absolutely unreservedly. This is strictly confidential talk between the three of us. It's about the late model and receptionist here, known as Margaret Mann. Before she came here to attend Mrs. Sigott, do you know where she was?"

"At the hospital. Or so I thought."

"She wasn't," I said. "She'd been attending a General Rimmell—"

She stared.

"Not the husband of—"

"That's right. The husband of the woman who was murdered at her flat, Mrs. Alysia Rimmell. She came here at the end of January and at the beginning of February to sit for her portrait." I turned to Sigott. "How many times?"

"Three in all. I'd have liked more but I didn't want to tax her strength."

"You begin to see the point, Mrs. Crewe? And you can assure me that you hadn't the faintest idea that Mann knew Mrs. Rimmell?"

"Not the least idea."

She looked away and she was moistening her lips.

"Now I come to look back, and considering what you've told me, there was something very peculiar. She didn't see Mrs. Rimmell here. She asked me to. I mean the first time."

I asked her to enlarge on it. Margaret, she said, had claimed to have a bad headache. That was the first time. The next time she said that as Mrs. Crewe had seen to her that first time it would be only right if she saw her the other times.

"By *saw* her, you mean admitting her. Anything else?"

"Oh, yes, taking her to the dressing-room and seeing her out when Mr. Sigott rang to say she was going."

"The dressing-room," I said. "I'd like to see it."

The three of us went. It lay along the widish corridor to the studio, the entrance door being about three quarters of the way down. It was a very pleasant room that looked over the small garden. Mrs. Crewe said it had once been a morning or breakfast room. A little annexe had been made to house wash-basin and lavatory, and there were easy chairs and a dressing-table with mirror and a tall cheval glass.

"And that other door leads direct to the studio?"

She opened it and there the studio was.

"Excellent," I said. "The arrangement couldn't be better. And just what happened when Mrs. Rimmell stepped in here?"

"Well, it would be beautifully warm, of course, so I'd hang up her coat and take her hat and bag." She smiled. "And then she'd do what everyone does—make herself presentable. Everything would be laid out on the table there. And when she was ready I'd open the door for her and announce her to Mr. Sigott."

"Good. I think I've got the routine," I smiled and held out my hand. "And I'm afraid that's all. I'm very grateful to you, Mrs. Crewe."

The corridor door closed behind her.

"A very competent woman," I said to Sigott. "And most helpful. I think she's given me all I want."

"And what *did* you want?"

"Just to clear things up. Very little beyond what you've heard. Shall we go back now? I shan't be keeping you more than a minute or two longer."

Back in the drawing-room I sat down on the edge of a chair.

"About Lister, or Mann," I said. "In case you've still got a warm spot in your heart for her, have a look at these."

I handed him the envelope of art studies. He began looking. He got as far as the sixth.

"Good God!"

He winced as he put the photographs back. I reached for the envelope.

"Even your art was prostituted," I told him. "And you might care to know that those photographs were taken while she was still with you. Wakes did them. The one she was having an affair with behind your back. The one who took the photographs of those sketches of yours."

He drew in a breath. I could see the whites of his knuckles as his hands clenched. I got to my feet.

"Well, that's all. Between you and me you've had a lucky escape." I gave a solemn shake of the head. "I hope I can keep the police out of this. I sincerely hope so."

"Anything I can do for you—"

The look on my face as I whirled round on him left the rest of it in air.

"One thing you can do, and you're going to do. You're getting into touch with Mrs. Penford and telling her the blackmail money's been recovered. Spin any yarn you like provided she gets a cheque for two thousand pounds."

He was trying to speak as I made for the hall. The blonde didn't appear. Near the other door he did find words.

"I apologise to you, Travers. I haven't come at all well out of this."

"Forget it," I said. "Plenty of things I haven't come well out of myself."

He opened the door, wondered if he should hold out a hand and knew, perhaps, that it might be ignored. He cleared his throat.

"You wouldn't like to tell me what else it was you found out? In the dressing-room, I mean."

"Afraid I can't," I said. "But you needn't worry."

I gave him a nod.

"Be seeing you, perhaps, sometime."

I was smiling wryly to myself as I walked towards Knightsbridge. I could have got anything from Sigott. I wondered what Bernice would have said if I'd told her, for instance, that Sigott was going to paint her portrait and it'd be exhibited in next year's Academy. Sigott would have done it—free of course—like a shot.

As for telling him what I'd discovered in that dressing-room, if he had a good memory he could work it out for himself. What I now knew was how Lister had got a key to Alysia Rimmell's flat. All she had to do was to slip into that dressing-room while Mrs. Crewe was busy elsewhere, and take the key from the handbag. But what happened afterwards was anybody's guess. Did she slip along to the flat herself or did she pass the key to the waiting Wakes? Or did she slip along to Knightsbridge and have another key cut? With the modern way they have of duplicating Yales, it wouldn't have taken more than a few minutes, and Alysia Rimmell's sitting would have been at least an hour. Maybe more, with a break.

Later that evening I rang Jewle with a pertinent question. He was out, but Matthews was in.

"What's being done about our lady friends?" I asked him.

"Leaving them guessing," he said. "Wakes is out of circulation and so's his car. Between ourselves the Chief wants just a little bit more information and then he'll be pulling them in."

"Maybe I can give him some," I said, and hastily added that it would be in the morning.

# 16

# CLINCHING THE NAILS

ALMOST as soon as I got to the office in the morning, Jewle rang me. He wanted to know if I had that information I'd mentioned to Matthews. I said it might come in at any time but I'd give him a ring before midday. He said he'd stay on tap.

"Any news from Montreal yet?" I managed to get in.

"These things take time," he said. "You know how it is."

When the time drew near for McGuffie's call, I moved to Bertha's office. She was to listen in on her extension and take the message down in shorthand, and afterwards I could fill in anything, like names, that she'd missed. And we were caught almost on the hop. The call came quite a time before we'd expected it.

It wasn't a long message.

"That enough?" asked Bob's night duty man. "Or do we go on digging?"

"Enough," I said. "It's perfect. Goodbye for now."

Once more we'd made it in time. Talking to New York is like spitting gold. But there was plenty of time to collate what we'd heard, and when we'd got it into shape I had Bertha make three copies. This is what it amounted to:

GROSS. Died 1952. Divorced his wife 1948. Vice-President Alaska Trading Corporation confirmed.

HELEN GROSS. Married Hod Keyser, band-leader, 1948. Divorced by him 1951. Now manageress dance hall, Montreal.

HERBERT RIMMELL. With Alaska Trading Corporation till divorce. Joined H.K.'s band as vocalist. On second divorce joined Leishmann Company, music publishers, as salesman. Embezzlement hushed up 1954. Living with mother 1278 La Croix Street, Montreal.

As soon as Bertha had those copies ready I rang Jewle. He was sitting at the end of the line.

"Got what I wanted," I said. "See you at the coffee-shop as soon as I can make it? We can go on from there."

"On to where?"

"The Court Hotel," I said. "You'd better make sure that Rimmell's available for us. No need to mention me."

Jewle was waiting for me at a table in the far corner. A police car with a driver was waiting outside. The waitress was bringing the coffee almost as soon as I'd sat down.

"Anything from Montreal yet?"

"Probably later in the day."

"Then we're ahead of you," I told him. "I got on to our New York agent some days ago. This is what arrived a few minutes before I rang."

He ran his eye quickly down the copy. He read it more slowly a second time.

"My God!" he said. "Of all the bare-faced liars!"

"Keep that copy," I said. "I've got another in my pocket. But you see the racket?"

"Sticks out a mile. Rigged up between him and his mother. She's pretty hot stuff herself by the look of it. The two of them realise the old lady's got no other real heir and much as the mother loathed the old lady, she can see a main chance when it's stuck under her nose. So Rimmell comes over here and gets in touch. If we have a look at last year's accounts I'll wager his grandmother started financing him on some pretext or other as soon as he got here. That yarn about breaking with his mother because of her would just warm her heart. And the will dates from during that first visit."

He gave himself a nod and then me a look.

"You see the implications? He couldn't go on milking the old lady and she might have gone on living for years."

"Yes," I said. "Looks as if you'd better bring the handcuffs."

He gulped down the rest of his coffee and snapped his fingers to the waitress.

"What're we waiting for? Let's go and get it over."

We went out to the car. The driver moved the car on: up Northumberland Street and into the traffic stream to The Mall. In under ten minutes we were drawing up at the hotel.

"You come with us, Harry," Jewle said to the driver. "Keep just behind and stay outside the door once we're in."

The three of us took the lift.

"You do all the talking," I told Jewle. "I'll just look on."

It was the biggest fiasco I've ever been at. Rimmell was all smiles for Jewle but he didn't look too pleased at the sight of me. Jewle said good morning, and followed it up with, "Take a look at that."

Rimmell had a look. Then he looked up at us and like someone suddenly struck dumb. He had another look but he didn't get far. Believe it or not he began to blubber. It was horrible. He just sat there on the bed and then he rolled over and was blubbering into the eiderdown. Jewle's lip was curling. I hardly knew where to look.

The blubbering grew quieter.

"You and your mother!" Jewle said. "What a scheme! And so that's why you killed the old lady. Thought she was going to live too long."

"I didn't!" He shrieked it at us. "I liked her. I was fond of her!"

"Yes," Jewle said. "Especially when she was dead."

He was blubbering again. Jewle waited for the racket to quieten.

"We'd better take him in, don't you think?" he said to me. "We can hold him for attempted fraud. There's the thousand he had out of her."

"I'll pay it back."

"Shut up!"

Jewle was towering over him.

"Murder for nothing," I said. "The solicitors must be seen and they'll get into touch with that other relative and she'll bring an action to have the will set aside. You won't get a single cent, Rimmell."

"He won't have to bother about wills," Jewle said.

Rimmell sat up. He wiped his eyes.

"All right," he said. "But I swear to God I didn't kill her."

"Just one little thing," I said. "There's a high-class dress shop in Butler Street called 'Simone'. You paid a visit there just after Inspector Jewle saw you the last time. Care to tell us why?"

He stared. He almost smiled.

"That proves I didn't kill her! I went there to see."

"To see what?"

For a minute or two he was almost his old self.

"Look," he said. "This is how I figured it. I rang Gran that morning just to see how she was and she said she was going out with a Mrs. Marrible. She's a friend she has at the flats. And there was something about this 'Simone', so after it all happened I saw this Mrs. Marrible and she told me about it—"

"Save it!" Jewle told him curtly.

He looked at his notebook and dialled the number of the flats. He gave his name and asked to be put into touch with Mrs. Marrible.

A minute or two and he was talking to her: explaining the visit and mentioning Rimmell.

"Better have a wash," he told Rimmell. "Before you do, though, I'll have your passport."

When the car moved off, I sat in the front with the driver, and I'd only to turn an ear to get each word of the story that Rimmell told Jewle. How Mrs. Marrible and Alysia Rimmell had gone to "Simone" but hardly were they in the shop than Alysia was saying they'd come back some other time and she almost hustled Mrs. Marrible to the door.

"And where do you come in?" Jewle wanted to know.

"I told you," Rimmell said. "The way I worked it out, it might have had something to do with—with what happened. I guess we all want to be detectives."

"You do, do you?" Jewle told him. "Well, don't begin getting ideas. You won't be the only detective who's taken a long drop."

There wasn't another word till we got to the flats. Mrs. Marrible's was on the ground floor too, but a smaller flat than

Alysia Rimmell's. She was a pleasantly plump woman of sixty, charming in manner and a first-class witness. Her husband, a gunner colonel, had been killed in the war. Rimmell didn't seem too much at ease when she greeted him. He was wearing a black tie and maybe it was that that prompted fresh condolences on his grandmother's death.

The preliminaries were over and she began telling us about her morning with Alysia Rimmell.

"We'd both seen those 'Simone' advertisements and had threatened to look in, and then the previous evening when we met each other at dinner, we really decided to go. We took a bus as far as St. James's and then had coffee and afterwards walked the short distance to Butler Street. There was only one customer when we went into the shop: an over-dressed woman who simply reeked of perfume, and she was being attended to by a youngish woman with long, very fair hair. I thought it was synthetic but perhaps I'm doing her an injustice." She smiled. "Am I going too much into detail?"

"The more detail the better," Jewle told her. "Just tell us everything."

"Well, the woman I was mentioning was looking at some artificial flowers—you know, for corsages or hat trimmings—and the saleswoman just looked up for a moment and said, 'Just a moment, madam,' and then went on attending to the customer. When I thought about it afterwards I knew it was me she was speaking to, because Alysia was just behind me. I'd wanted to look at the corsages or whatever they were myself, and then, when we were both practically at the counter, the saleswoman looked at us again and all at once Alysia fairly clutched at my arm and then she said, out loud, 'I don't think we'll stay now. Well come back later,' and then she literally hustled me out of the shop! But the funny thing was that the saleswoman didn't tell us we could be attended to at once, which she might have done because there was another saleswoman just coming into the room from upstairs. Now wasn't that odd?"

"It certainly was," Jewle said. "And what happened then?"

"Well, we went out, of course, and then Alysia said she was feeling a bit tired and we'd take a taxi home which she insisted on paying for. Of course, I asked her what it had all been about and had it been that over-dressed woman whom she recognised and wanted to avoid. 'I just didn't feel well, my dear,' she said, and of course I couldn't say any more. I ought to be ashamed of myself, I know, but I really didn't believe her. She liked being secretive in all sorts of little ways. And then when I saw her at lunch she was eating her meal as if she enjoyed it and looking just as well as she ever was. 'I think you're up to some trick or other,' I told her, and she gave me a queer look. It was as if she was very pleased with herself. 'You mustn't imagine things, Alice,' she said. 'I just didn't like the look of the place.'"

That was about all. We thanked her and said good-bye. Once more she was very affectionate with Rimmell. Doubtless he'd contrived to insinuate himself into her good graces, too. Jewle made him sit in front with the driver, then nodded to me. We took a turn or two along the street.

"What d'you make of it all?" he said. "Was it just that Mrs. Rimmell recognised her old friend Nurse Lister?"

"Undoubtedly she recognised her," I said, "but the reactions were all wrong. What would the average woman have said? I think this: 'Why! if it isn't Nurse Lister! And what on earth have you been doing to your hair?'"

"Yes," Jewle said slowly. "And there's what she told you, that she'd misjudged you over something. And how she sort of hinted she'd led me wrong. Both remarks could only have arisen out of her recognition of Nurse Lister. But why didn't she explain further? I don't see it. How could a recognition of Nurse Lister tally with having misjudged you and misled me? It just doesn't make sense."

"I know," I said. "I'd hinted to her that Lister might have stolen that jewellery and I guess you had too, so the terms *misjudged* and *led astray* couldn't possibly apply to merely having recognised Lister in that shop. There must be more to it. What do you say if we think it over?"

The car took us back to the Court Hotel. Jewle told the driver to stop well short.

"You can get out," he told Rimmell. "But don't go thinking you're in the clear. You're in it up to the neck. And no monkey tricks. You're going to be watched from now on."

We watched Rimmell move off. He wasn't so jaunty as when he'd walked with us to the car from Mrs. Marrible's flat.

"Honest to God I don't know if he had the guts to do that job," Jewle said. "And what do we do now?"

"What about getting a search warrant and having a look at Wakes's flat?"

"Matthews did it soon after we pulled Wakes in," he said. "What's in your mind?"

"He was looking for stuff to incriminate Wakes. We might find something to incriminate Lister."

"Haven't we got it? Didn't she go to you to get Hover's address the day he was done in?"

"I think there's more to it than that," I said. "But why not give it a try? You're going back to the Yard?"

"That's right," he said. "What about you?"

"If it's not too much bother I'd like your driver to take me on to Broad Street. And what about meeting you at the far end of Northumberland Avenue at about two o'clock?"

Jewle had guessed that I had something up my sleeve. That was why I didn't want the driver questioned. As soon as the car had set me down, I made for Lombard Street. Hill wasn't in and it took a subordinate far too long a time to get me a descriptive inventory of the Rimmell jewellery. After that there was getting a taxi and going to Marlbury Street to find Hallows. I ran him to earth in a restaurant. There was just time for me to have a single course and tell him what was in the wind. By the time we were at Northumberland Avenue he knew as much as I.

The police car drew up.

"You know Hallows," I said to Jewle. "I brought him along because he might help."

Hallows was at the front and I in the back with Jewle. The car had hardly moved off when Jewle was wanting to know just what was in my mind.

"I don't say I can read you like a book, sir, but I've got a pretty good idea by now of what's meant by one or two of your looks."

"You're too clever for me," I said. "All the same, it's only an idea. The way I worked it out is that Mrs. Rimmell must have seen more than just someone she knew for her old friend Nurse Lister. Suppose, for instance, Lister did lift that jewellery—and I virtually know that she did—then mightn't she have clung to something she liked? A ring, for example, and that's what Mrs. Rimmell also saw?"

"You're right," he said. "It hits the nail clean on the head! We'd both tried to suggest the Lister woman for the thief and then Mrs. Rimmell *knew* she was. That's how she misjudged you and misled me.

"But wait a minute," he went on. "Would Lister have risked keeping anything like that?"

"With three years gone by? And a change of hair? And working in a dress shop?" I laughed. "Where was the risk?"

"I didn't mean that," he said. "Wouldn't she have got rid of whatever it was when she saw Mrs. Rimmell had spotted her?"

"I know," I said. "I know it's a gamble, but I'm taking a chance on the jackdaw element. I don't see a woman parting with something really good in the jewellery line until the very last moment."

We left it like that. The car was circling Lord's and in a couple of minutes we were at the flats. Hallows and I waited while Jewle had a word with the manager, then we took the lift.

"Everything's being very discreet," Jewle said. "The women don't know the flat's been gone over and they won't know now. Unless we find something."

He waited till the corridor was empty and then nipped into the flat. It was the usual furnished flat, room service provided and a restaurant for meals. We had a preliminary look at all five rooms: living-room, single bedroom, double bedroom, small kitchen and bathroom.

"We'll split up to save time," Jewle said, "and see everything's put carefully back. You do the single bedroom, Hallows, and then shift to bathroom and kitchen. I'll take this room and Mr. Travers the double bedroom."

I went over my room with a small-toothed comb. I even took the drawers out of the large dressing-table and felt round the woodwork, and I did the same with the reproduction Sheraton chest. There were twin wardrobes, both of them large. Wakes had everything: black tie suit, tails, tweeds, handmade shoes in trees, beautiful silk ties, monogrammed handkerchiefs, two whole drawers of beautifully tailored shirts, underwear of sheer silk—the whole caboodle and everything with the best labels. I took a breather and tried to calculate what the lot had cost. Believe it or not, including the overcoat with the sable collar, I couldn't see how Wakes could have got clear with a thousand pounds.

I set to work on the other wardrobe. It wasn't too badly stocked, but nothing like Wakes's, and that wasn't surprising considering that Elizabeth Lister was half of "Simone". I left till last a conglomeration of what looked like old magazines and papers on the long top shelf of that wardrobe. I'm tall, as you know, but I had to get the dressing-table stool to stand on before I could see what there really was.

There were copies of *Harper's* and *Vogue*, cheap magazines dating from weeks back and even some invoices for things for the shop. I was grubbing among them when I found something. Another minute and I wassailing to Jewle. Hallows came in with him.

"Well I'm darned!" Jewle said. "Isn't that the photograph that General Rimmell wrapped up with that Russian Cross?"

"Must be the one," I said. "I've got the other one myself."

Jewle tore a page from his notebook and wrote down what it was and how it had been found. Hallows and I signed it.

"Worth the trip," Jewle told us, and treated himself to a nod. "This makes a holding charge for Lister."

Hallows was now in the small kitchen and so far he'd found nothing. Ten minutes later I'd finished with my room and I went in to help Jewle. He'd practically finished and he'd had no luck. I asked him if he'd taken the drawers out of the writing desk and he said he had.

"Nothing on the partitions between or the backs?"

"I didn't try them," he said. "Do you think we should?"

He took the drawers out and laid them on the carpet. His fingers began probing the undersides of the woodwork.

"Something here!" he said. "A lump of some sort. Seems to be stuck. Two lumps."

He got down on hands and knees. The light wasn't good as he flashed his torch. Then he opened the big blade of his pocket knife.

"Maybe I can prise 'em loose with this. You hold the torch."

In less than a minute he was standing up, those two lumps in his hands.

"Well I'm damned! Stuck on with chewing-gum! Better see if we can get them cleaned."

They were a pair of earrings. One way and another he got them fairly clean in the bathroom. Hallows had the inventory ready.

"Here it is," he said, and showed it to Jewle. "*Pair of circular, Indian work, gold earrings with ruby centres and diamond clusters*. Valued at eighty pounds. And that was long before the war."

Jewle chuckled. Then he sobered and held out a hand.

"Shake hands, sir."

"Why?" I said and felt a bit of a fool.

"Just because," he said. "How you get these hunches beats me. You must have a crystal or something."

"You tell that to George Wharton," I said. "He'll swear blind that nine out of ten of my hunches go wrong. This one happened to be the tenth."

"Well, we've got what we want," he said. "We know what Mrs. Rimmell saw. And we've got Lister just where we want her."

Another page from the notebook and more signing. The earrings went into an envelope and the envelope into his pocket.

"Better leave everything much as we found it," he said. "She certainly won't miss that photograph and I hope she won't try seeing if the earrings are there."

A few minutes later and we were having a last look back at the sitting-room, then Jewle glanced along the corridor and we went quickly out. Hallows and I waited in the car till Jewle came back from another interview with the manager.

# 17

# CODA

"BEFORE we move off I'd like to get something cleared up."

"And what's that?" Jewle said.

"Well, first of all, are you pulling Lister in?"

"That might be out of my hands," he said. "Wheels within wheels. Take Wakes, for instance: up to the moment he hasn't done any singing. He's waiting to see just how much we know."

"Which is the devil of a lot."

"Admitted. But we haven't got him for murder. Everything's circumstantial and there isn't enough of it. Defending counsel would knock the whole thing cock-eyed."

"The very point I'm trying to make," I said. "Pull Lister in and she'll start singing."

"You think so?" He smiled. "We can't even prove she did the jewel job. All she could be charged with is possession. For that she might get three months or six: depends on what yarn she spins. She might even wriggle clear. In any case, we haven't enough on her to use it as blackmail and make her start singing about Wakes."

I granted.

"I've listened to some pessimists in my time, but, as Wharton says, you take the cake. But what about this one? As soon as Lister knew Mrs. Rimmell had recognised her—and the earrings—she had to do something about it. And something *was* done about it."

"By whom? Admitted Lister had a key and knew the old lady's habits, but she could have rung Wakes or gone to see him. She almost certainly did, but that doesn't tell us beyond any reasonable doubt which of them did the murder."

"But you're going to question her?" Hallows put in.

"If you mean about what we've found this afternoon," Jewle said guardedly, "then the answer's yes. But I doubt if she'll be held. I don't have the final say, you know. It might be decided to keep her loose and nag at her till she loses her nerve."

He motioned to the driver to move the car on. I knew he was right and I hoped he was wrong. He didn't have a free hand. He might advise but Wharton and then Forlin would make the decisions. And the Director of Public Prosecutions would want more than we'd got to decide on putting Lister or Wakes or both in the dock for murder. And to decide too soon was far worse than delay. Once you're acquitted on a murder charge you can't be tried again.

But I did think of something else that might help.

"I've been thinking about Wakes," I said. "When you work it out, he's spent the very devil of a lot of money. I know the total value of those jewels"—I didn't mention the Sigott money—"and they wouldn't have gone half way to buying those things he had in his wardrobe. So doesn't that mean he had the diamonds from the Russian Cross?"

"Looks like it," Jewle said.

"And would he have disposed of the whole lot at once? I don't think he would. He could sell one at a time more or less in the open market instead of through a fence, and he'd get nearer the value. There's the possibility he still has some left."

"That was thought of," he said. "If he has a safe-deposit box, then there was nothing on him to show it. And we searched the studio. And Matthews looked for something of a clue at the flat."

We were very near Piccadilly and I had to think fast.

"Look," I said. "Why not play out our hand? We're in luck so let's give the wheel another whirl. Wakes would never have kept any diamonds where Lister might find them."

"You mean, go over the studio again?"

"Why not? We've nothing to lose."

He shrugged his shoulders. He gave the driver new orders and the car turned towards Daventry Street. There wasn't an inch of parking space near the studio so we got out. Jewle said he'd take a bus to the Yard and the car moved on.

A "closed" sign was on the studio door. Jewle had a key ready and we went in. The man on duty was in at once. He'd been brewing some tea on a ring in the receptionist's office.

"It's all right, Fred. We're just having a look round."

"Well, where do we begin?" he asked me.

I thought I'd like a look round myself. The place was certainly worth it. Everything was regardless and always in good taste. The waiting-room was even better than Hallows's description—modern but comfort itself and the last word in chic. The studio itself was perfection and maybe Wakes had had it designed to give expression and impetus to his art. It had every modern device, and some I'd never seen. The walls were gold and cream. On them were framed photographic studies and, to reveal them, tiny fluorescent, built-in lights. A perfect touch of colour was lent by a scarlet cyclamen in a large black enamelled kind of pot that stood on a small painted table in the window recess.

"Is there a safe anywhere?"

"In his office," Jewle said. "Nothing in it that looked like helping much. The whole bag of tricks is at the Yard."

He went to the end of the room, peered round, and listened. He came back and his voice lowered.

"Tell you what we did find in there, but keep it strictly under your hat. There were about twenty sets of what was called art studies. A nude in various poses. Not exactly pornographic but very suggestive. And something else. A set of photographs of some stuff that was really hot. Photographs of some drawings by the look of them. And each was signed with a kind of sprawling signature in the bottom corner. I daren't look at Hallows. And I was hoping my face had no flush. I took out my handkerchief and blew my nose. And I had to know how much he knew."

"Wakes's signature?"

"No," he said. "The name of a chap called Sigott."

"Sigott?" I frowned. "Sigott? You can't mean the portrait painter?"

"That's what we think," he said. "Keep it under your hat for God's sake but apparently he must do that sort of thing as a kind of hobby. Where Wakes comes in we don't know yet and we don't want to have to go to this Sigott direct. Now you see what I meant when I said 'wheels within wheels'."

I hardly heard him. I wondered how long it would take him to find a connection with Lister. And whether he'd discover—if Sigott were to tell—that I'd known that much all along.

"Extraordinary!" I said. "But what about a look for those diamonds?"

We gave the whole place the treatment. Over an hour and we'd found nothing. Even the developing room had been turned inside out.

"Well, there it is," I said. "If ever they were here they'd have been where no burglar'd have thought of looking. Not in the safe, for instance."

"What about that plant?" Hallows said. "It's the only thing left."

It was one of the new cyclamens. I was intending to give one to Bernice at Christmas. From what I'd read about them they were as much as two feet across and carried an enormous number of blooms. This one was about eighteen inches and had about twenty blooms.

Hallows hadn't waited. He'd found some paper and was loosening the edges of the soil with his knife. He turned the pot—it was more of an oblong container—on its side and gave it a punch or two with his fist. The whole thing began to move. He turned it almost over and punched again. He almost fell over as the plant and soil came out. At the very bottom, still adhering to the last of the soil, was a yellow something. It was one of those waterproof, fold-over tobacco pouches, rolled to a thin cylinder. Jewle grabbed it and unrolled it. Something fell on the table. Four things. Four flattish things, each as big as a hazel nut. Four twinkling things.

"My God!" Jewle said. "So there they are!"

As though they were fragile, he touched them with the tips of his fingers. He picked one up and looked at it through his glass. Hallows looked at one.

"What are they worth?" Jewle asked.

"Can't say," Hallows told him. "I'm only an amateur. A thousand apiece? Perhaps a lot more."

"Right," Jewle said. "Better get 'em to the Yard."

"Just a minute," I said. "To the Yard by all means, but you know whose they are?"

He looked surprised.

"The property of the Rimmell estate."

"Oh no. You tell him, Hallows. You're the expert."

"They're the property of United Assurance," Hallows said. "Work it out for yourself."

Jewle didn't see it.

"This is the position," Hallows said. "There was a valuation that was agreed to by both sides and the policy was issued. It doesn't matter how long ago that policy came into force. It'd stay valid as long as premiums were paid and its terms weren't altered. Right. The company has paid and the whole thing's over. Mrs. Rimmell got full payment. The fact that some of the property has now been recovered doesn't enter into it. As far as the Company's concerned, that's just a stroke of luck."

Jewle grinned.

"This chap talks like a lawyer. Sounds a bit fishy to me but maybe you're right."

"Of course he's right," I said stoutly. "So, strictly without prejudice, I think you should give me a receipt. After all, I was in charge of the investigations for the company and our contract says we're their agents."

He wrote the receipt, then he wrapped each diamond in paper, put the four back in the wrapper, and put the wrapper in his inside pocket. He even took a pin from his lapel and fastened the pocket flap.

"Just one thing," I said. "Do us a favour. Let me handle this with the company. Don't notify them till I give you the word."

He gave me a look. He smiled.

"I told you it was fishy. What's the idea? You two hoping for a bonus?"

"Why not?" I said. "Free to hope, aren't we?"

"Right," he said. "And, by God, you'll have earned it."

"If we' ever get it," said Hallows. "And that reminds me. We ought to have another receipt: for those earrings."

It was far too late that night to ring John Hill, so it was put off till the morning. Hallows was listening in.

"That Rimmell robbery case," I said. "We managed to pick up a lead and we're hoping to do a lot more about it—purely as a speculation, of course."

I caught the rather patronising chuckle.

"You know if it's worth your while."

"We think it is," I said. "The jewellery's probably gone long ago but there might be a diamond or two left from that cross."

"That's interesting. You mean that?"

"We're more than hoping. So tell me: if we recover only one diamond, will it do you any good?"

There was a pause. He was ready to hedge.

"Well, if the stones are what we think they are, it would go some of the way to recovering our losses."

"And two stones would clear you?"

"Well—yes. I think they would. The whole thing would be gone into, of course, and you might even get a small contract bonus."

"Thanks," I said. "That sort of heartens us, if you know what I mean. Two or three days and we might have some news."

That was that.

"'Heartens is the word," Hallows said. "I feel heartened already."

"So I guessed," I told him. "Your own bonus isn't to be sneezed at. But Hill's a tough nut where business is concerned. It's nice to know he's got the situation in mind. And we certainly ought to wait a day or so before giving Jewle the word. Now you'd better have the day off. Take your wife somewhere and celebrate."

"I've got to explain away those posh photographs," he said. "I'd had the rough proofs and she'd picked the one she wanted. Looks to me as if Wakes is out of business for life."

"We'll get Jewle to find the plates," I said. "I don't know that I wouldn't like one myself."

I took Bernice out to lunch and then we saw a new Italian picture at the Curzon. We had tea in town and came home to a domestic evening. We were just going to bed when Jewle rang.

"Thought you'd like to know that a certain lady was in for questioning this afternoon. Asked about the earrings, she said Wakes gave them to her. And why did she hide 'em? Because Wakes had been pressed for money and she thought he might help himself to them. The photograph she swore blind she'd never seen before. Asked about Mrs. R., she said she'd never even known she was in the shop. She'd been too busy attending to a customer."

"She's got all the answers," I said. "But it oughtn't to be too hard to tie her in knots."

"You think so?" He gave a grunt. "A certain gentleman was brought in again this evening. Just one mention of earrings and he clamped down. We can't get a word out of him. Just, 'Nothing to say. Nothing to say.'"

"I see. And what's your next move?"

"Keep on at her and throw him to Norwich. Once he's inside we can always get him out. And we'll start that nerve attack on her."

There were other questions I'd have liked to ask, but I didn't. In any case I was virtually out of things—semi-officially, that is. For my own reasons I wanted those two to get what was due to them. Doreen Lister too, perhaps, though she was someone far too shadowy. But the night brought no new ideas. The very reactions after the days of inquiry and the previous day's excitements brought a kind of lassitude and somehow I didn't feel like going to the office.

I rang Norris and said I mightn't be in till late. Hallows was his, I said: at least I had nothing for him at the moment. That done I read the papers and did a crossword. Bernice brought coffee and said she was going out. I caught sight of my desk and thought I would do some tidying up and discarding of the unnecessary. It was a job I'd been threatening to do for weeks.

And that was how I came across those two magazines I'd bought, thinking they might contain some publicity for Wakes. I turned the pages over again and came across that article on old-time photography. It was by a genuine old-timer: his age was given as eighty-seven. And that article looked interesting as I began to read it.

About ten minutes later I very slowly picked up the receiver. I actually didn't know that I'd dialled, but apparently I had.

"Ludovic Travers here. Put me through most urgently to Chief-Inspector Jewle."

In less than a minute he was on the line.

"Can I see you?" I said.

"Of course," he said. "Where?"

"Better be here, at the flat."

"At the flat," he said. "Why? What's on?"

"Something that might be important. I think I've found the way to make the Lister woman sing."

As I waited in Butler Street that night for "Simone" to close, I was still pretty sure of everything but one thing. The problem would be to get those two women to my flat. I hoped, and I'd never hoped harder, that the scheme I had in mind would work.

The moment was getting near. The saleswoman came out and made for Marlbury Street. She was, we learned later—and if it brings anything back to you—of Danish extraction and had lived as a girl in Odense. Lights went off on the second storey and two work-women came out. Then another came out. The window lights went off and there was only a dim light at the back of the shop. I crossed the street and went in.

Only the Lister sisters were there: Doreen waiting and Elizabeth preening herself at the cheval glass.

"I'm afraid were closed," Doreen said.

"But not to me."

Elizabeth looked round. She stared.

"That's right," I said. "The name's Travers as you know. You're no longer Mrs. North. You're Elizabeth Lister. This is Doreen."

"What d'you want?"

She was glaring at me.

"Just a friendly talk," I said. "I think I can do you both a good turn."

"I don't understand what you mean." That was Doreen, the sharp-faced one.

"You will do," I said. "I know a whole lot the police don't know. Enough to land you both in jail. Even a bit worse. They still hang women, you know."

Doreen bit her lip. The other sneered.

"You've got nothing on me. Nothing the police don't think they know."

"Haven't I?" I tried a sneer. "What about a few names? Just as a sample: Margaret Mann, Sigott, Mrs. Crewe who was asked to see to Mrs. Rimmell, the man you called Jack who was supposed to be your husband—"

"How much do you want?"

"Don't know yet," I said. "We've got to have a chat."

She was hard. The other looked scared.

"All right then. Chat."

"Not here," I said. "The police have got this place watched. We'll go out the back way and talk in my flat."

She laughed.

"Oh no. You don't try that trick."

"Very well, either that or I'll go straight out of here and ring the Yard. But there isn't any trick. I've got something to give you, for one thing, and it's at the flat. This is the address. There's a taxi waiting round the corner. You tell the driver where you want to go."

She frowned.

"It can't do any harm," Doreen told her.

"Just the opposite," I said. "It's about the one chance you've got left. And you'll both be there."

"All right." That was Elizabeth. "But you'd better mind your step."

There wasn't a word spoken till we reached the flats. I settled with the driver and the three of us went through the swing doors. I was glad George, the hall porter, was there to flick his hand to his cap and tell me it was wonderful weather. It gave me a standing in the place and I wondered if Jewle had put him up to it.

"Just a couple of doors along," I said as we got out of the lift. I moved on ahead to unlock the door. We went into the living-room. Matthews and a stenographer were in my den. I looked in. I looked in the main bedroom, and nodded to myself.

"Right. We're absolutely alone. Perhaps you ladies'll sit down. And may I get you a drink? Sherry? Gin and something?"

"Never mind the drink," she said. "Let's have the chat. Plenty of time for a drink when we know what we've got to pay for it."

She was the dominating one. Doreen wasn't even an echo. Lizzie—that was the only way to think of her—sat on the edge of the chair, handbag on her knees, eyes on my face and the lip always curled. Doreen, just to the side of her, couldn't keep still.

"You've surprised me, you know," Lizzie said. "I didn't think you were that kind. Quite the gentleman when I saw you before."

"Which just shows," I said. "But suppose I tell you some of the things I know. If we're going to make a bargain, you ought to get good value."

"And what *do* you know?"

"Plenty. Right from the village to the big city. All your men, or most of 'em. Wakes, Hover, Dr. Kossack, Sigott. I've got a dossier on you the police'd give their ears for. But let's get down to cases.

"The police aren't on to the Sigott business yet and I'm in a position to head them off. That job netted four thousand pounds and whether you got your share or not I don't know. What I do know is that I can get Sigott to go to the police. That'll mean a pretty long stretch."

"How much do you want?" She was ice-cool: the voice part sneer, part contempt. If there'd been a gun in her bag I think she'd have pulled it. That's how she looked.

"I'm going to surprise you," I said. "I don't want a penny. The one I want is Wakes. Let's say he did me a dirty trick and I've been waiting to get him. That's why I dug right down into your history, and his. No one's going to double-cross me and get away with it. And now I'm going to prove to you that you were double-crossed too."

"That's what *you* say."

"It is. And it's what I'll prove. But let me tell it in my own way."

I went across the room and brought back the sherry decanter and three glasses. I filled my own and took a sip. I filled a second and put it near Doreen. Lizzie didn't even bother to look.

"Let's begin with the Rimmell jewellery," I said. "And, by the way, I know the very day when it was taken: the day when Hover was being shopped at Hurst Park. Wakes had a couple of paying propositions in mind once Hover was safe inside—the Sigott blackmail job and the Rimmell jewellery job. You don't mind my saying it but you were the one who provided the information, and you were entitled to your share. But you didn't get it."

She'd nothing to say but her lips were tight together and she was watching like a cat at a hole.

"Let's take Wakes for a minute," I said. "Look at the money he spent. New car; new studio and up-to-date equipment; the lease; hundreds of pounds' worth of clothes; his share of the flat—everything. Where'd the money come from? The whole Sigott four thousand wouldn't have begun to cover it. Nor would the Rimmell jewellery. I've got the valuation in my pocket if you'd like to see it."

"You know a lot."

I refused to be nettled. Then Doreen cut in.

"The money came from the studio. He was coining money there."

"You've seen the books?"

"Well—no. But it *must* have been coining money."

"You're wrong," I said. "Wakes was spending every penny." I switched to Lizzie.

"I'll tell you where Wakes's money came from. It came from you."

"Me!" She laughed. "You must be mad. I never gave him a penny. It all went into our shop."

"You think so?"

I took that magazine and the Rimmell photograph from the table drawer.

"Read this. Read it together. It's an article by an old-time photographer on the troubles of old-time photographers, and remember that this photograph of Mrs. Rimmell wearing the Russian Cross was taken sixty years ago."

I opened the magazine at the place and indicated the marked paragraph.

"Read that. Remember also that Mrs. Rimmell agreed that the photograph showed no diamonds in the cross, even if she was certain they actually were there. Now read why."

Their lips moved as they read. It was Lizzie who looked up first.

"I think I get it. I'm not sure."

"Let me explain," I said. "That old-time photographic apparatus was pretty crude compared with modern stuff. Those flashing diamonds under artificial light would have made the whole cross come out as a big, white blur and spoiled the photograph, so what the photographer did—Mrs. Rimmell wouldn't know it—was turn it quickly back to front. It was the back that was photographed. Now read that paragraph again."

This time she had it.

"Wakes knew that," I said. "He was an expert. What he did was take the diamonds out of their settings and show you the cross, and the photograph, to prove they'd never been there. And you fell for it. And he probably kidded you that Mrs. Rimmell's memory must have been faulty about the whole thing. And now do you see where Wakes's money came from?"

"Perhaps." The lips clamped together while she frowned. "Sounds good, but how can you prove it?"

"Because I happen to know that the police searched his studio. Wakes had cashed in on only three of the diamonds, and that might have brought him anything up to four thousand pounds. The other four were there. You know his studio but you'd never guess where. He probably changed the hiding places around but the police found them hidden in the soil of the pot that held that scarlet cyclamen. The one on the table in the window."

She stared.

"And if you want absolute proof, I've got nicely parked downstairs the very one who found them. I'll get him to come up. And now do you know where Wakes's money came from?"

"The double-crossing bastard!"

I gave the signal down the house telephone.

"He was all that. But we've got him. All you have to do is talk."

"Talk?" She laughed. Her hand went out to the decanter. "You bet your life I'll talk."

"Fine," I said. "I've waited a long time for this. You two owe nothing to a cheap crook like Wakes. He double-crossed you then and I happen to know he's ready to double-cross you now. Play your cards right and you might stay in the clear." There was a tap at the door. Jewle came in. I went out and left him to it.

## FINAL CADENCE

BERNICE and I always have meals brought up to the flat but there's a small restaurant on the ground floor and that's where I went. I'd hardly begun dinner when George, the hall porter, came in with a message. Everything upstairs was clear.

Jewle didn't ring me till about nine-thirty the next morning, at the office. He apologised for the delay in letting me know what had happened. And he'd been up till the small hours making his report to date.

"We didn't stay in your place," he said. "We got those two to come to the Yard."

"They sang?"

"Like a couple of nightingales. Soprano and contralto duet. Everything pushed on Wakes. He rang Hover at the hotel, for example, and got him to come to the shop. Said all three had been lying low and on the run from the police. Hover didn't swallow it and pulled a gun and got shot in the struggle. That was Wakes's account to the women. By the way, that sprained ankle of his was a fake. Suggestive, don't you think? Proving beforehand that he couldn't possibly have handled Hover's body."

"And the Rimmell job?"

"Wakes again. But Lister's put a rope round her own neck. You know why?"

"No," I said. "Unless it was because you had Wakes under observation at the time."

"Got it in one. We sure did have him under observation. We give him his alibi. But we'll talk about that later. What I wanted to ask was if you could join Wharton and me for lunch. We're standing you one."

"No, no," I said. "You mustn't do that sort of thing. Honestly you mustn't. Besides, I owe you a lunch."

"Listen," he said. "Wharton's in this too. Wouldn't you like to see him open that purse of his for once?"

"It'd certainly be an experience."

"Right. Be in his room at about a quarter to twelve."

"Just a minute," I said hastily. "I want you to do something. Ring John Hill straightaway. Tell him that, thanks to various clues and information provided by us, you found four diamonds and you've given me a receipt. Don't mention any dates. You'll do that?"

"Glad to." He chuckled. "When you're sending that case of whisky at Christmas, I drink Haig and Haig. As if you didn't know it."

Half an hour later Hill rang me.

"Great work, Travers. Chief-Inspector Jewle just told me about it."

"Jewle?" I said. "Oh, you mean the recovery of those four diamonds. But you realise the police may have to keep them for some time if they're evidence."

"I do realise it. When shall I be seeing you?"

"To-morrow morning? And I'd like to bring Hallows along too. The credit's as much his as mine."

"A nice fellow, Hallows. Well, I'll be seeing you both. At about ten-thirty?"

I wasn't exactly dressed for a celebration lunch so I went home and dressed again and generally dolled myself up. It was a quarter to twelve to the dot when I walked into the old familiar room. Jewle was there and, of course, the old maestro himself: huge shoulders, vast moustache, peering look—everything but those antiquated spectacles. He didn't smile as he held out his hand.

"Sorry it's come to this. You got the bracelets, Jewle? If so slip 'em on."

George's jokes are always a bit ponderous but I was in the mood to play along.

"What's the charge?"

"Attempting to blackmail two innocent women."

"Right," I said. "I'll come quiet. I thought you were having me for rape."

George chuckled.

"I wouldn't put it past you. Better get out some beer, Jewle. We'll have a drink before we go."

On his desk was what was almost certainly a copy of Jewle's report: that was why I couldn't understand why I had to go over things again. There was something very peculiar about it: almost as if those two were playing for time. And then the buzzer went. George reached for the receiver.

"It's for you," he said.

I wondered who on earth could be ringing me there. It wasn't long before I knew.

"Forlin here, Travers. How are you?"

"Very fit," I said. "And you?"

"Can't grumble," he said. "I heard you were going to drop in and I wondered if you could see me."

"I'd love to. Unfortunately I have an engagement."

"I promise not to keep you for more than five minutes."

"Hold the line a minute, will you?"

I cupped the receiver.

"It's Forlin! Wants me to see him for five minutes."

George shrugged his shoulders.

"You there, Forlin?" I said. "I'll be with you straightaway."

I put the receiver back. Wharton gave one of his grunts.

"So you're trying to get in again with the Big Bugs, are you?" I caught the wink he gave Jewle. "What's the idea? Going to lever Forlin out of his job?"

I laughed.

"God help you if I do."

As I closed the door behind me I heard George laugh. He chuckles, he guffaws, he leers and he grimaces, but not once in a blue moon do you hear him give an honest-to-God laugh. As I walked along the corridor I felt like laughing too. For one thing it was a grand morning and the sun was positively glaring through the windows. And I'd left Norris happy too about the Assurance bonus. And I was going out to lunch with two of the best friends I had. And, as I actually had to remember, I was on my way to see Forlin!

THE END

Lightning Source UK Ltd.
Milton Keynes UK
UKHW012007130123
415315UK00001B/134